NASOMI'S QUEST

....

LEGENDS OF AO #1

ENOCK I. SIMBAYA

MVmedia, LLC
Fayetteville, Georgia

MVmedia, LLC
Fayetteville, GA 30214
www.mvmediaatl.com

Publisher's Note: This is a work of fiction. Names, characters, places, and incidents are a product of the author's imagination. Locales and public names are sometimes used for atmospheric purposes. Any resemblance to actual people, living or dead, or to businesses, companies, events, institutions, or locales is completely coincidental.

Book Layout ©2017BookDesignTemplates.com
Cover art by Odera Igbokwe

Ordering Information:
Quantity sales. Special discounts are available on quantity purchases by corporations, associations, and others. For details, contact the "Special Sales Department" at the address above.
Enock I. Simbaya\Nasomi's Quest. -- 1st ed.
ISBN 978-1-7346279-0-9

Contents

For my lovely wife, Bumbe.

There's greatness in you.

However long the night, the dawn will break.
—AFRICAN PROVERB

CHAPTER 1

LORD TAMBO

Nasomi uncovered the basket to admire her work. She inhaled the aroma that wafted from it, reveled in Father's yet-to-be-given compliments. "This is wonderful, my daughter," he would say, his mouth full. She'd prepared his favorite: pumpkin leaves mixed with powdered peanuts and dried chili; she'd included a piece of hard bread.

"Nice!" she said out loud, proud of the extra attention she'd put into her work.

"I'm sure it is," someone behind her said.

She started. "I'm sorry, I didn't notice you were behind me," she told the man.

He was dressed in a rich brown sleeveless tunic adorned with patterns of red and green, and baggy breeches fastened at his shins. His sandaled feet were dustless, like he'd walked on the air. All his fingers had rings of copper, all studded with various gems, marking him as a tribal lord. He had searching, teasing eyes and a long handsome face. He had much hair on his head, and although it was unkempt, it suited him well.

Nasomi performed her act of courtesy: she touched her chest, curtsied. "My Chief. Please pardon me."

"That is good smelling food there." He returned the greeting by touching his chest and dipping his head. He gave her a sweet smile.

"It's for my father. I am sorry I blocked your way, My Chief."

The path at that point was too narrow to let him pass by her. It wound through tall grasses and bushes. She covered the basket and walked on. She couldn't seem to walk fast enough. His strides were long and he was but a pace behind her.

After a while, he said, "I think the path is now wide enough for us to walk abreast."

They had gone past the thicker section, and the grass and wild flowers in the sides were easy to tramp upon if more walking space was to be required. She ignored him and tried to walk faster.

"I mean you no harm," he said.

"Isn't that what a robber or rapist would say?"

He gave a short laugh. "You're right. I am sorry. I think I am lost," he said. "Someone pointed the way, but there are too many forks, I misremember."

She paused to let him catch up. They were now by the first field and a number of people were in sight. She felt safe enough. "You are a tribal lord," she said, "but where are your attendants?"

"I didn't need my own today. I am in my father's company."

She didn't pry. "Where is the lost lord going?"

"To a field."

"That's not saying much."

"All I know is my father will be there, to attend to some dispute."

"The fields begin here, My Chief. You can go along this path until you come to the one you are looking for."

He gestured for her to continue walking. "What is your name?" he asked.

She could lie, but she wasn't a good liar and it was just her name. "Nasomi."

"Nasomi," he said, stressing the 'o' in a thick accent that revealed he was of the Somebo tribe. "Lovely name. Mine is Tambo Mwanakepe Go."

"So you belong to the Kepe clan. It must be nice being the son of a Chieftain."

"It has its good days... Ah, I see you don't believe me because I travel alone. Why would someone impersonate a tribal lord?"

"I'd expect a palanquin and at least half a dozen attendants, maybe a singer or two to sing your praise as you move to the admiration of the people."

"I like walking around alone. Helps me see things I would otherwise miss. Like finding a woman in the bushes talking to herself. Look, my breeches have pockets. Sometimes I put my hands in them to not be too conspicuous." He demonstrated, grinning as well.

"Your clothes, though. They scream rich and lordly."

He shrugged. "Not as much as the rings."

They walked on for a moment in silence. "Some people I know talk to themselves," she said defensively. "You crept up on me."

"I didn't. You were minding what was in the basket to hear me come. I only wanted to ask for directions."

"But you're not a rapist?"

He laughed, and so did she. She found herself mimicking his laughter.

"I hate such people," he said, with all seriousness. "You'll forgive me for saying this, but if I were a spirit, I would haunt them at night and rip out their innards and let their bodies rot in the streets."

"So would I."

There was a dozen more people than she expected on her father's field. Even the lowest among the strangers looked richly dressed in the manner Tambo was. Her father looked drab against all that finesse, as he argued with another elderly man who was obviously Tambo's father.

"It seems we were coming to the same place," Tambo said to her.

She rushed to her father's side.

"You keep disputing the deed," Chieftain Go said, waving a parchment in Nasomi's father's face. "Would you like me to read it again?"

"I have a deed also," Father said. He leaned on his hoe and looked eager to get back to the digging. "It has the monograph of the king himself and his scorched symbol. And it says my land extends four gardens, from there to there"—he indicated with a shaking finger—"and five the other way. I've had it for five years, My Chief. Five years. Ask Chishala, my neighbor, there. There are beacons set. I was there when they were being laid by the architects themselves."

"You haven't shown it to me. My deed here reads that—"

"Yes, yes, you repeat yourself. Your deed describes your land being seven gardens long. A good part of that lies in the farms of Chishala and the other idiot over there. I do not see you harassing them to hand over the land. Why only me? Because I am a poor farmer who has nothing but a few grains to plant?"

"Harassing you? I am here only to claim what is mine."

Father touched Nasomi's hand. "Quick, my daughter, rush to the house. Get the deed to this land. It will be folded neatly in the small chest beside my pallet."

"I am not leaving you alone," she said.

"I need the deed, Somi. My Chief here seems to think this is his land." He looked the chieftain straight in the eye.

"Are you saying I am trying to steal from you?" The chieftain was breathing hard, near wheezing.

"Father," Tambo said, so coolly like tempers were not flared. He knelt before the chieftain.

"Son. Did you get lost like I knew you would?" the chieftain asked as though only just noticing that Tambo was there.

"No. I took a different route."

"Stand, my son. Now, I want these people arrested and tried."

"May I propose another way to solve this, Father?"

Chieftain Go sat on the seat of his palanquin. "I'm impatient, boy. What other way is there? This is our land here."

"Hear my proposal. Let us invite these people to our table and we can examine both parchments, and we can call experts to help us. Perhaps there has been a mix-up, but a good-natured discussion over a meal can set things right."

The chieftain grunted. "Now they must eat my food as well? A good few days in a dungeon will bring senses to this man." He pointed at Nasomi's father, who scowled at the insult.

"I am not an interpreter of the law, and neither are you, Father," Tambo said. "We need someone to examine both documents. If it turns out we are right, this man here would have no objections about it. And we might even employ him to look after the farm."

"Or have him imprisoned."

"And if it turns out we are wrong," Tambo continued, "we would have not condemned an innocent man. And people will still say good things about us in either case."

"Good things. Good things! *Pa!*" the chieftain said bitterly, shaking his head. "I should have come with one of your brothers instead. They know how to act quickly. You talk too much."

"But you must admit I have talked well."

His father gave him a long look. "Perhaps you have. Have it your way, for now. Take charge of this dinner yourself, and see that this is brought to a quick end. The sun is hot on me, I would go home now."

The attendants immediately took their places around the palanquin and hoisted it to their shoulders in a well-rehearsed synchrony. A poet strummed his string instrument, prepared his voice as the palanquin began to move. Tambo gave a small wave to Nasomi and mouthed something she couldn't make out, then followed after the chieftain.

Nasomi and Father went home without working on the field. When he spoke, it was to mumble about how greedy some people in the world were, how unfair life was, and how this was the work of the *Tumina*, the spirits beneath the ground. Nasomi had seen him bitter, but this was deep, this was fury. He kicked the dirt and picked stones to throw at trees. He dropped the hoe and Nasomi had to carry it.

At home, he refused to eat, refused to wash, no matter how many times Nasomi pleaded. He muttered to himself when he thought he was alone, and complained to Nasomi and her cousin, Naena, when they were anywhere close to him.

"We've lost everything," he said. "Everything! All because of some greedy man. He has more than generations after him will need. Why does he want to also get my crumbs?" He coughed so terribly Nasomi thought he'd cough himself to death.

"I can start selling things at the market," she said. "We can sustain ourselves."

"What things, if we will have nothing to reap? And what will I do? Sit on my rump all my days till I die?"

"Father, you're being so anxious. What would Mother say?"

"Don't bring her up to try to control me." He coughed. "You know how hard she and I worked to get that piece of land."

Nasomi looked to Naena for help, but her cousin, who usually knew what to say, was quiet.

"We mustn't lose hope, Father. I think things will go well. The young lord will make things well for us."

He sucked through his teeth, and went to his room, muttering to himself.

"Young lord?" Naena said. "You must tell me about him."

"Now you have found your mouth?"

"What did you want me to say, Somi? You've seen the mood he is in. Just tell me about this young lord."

CHAPTER 2

THE WALK

Nasomi and Naena were scouring pots the next morning when Tambo appeared at the gateway. Naena was the one who saw him and she nudged Nasomi. They both stood and wiped their hands on their wrapping cloths as he entered. He was smiling.

"I found the place," he said, looking quite pleased with himself.

"My Chief," Nasomi and Naena said together, curtsying.

"You came here, My Chief?" Nasomi asked. She became conscious of her and Naena's appearance: un-oiled skins, undone hair, wrapping cloths with sodden patches. And also the small drab house, the unremarkable yard with a falling fence around it. Two hens chased another right past Tambo's feet, clucking too loudly.

He returned the compliment. "Ladies." He didn't seem bothered by the poor surroundings. "I asked around for a farmer with a daughter called Nasomi. I got lost through some of the ways, but I persisted."

"You have to forgive us, we didn't expect this," Nasomi said. "We were going to come to your home this evening for the meeting."

"I told you I'd come to find you. There's no need for the meeting now. I have set things right."

"You mean the farm? It is ours?"

"Yes. Entirely. I convinced my father to let the matter go. We have more than enough land, and it was a matter of inquiring about the deed. Is your father home?"

"Let me get him. He will be glad of this." She rushed into the house and found Father dozing on a stool next to his pallet. He had said he needed to pray. It seemed he needed sleep more.

She knelt before him. "Father?"

He lifted his head to look at her like he'd been expecting to see her there. "Mhmm?"

"Father, Lord Tambo is here. He has some news about our land."

He opened his mouth and paused, as if not comprehending. "Lord Tambo? Who is...? He's come here? He's outside our house?"

"Come, Father." She took him by the hand and led him outside.

"My Chief," Father said, touching his heart and dipping his head.

"The *Mara* bless you," Lord Tambo said, gesturing for the man to be at ease.

"When my daughter told me there was a lord at the door, I thought it was your father. Where are your attendants, My Chief?"

Tambo stole a glance at Nasomi, gave a dismissive laugh. "I sent them on an errand. I thought to personally bring this news to you. The land..."

"Yes?" Father shuddered.

"It turned out our deed was old and invalid. We didn't realize my great-grandmother had gifted the land to the king and somebody forgot to get rid of the deed. When Father stumbled upon it... Well, he thought we had land no one had reminded him of. But it is all yours now."

Father did a stiff dance of wiggling his shoulders and pumping his fists. "Ahhhh! This is so wonderful! I don't know how I can thank you, My Chief."

"No need," Tambo said. "My father was quick to understand and leave the land in the hands of a hard-working citizen like you. I have also provided you with two workers to help you with the season's growing."

Father couldn't help but take Tambo's hand in both of his and shake it. "You are a good lord. Nasomi, I will go to the field now. The weeds won't pluck themselves."

"But you need to eat first, Father."

"You will bring me the food. The sun won't wait. Give Lord Tambo some cornwine." He dashed back into the house.

"You have brought joy to Father," Nasomi said to Tambo. "He was sick and worried."

"I'm only happy to." A moment of heavy silence fell upon them, the three exchanged looks.

"This is my cousin Naena. She is the daughter of my mother's young brother..."

Naena nudged Nasomi in the ribs. "You don't have to say everything, Somi. You will bore the lord."

"Please, you can tell me everything," Tambo said with a laugh. "I wouldn't mind listening to your family history."

"Sit for some cornwine," Nasomi said. "I will bring it shortly."

"No, no. Don't trouble yourself. I've had a lot to eat already."

Another bout of silence.

"I will go now," Tambo said.

"Thank you, My Chief," Nasomi said. "For this gift. It is a good thing." Naena gave her a disbelieving look, as if to say, Are those the best words you can speak?

He smiled and turned. He walked away slowly, deliberately. He was in no hurry. He placed his hands at his back, turned his head left and right and skyward to study whatever caught his attention. A man with few troubles in his life, Nasomi thought.

Naena poked her. "How can you be so dim, Somi?"

"What?"

"He wants you to follow him."

"That can't be right."

"Don't be silly. Learn to understand the clues. Go after him, now, or I will."

"You wouldn't."

Naena took two steps forward. Nasomi grabbed her hand.

"I will go. Stubborn you."

She trotted some of the way, walked the rest. When she was almost upon him, she felt so stupid. I shouldn't have come, she thought. When he turned and saw her coming, he stopped. She would tell him she was going to see an uncle and walk past him.

"Nasomi," he said, sweetly and without surprise. "Have you seen the new aqueduct being made?"

"Glimpses of it as I move about the city. I have meant to take a good look one good day." She lied. She didn't care about construction.

"Today is a good day then," he said.

"Well, I can't go like this."

"I will wait."

She hesitated, thinking he was jesting. But he smiled reassuringly. "I won't be long," she muttered, and she ran back. She rushed past Naena even as her cousin asked why she was back so soon. She went to her room with Naena in tow.

"What are you in a hurry for?"

"He's taking me to see the aqueduct."

"Ooh. Let's get you dressed properly."

Nasomi chose a supple seamless dress, the fabric brown from years of being worn. It was her favorite, and she thought the fading made the dress look better. Naena was about to comment when Nasomi gave her a look that said, I am wearing this!

Naena shrugged. "Your hair."

"Have you seen his?"

They both laughed. "Let me do something quickly," Naena said. "And wear my sandals. Yours will break before you take five steps."

"They never break."

"Wear mine still. You know they're better."

ENOCK I. SIMBAYA

Nasomi tied the sandal straps around her shin as
Naena worked on her hair. Naena gathered and wound
Nasomi's hair into a high chunky bun. "You look like a
tree. A tree in love."

Nasomi poked her. "It's only a walk. Don't be too
quick about things."

Father called from the living room that he was
going, singing and whistling as he went. Nasomi waited
for him to get to a good distance before dashing out. At
the gate, she called back to Naena, "Take some food for
Father in case I am gone for long."

Naena scowled and folded her arms, but Nasomi
knew she would do as asked.

She fell in by Tambo's side. With his hands in his
pockets most of the way, they walked through the streets
and alleys of the district. Ninki Nanka was a middle-
class district, the abode of farmers, merchants, fishers,
workers of cloth, and messengers. Although she had
lived her life there, Nasomi thought it was a good place
to stay. Even as she and Tambo walked into the next district, Mokele, the differences were obvious: Mokele's
streets were narrower, winding and cutting and veering
in undefined patterns; the huts were smaller, clustered;
and every few paces, a vendor was trying to sell them
something: fresh mangoes, sweet potatoes, sandals,
goats, chickens, "sticks that catch fire quicker".

The new aqueduct passed over the edge of Mokele, held thirty feet in the air by towers that were being
constructed twenty feet apart.

"It goes higher as you get closer to the North
Gate," Tambo said. "It is more stable than the old one,
longer even by fifteen gardens. When it is complete, they
will set to renovate and extend the first one."

Father used to take Nasomi to the first on numerous times when she was young. He lifted her onto
his shoulders, told her to look up. The aqueduct had
looked like it would topple on her, and the dizzying effect was excitingly terrifying when he spun her around.
Beneath a part that leaked, she had held her mouth open

for a drop of water that fell every four heartbeats. Most of them hit a part of her face other than her mouth, and she enjoyed adjusting her position in the hopes she would get ingest the next drop.

"Imagine climbing up there and going all the way to the wall," she said.

Tambo raised a brow. "Who would want to?"

She shrugged. "I don't know. I am just imagining things: people are chasing you, the gates are locked, and that's the only way out."

"I'd go to the parts of the wall with gaps, try to squeeze myself through one."

"The gaps are being guarded by soldiers. Soldiers who have been bewitched to do nothing but kill you."

"That person should be brave then, climbing so high and going against the water flow. And you do have quite an imagination. I like it. If only we were younger. We would have tried it."

As her eyes followed the winding of the duct, her hand brushed against his. She flushed, but when she looked at him, he didn't seem to have noticed.

"The whole thing has needed over five thousand bamboo trees, fifty-six gallons of tar, miles and miles of timber, I-don't-know-how much stone-weights of rocks, and the rope required could be thirty-eight miles long."

"Impressive," Nasomi said. She touched one of his rings with her finger, feeling the texture of the ruby gem.

He looked at her and smiled. "The amount of labor is staggering. It has needed three hundred men and women, thirty-seven oxen, forty horses. The wagon that brought the largest boulder - for the pillar over there - was so long it had a dozen pair of wheels—"

And I thought I was the shy one, Nasomi mused. She gave him a slight pinch on his arm above the wrist.

He reached out to her and she evaded his hand. He reached again and she jumped out of his way.

"Oh, you think you're clever," he teased. He lunged for her. She ran, he chased. When he caught her, she was giggling like a little girl. He pinched her and she chased him through narrow streets of clustered stalls, among mud houses, and through a throng of workers hefting planks. Some of them spouted curses, but upon realizing Tambo's status, they gave the gesture of respect, saying "My Chief."

He pretended to be tired, to let her catch up. He took her hand and in silence, they watched the raising of a massive scaffold.

"It's lovely," Nasomi said. "The structure."

"It's magnificent."

He escorted her home and went his way.

Later in the night, after a hearty supper of corn pap and cow trotters boiled in beans and pumpkin leaves, Nasomi and Naena sat outside to watch the moon and stars. All the four stars of the Bowl were bright tonight, signaling the advent of the rain season. The moon's splotches were vividly gray against its luminescent silver. As Father snored loudly in the house, Naena, poking her teeth with a stick, said, "You just have to tell me what happened."

"We talked and walked and saw the aqueduct. Then I came back home."

"That's not saying much, you. What did you talk about?"

"He knows all these things about the aqueducts... you should have heard him talk. Numbers and all that. On our way back, he asked me about my family. I told him about you and Father. I told him Mother died four years ago from ulcers. He asked me if I had been close to her. I said 'Yes, very. I enjoyed it when she carried me on her back and sang for me when I was ill."

"'Sounds like a wonderful woman,' he said. 'I said she was."

"He talks sweetly, doesn't he? One word at a time." She mimicked his speech: "'Sounds like a wonderful woman.' I can just imagine you there by his side, falling for his voice."

Nasomi shoved her. "That's just his accent. They all talk like that."

"But he does it so well. What did he say about your eyes?"

"He didn't mention my eyes."

"Oh, swallow him! How can he not talk about your eyes?"

"Watch your language, Nae. How is he supposed to notice my eyes on the first day?"

"Second day. Your eyes are the first thing everyone loves about you. Is he timid?"

"Not particularly."

"You asked about his family?"

"Yes. He has two brothers and a sister. I can only remember her name, Teeyana. The other two I forget. He's firstborn, and will inherit the lordship."

"That's too shallow. Give me the intimate details."

Nasomi shook her head as she laughed. "What surely can I know in just a day about someone?"

"You're afraid of asking questions. Take me along next time and I'll show you how to talk to boys."

Nasomi pushed her again. "He'll get bored with me."

"It shows that he likes you. He must be on his lordly bed right now looking at his ceiling and thinking of you."

"I doubt it, Nae. What have I got to offer?"

"Well, let me count." She brought her palm to Nasomi's face and folded the first finger. "First, your eyes."

"What with you and my eyes, please?"

"They are lovely Nasomi. So brown and shiny."

"And my face? The rest of my figure?"

"Look at you saying figure. It is not so bad, with your thick hips and tall legs. Good enough to attract a lord."

"You're full of teasing, Sister."

"Second, you cook well. Who doesn't like good food? Thir— What's with your face?"

Nasomi was squinting at the gateway. "I'm having that feeling again like I've dreamed this before. It was exactly like this, you and me talking, and at the gate, a small cat passed."

Naena looked at the gateway and back at Nasomi. "And third is this," she said, making a sweeping gesture with a hand of three folded fingers. "This weirdness of yours. He's going to love that, I tell you. You and your deja vu."

Nasomi shrugged. She yawned, and so did Naena. "You'll do my hair tomorrow?"

"Of course. First thing in the morning, before your boyfriend comes." Naena escaped from an impending pinch.

"He's not... Ah, there's no convincing you."

"No, there isn't." Naena stood up and stretched. "Let's go to sleep."

Nasomi stood and followed her cousin into the house. As she closed the door, she lingered a while, looking toward the gate. A ginger cat with white stripes appeared. It scratched at something on the ground, waited, and bounded out of view.

CHAPTER 3

THE KISS

He was waiting for her on the narrow path that led toward the fields. He took the basket from her hands and sniffed at it. "Mhmmm. This smells good. Bring me some of your cooking one day." He gave it back.

"Maybe I will," she teased. "Are you coming with me to greet Father?"

He shook his head. "Take the food to him, you will find me here. I like your hair."

"I thank you. Naena did it so."

When she returned, he stood where he was, watching her walk up to him with a smile on his face. He said, "Today we're going to a dismally romantic place."

They walked up to the new aqueduct where one of his servants was waiting with a horse. He mounted and extended his hand to Nasomi. She took it and he helped her up.

"I will ride home soon," he told the servant. "As usual..." He put his first finger against his lips.

"Yes, My Chief," the servant said. "My lips are sealed." He waved and walked away.

"Hold on tight," Tambo told Nasomi. "Have you ridden on a horse before?"

"No. I've been meaning to. On a good day."

He gave a short laugh. "This is a good day, then." He kicked the horse into a trot, then to a gallop when they were on a wide path. Nasomi enjoyed the wind upon her face, the view of the city zooming past, and holding Tambo's waist.

"Out of the way! Out of the way!" Tambo screamed to people. He nearly knocked down a merchant's cart. They went down the road through the opulent Nkuku District, followed along the old aqueduct for a while and branched off into The Dragon District. Although The Dragon was in the middle of Nari, it contained nothing much but a barracks for young warriors, a guild of woodworkers, the palace of the Jaad clan with a few residential spots about it, the amphitheater, and the cemetery.

She was seven years old when she asked, "Father? Why is it called The Dragon?"

"Every district in Nari is named after a creature," Father had replied. "Some of these creatures are real, like those Kwindi, Kowasa and Nkuku districts are named for. Others, as far as we know are myths, legends, and scary bedtime stories. Ninki Nanka is a gigantic water creature said to be protecting the big swamp of the Shodishu people. Let me tell you about this beautiful beast—"

"Start with The Dragon," young Nasomi said.

"Indeed. Some say the dragon used to be an Ao'Pan warrior named Yanga. Everyone coming from the south will have heard of his story. He was a mighty warrior, going on quests to kill monsters that troubled villages. He heard of a dragon that couldn't die, and he said to himself 'There is no dragon Yanga can fail to kill.' He traveled to the troubled place and found the dragon. A monster so big you think it's a tower."

"Taller than our walls?"

"Taller than the walls! And it breathed fire upon him. But he fought and defeated it. The proud warrior killed the dragon that couldn't die. And then he became it. That's why it cannot die because whoever kills it takes its place."

"That's scary."

"Very much so. Many believe the dragon is real is because, so many years ago, before the walls of Nari were built, before the kowasa emerged and our tribes united, the dragon flew over these lands, snatching our ancestors' livestock and burning those who tried to fight him. But he flew away and has never been seen or heard of again."

Tambo and Nasomi reached the cemetery. He tethered the horse to a small dry tree and led her by hand onto a black piece of land. Every Season of the Sun, the grasses and shrubs that grew upon the cemetery would be put to the flames. Few people these days really bothered to attend this burning ceremony called Respecting the Dead, or Responding to the Taunt. Nasomi had witnessed it once in her lifetime.

Tiny green plants and tufts of grass mottled the ashen ground, signs of the new life that would be fuel for next year's burning. Tambo was right about the place being dismal and romantic at the same time. It made her reflect on death, desolation, but it also made her think of the life that carries on after, of the sunrise after night, of the impending rain after months of heat. She experienced again the emptiness of missing Mother, but she also felt the companionship of being with Tambo.

"Mother is buried there," Nasomi said, pointing to a distant group of mounds.

He took her hand in his and squeezed gently, saying nothing, and Nasomi loved him for that. Their sandals crunched the ashes beneath as they walked, the rising particles clinging to and blackening their feet. He listened to her.

"I sat by the grave the entire day after we threw her body in, but I didn't dare look in. Father and Naena insisted that we go home, but I stayed, even though I didn't want to look at her body. I hated myself for it, but I had no strength. I didn't want her to be dead. I wanted her to rise up from the hole and say 'Let's go home, my daughter, I am well now.' She used to say that a lot. 'I am well now.' Even when it was clear to see she wasn't. I guess she wasn't strong enough for death.

"It stunk, the grave. There were four other bodies in there. Balsams and other noisome herbs, and a hint of rot from some older corpse or two. But I didn't move, the stink was nothing compared to the pain in my heart.

When evening came, so did the people, families of the dead, Father, Naena, too. For the first time, I understood the collective grief. We were all one person when it came to our dead loved ones. Father cried, Naena cried, I cried and I couldn't stop even after we covered the grave. We embraced each other, embraced the other families. Father had to carry me home and I cried all night. All I wanted was to die, too. Being alive was painful."

"I am glad you didn't," he said.

She chortled. "I am glad I didn't, either."

They walked past mounds, the older ones as ashen as much of the cemetery from burned grass, the newer ones barren and awaiting the Taunt of the *Tumina*. These underground spirits were what gave life to what grew on the land, but they were sly spirits, too. They demanded that you had to till the land and plant seeds and water the ground to get any crops out. And even then, you'd be lucky if insects and locusts don't come to devour your crops. The *Tumina* also accepted the dead, ate up their flesh with worms in order to continue giving life to plants and to cause less trouble in the world. When grasses and plants grew on the graves, the Narites considered this a taunt, a spiritual jest by the *Tumina*. That was why Narites performed the Response, burning the cemetery out of respect of their dead and to say: we will not demand anything of our loved ones in their death.

A group of people, four boys of which the youngest looked five and the oldest fourteen, a teenage girl and an elderly woman stood beside a newly dug grave. The girl and the three older boys hefted a body wrapped in cloth and tossed it in. Then they moved back a few paces and all began to weep.

"Let's comfort them," Tambo said. They approached and spoke words of comfort to the elderly woman, praying the *Mara's* blessings on the family, wishing them well in life. This reminded Nasomi of her grief and it gave her the sincerity and kindness to give the children each a hug and to urge them to live a good life as they remembered their dead brother. Burial day was two days away, she could imagine how hard this would be for them.

"I must go now," Tambo said when they left the mourners. "Father would be looking for me. Let me take you home." He let her ride the horse. She was nervous, thinking the horse would throw her and Tambo off, or gallop into a ditch. But Tambo's gentle guidance eased her fears and she felt comfortable enough about riding by the time they got to Mokele District. He left her there and she walked home, rehearsing what to tell Naena.

From then on, she met with Tambo as often as four days a week. He would take her to places she would otherwise not think of going, some of which she had last been to as a child. They scouted for spots they could be alone: in the unoccupied cave houses of Kwindi District, behind stalls in the marketplaces, under trees and beneath bushes, and in the shadows of the towers holding up the aqueducts.

Once, he took her to the amphitheater. Dark clouds were gathering and rain smelled in the air. The wind wafted her skirt, prickled her skin with goosebumps. The amphitheater stood tall and majestic, and it looked like it was moving against the gloomy clouds. The gargoyles perched at the top, rimming the entire structure, looked as though they would pounce down. They were statues of previous kings and warriors of Nari, some of them winged or having limbs of lions. Nasomi's head span looking up at them, just as it had the numerous times she'd been there for New Year's festivities.

Tambo and Nasomi walked around the amphitheater, naming parts of the panorama of the city that revealed themselves. They stopped halfway around; he took her by the hand into an alcove behind a pillar. He turned to face her.

"Your eyes," he said.

"What about them?"

"They make me want to do this." He cupped her neck and part of her face in his palm, drew close and kissed her on the lips.

His lips were soft, full, ravenous with desire. Resistance welled up in her, but she pushed it down, let her own desire swell and meld with his. And as though the kiss unlocked the heavens, rain began to fall.

CHAPTER 4

THE CONFRONTATION

"He has a woman!"

A hard wind was blowing and rain slanted down in torrents. Parts of the house leaked. Nasomi went around patching the walls with tar. For the roof, she had to climb onto a rickety tripod Father had made for the purpose. If hunting for leaks was a tedious task, trying to control the ants was irksome. They bored through the floor and raided the kitchen in their hundreds. She had blocked their holes of entry but they kept making more. Flying termites had flown into the house earlier and died in scores. She needed to sweep them away. And a dozen beetles buzzed around the house. The stenches of wet timber, fresh tar, and dead insects were thick in the moist air.

She was already in a bad mood; this news wasn't helping.

"He has a woman," Naena said. She had returned from the market with some meat. She was drenched, her clothes clinging to the form of her body. She went to the bedroom to change.

"Naena, what are you saying?"

"I am saying that your boyfriend has—"

"I get that. I mean, are you certain?"

Naena emerged into the kitchen, drying herself with a towel. "I was boasting to some woman that my cousin had won the heart of some tribal lord." She sat before the clay oven, shivering in the heat it effused. "When I mentioned he was Tambo and that he wanted to marry you, she told me I was wrong, that he was betrothed to some high girl. She's already wearing her brideclothes."

"Nae, Tambo didn't say he would marry me."

"He might as well have from the way he's been around you. You remember Maampi? The girl with big cheeks, the one who burned down her father's house? She also told me the same thing. That not two weeks ago, Tambo was officially engaged. I asked around. The bride's called Reema, daughter to the Nyate Chieftain. She's my own clansmate! I've seen her many times, Somi."

Nasomi sat down, harder than she intended. Her hand was sticky with black tar, but she was too upset to wash it off.

"She's beautiful," Naena continued. "Her skin is as dark as ebony, smooth as midnight. She wears gold bangles on her arms and neck, and one in her forest of hair. Gold, Somi, gold!"

"He could have told me," Nasomi muttered, more to herself.

"I'm so sorry, Somi. This is hard to bear. I was so happy for you. I was planning to buy some fabrics and wool to start making baby clothes."

"This is not funny."

"I know. I can imagine how difficult this is to you."

"It is heart-rending. What should I do?"

"Go see him, talk to him. Tell him you know."

Nasomi couldn't go to him. He'd told her he would send someone to call her whenever he wanted to see her, or he'd wait for her on the path to Father's field.

She went there the next morning, but he didn't show up. It was two days later when a boy walked into the gate, hesitated, and said he had thought this was Nundu's place. That was the arranged signal. A few heartbeats after the boy was gone, Nasomi dressed up and rushed to the hill that separated Ninki Nanka from Nkuku.

Tambo was seated on a rock. As she approached him, Tambo beamed. "Nasomi," he said sweetly, standing up to take her hands in his. When he saw her crestfallen face, his smile died. "You look sad. What is it?"

She half-turned her body away from his. "I have something deep on my mind."

He touched her waist. "Come, sit with me and tell me all about it."

She sat, not facing him and not talking. She pursed her lips, trying to find a way to say what she had to.

He made a small laugh to make a light moment of the situation. "I used to put my thumb in my mouth when I was angry. Sometimes I'm tempted to do so even up to now, but I fight it. You should have heard how my siblings laughed at this, as if I wasn't the eldest brother. And I'd be upset more and suck more. It was a silly habit."

"Sometimes I have vivid memories of the past when I'm upset," Nasomi said. "As though they happened yesterday. I can even remember details I should normally forget, like a smell or what someone who was only passing my way was wearing."

"Interesting. That sounds deep."

"Right now, I can almost feel the hurt when my friend Des stole a piece of meat from her mother's pot and said it was me. Her mother was furious. Her skinny hands were pale from some disease which made her smell like dead people. She was using some kind of perfume to disguise the smell of the disease. I can almost smell and see her right now. She looked so mean and old when she was shouting at me. I can still hear her terrible voice: 'Get out of here, you little thief! If I ever see you again, I will hit you so hard with a cooking stick your head will come out from your buttocks.'"

"What?" Tambo broke into laughter. "She said that?"

"She was foul-mouthed like that. It was always funny when she said it to other people. But that day when she said it to me... The only thing that's stopping me from crying right now is realizing it was so many years ago. I must have been four. I never wanted to talk to Des ever again."

"Sorry about that. Now tell me. What's upsetting you?"

She turned to look at him. "You are betrothed."

He said a soft "ha", finally seeing what this was about. He was silent for a moment. "You found out?"

"It's news around the city, Tambo. And she is already wearing her brideclothes, do you deny it? Show me your band."

He lifted the left leg of his breeches. Below his knee was a white cloth tied around his leg.

"Why Tambo? Why didn't you tell me? How long did you think you could hide this from me?" Tears fell from the corners of her eyes. She wiped them away; they came again.

"I have wanted to tell you. The truth is I do not want to be with her. The thing between Reema and I was more of an arrangement between our parents, but I do not love her. It is you I love."

He took her hand and she yanked it free. "I am not a child, Tambo. Speak straight to me. I've been stupid, Oh *Mara*, I have been stupid."

"No, my dear. How can you say that?"

"I only see you at your convenience. I cannot walk into your palace gates and say 'I want to see my man.' Can I?"

"Not yet. But when I—"

"But she can, can't she? And your people will praise her and offer her wines and kiss her feet and talk about all the children she will have. If I dared to even come near to the gate, I would be kicked and spat on and called all sorts of names, even before I said anything."

"You're too harsh on yourself—"

"I am being honest. Tell me the truth here, My Chief. All you want is to fornicate with me."

"Nasomi! Please, it is not like that. You are my heart's desire. I knew I had found the one I could love, the one I could build my life with, when I met you. You wrenched my heart from Reema."

Nasomi stood up to go. He grabbed her arm and stood.

"You have to understand, Nasomi. My father is a harsh man. He wouldn't let us... I need to talk to him, to set things straight."

She opened her mouth and, at first, couldn't put words to the anger boiling inside her. "I am not the kind of girl who... Forget it. Forget me. Leave me alone. My life is not grandiose, but it is a life. I have Father and Naena to look after. I cannot waste it on this folly. Find another girl for your fancies."

"Nasomi. There's no other girl for me but you."

"You have a damn wedding band on your leg! And she is in her brideclothes, for the whole world to see. How long till the wedding?"

"First day after next Burial. Seven days from to-day. But that's not important. I will have it canceled."

"Is that so?" Nasomi found a sarcasm she never knew she had. "You will cancel your wedding to a wealthy, beautiful bride? For me? You will break down your engagement vows, go against the wish of your par-ents?" She felt like slapping him, and she knew he would take it. He was a gentleman. But he was a liar, too.

To her surprise, he knelt before her. "Wealth dwindles, and beauty fades. Nothing is compared to the love I have for you. I will cancel the wedding, and show everyone that I truly love you. Meet me here after to-morrow. At noon. I will have made things right by then. I will take you by the hand through the palace gate, I will introduce you to my father as the woman I want."

Noon of the said day came, and Nasomi stood on the hill. Tambo didn't show up. Lightning split the sky; thunder rumbled the world. Rain came. Tambo didn't. Tears came. Tambo didn't. She went home sodden and broken.

"Where have you been?" Father asked. She ran to her room without answering. She stared blankly at Naena who eventually got tired of asking what happened.

That night, she dreamed Father died in his bed from his coughing. She was by his bedside. There was a young girl beside her, whose name the Nasomi in the dream knew but the Nasomi dreaming didn't. They both wept when Father coughed his last, died with a smile on his face.

CHAPTER 5
TAMBO'S CHOICE

The dream of Father's death persisted over the
next four nights; exactly the same: a young girl with her,
Father coughing, dying with a smile on his face. Nasomi
spoke to neither Naena nor Father about it. She spoke
little about anything else, anyway. She bit and plucked at
her fingernails, nibbled at her food, lolled her head,
sighed incessantly.

Naena let slip to Father what was bothering Nasomi. He called her and Naena to sit with him outside
when the rains stopped and the sun burned. Naena prepared boiled peanuts and wheat beer, and they talked as
they ate.

"He's a good man, isn't he?" Father said.

"Yes, Father," Nasomi replied. She gave Naena a
look of impending retribution.

"We were strangers to him but see what he did
for us. And Gani and Nas, the two men he sent to help at
the farm, always speak good things about him. They can
go on and on about his kindness, his well-cultured manner of speech. Not so his siblings, they tell me. You'd almost think he was born of a different family." He
cracked a peanut shell, tossed the seeds in his mouth,
chewed with patience. "If I'd known about his interest in
you... Well, I wouldn't have refused him if you told me
you wanted to marry him."

"You wouldn't?" Her eyes watered but she didn't
let a tear fall.

"I wouldn't. He's kind and thoughtful of others,
and, to add honey to a hot brew, he's a tribal lord. Imag-

ENOCK I. SIMBAYA

ine my daughter a tribal queen. Maybe you can go for
one of his brothers."

"Father!"

He laughed, then sighed and looked at her like he
always did when she had come to him with a problem. It
was a look of pride in her. "You're a grown woman, my
daughter. Your mother would have loved to see you grow
stronger each year. You're generous, mature, thrifty,
helpful. No matter our circumstances, I am glad you're
my daughter. I'm proud of you too, Naena."

"Thank you, Father," Naena said. "What would
you be without me?"

"Indeed." He laughed. "You girls bring joy to my
heart. Good men will come your way. The *Mara* will
bless you with good families and wealth, and lots of
happiness."

Both girls clasped their palms together, to indicate they received the blessings.

"Nasomi, heal your heart."

"I thank you, Father. I cannot weep forever about
it. I am well now."

"I hope you are. Now give your father a warm
embrace." They stood to give their hugs.

Nasomi felt better, the gloom of her brooding
was fading. She found herself singing throughout the
day, and there was a lightness within her. That night, the
dream changed: she floated through a majestic palace.
The walls were white, adorned with black and ochre
sketches of warriors, winged creatures, and red blobs
that looked like suns. She was in a cavernous corridor, lit
by bulbous firestones hung from the ceiling. Two people
came up from behind, talking. She couldn't hide even if
she tried. She was like a ghost there, formless, an unseen
presence, an awareness. They couldn't see her. They
walked through her and she followed after them.

"...is not just right," the young man said. He re-
sembled Tambo, but it wasn't him. This one was younger, perhaps twenty years old, and slimmer. And he
groomed his hair better than Tambo. "It just isn't."

"I hear you," the girl replied. She looked to be about fourteen years old. They both had rings on all their fingers. "It isn't like Big Brother to behave like this. I know he isn't into Reema as she's into him, but—"

"What? How can you say that? Of course, he loves Reema."

"Oh please, I know what I see. She's a duty to him, not a stars-bright-in-the-sky kind of love."

He laughed, with a meanness to it. "You're too young, Yana. A man can love a woman and still need... you know, a friend by the side. But this girl I hear about... She's a dirty farm girl. Tambo should not stoop so low. It just isn't right."

"That's just wrong, Kukalo. A man must be faithful to his woman."

"You're too young."

"Too young to see that you're the one who fawns over Reema?"

He scowled at her. "Watch your lips, Yana. "Don't accuse me of such things. We're on the same team here. We must expose Tambo... So that he sees the error of his ways and make him focus on his bride and royal duties."

"I am only interested in this because I want to see this other girl. We shouldn't take it too far."

"It's already gone far enough." They reached a door and he opened it as he said, "This is the one who will take us to the slut."

In the gloomy, smaller room — a storage room, from what Nasomi could make of it — a man lay on the floor. He jerked at the opening of the door, raised himself languidly. His face was bruised, an eye swollen. Nasomi recognized him as the servant who brought and held Tambo's horse when he came to see her.

In the morning, as she was going about her chores, Nasomi reflected on the dream. She was stunned when the people in it actually walked through her gateway. The young lord and lady, as well as four muscular men. They pushed forward the beaten servant.

"My Chiefs," Nasomi and Naena said, performing their acts of respect. A crowd was gathering at the gate.

"Which one is it?" Tambo's brother asked the bruised man.

The servant pointed at Nasomi. The muscular men stepped toward her as Father emerged from the house. "My Chiefs!" he said. "The *Mara* bless you for visiting my home." He eyed Nasomi, but she shook her head to indicate she didn't know what was going on. She knew but was too bemused to accept that her dream had been real.

"And you too, old man." the young lord answered impatiently. "Get her quickly."

Father jumped in between the men and Nasomi. "My Chief! She's my daughter."

"She's been summoned," the young lady answered. "Father means to question her."

"Over what, My Chief? Perhaps if we can sit here and discuss—"

"We'll discuss nothing with you, old man," the young lord said, pointing a warning finger at Father. "Move away, don't try my patience. You know what this is about. You even cajoled my brother into giving you two workers so he can have a way with your daughter. Don't think I don't find out things."

"I would never... My daughter would never—"

The young lord came forward and shoved Father away. Father fell to the ground. Nasomi and Naena jumped to his aid, but the big men grabbed Nasomi, carried her off. She kicked and bit at them, and received a head-throbbing slap for all her efforts. Father, after being helped to stand by Naena, ran after her.

"Please, My Chiefs, let me come and talk to the big chieftain. As one father to another. I will tell him the truth."

He continued pleading with them as they threw Nasomi into a wagon outside the gate. The lord, lady, and brutes got into the wagon as well. Father followed at a stumbling trot when the rider kicked the two horses to start moving. "Please. My. Chiefs," Father begged, panting. "It is not. The way you think. Let me talk. Listen to me please."

Teeyana, as Nasomi remembered was the girl's name, said to her brother, "Kukalo. We must let him come along, or he'll fall from exhaustion."

"Let him fall... Don't look at me like that... Alright. Stop the wagon!"

One of the brutes helped Father into the wagon. His thanks came out as a cough. Kukalo waved him to sit and be quiet. The journey was conducted in heavy silence, Nasomi keeping her face down under the incredulous gazes of Tambo's siblings. Kukalo's was laced with fury, Teeyana's with cheerful curiosity.

The palace, in the heart of Kwindi District, stronghold of the Kepe clan, was as grand outside as it was on the bit of inside that Nasomi dreamed about. In all her life, she'd come close to three of the eight tribal palaces in the city, but this was the first time being ushered through the gate of one. White walls, wide cobbled paths, a grand lawn, tall rondavels, long bungalows.

She was lifted off the wagon and dragged by two of the brutes.

"Let her go!" a voice shouted, and Tambo came running out of an arched garden. "Kukalo! What is the meaning of this? How can you do this?"

"Father wants to see her."

"May the *Tumina* swallow you! This is none of your business!" He chased Kukalo around the wagon.

"Father sent us to get her—"

"This is none of his business, either. Yana, even you?"

The girl seemed ashamed.

"Let her go, I said!" He came to Nasomi, took her by the hand. "Get in the wagon. They will take you home."

"It is my business," another voice said. It was the chieftain himself, emerging from the garden in the company of three people. And *she* was among them: the dark beauty with gold on her neck and arms and feet and hair. She was in a seamless blazing white dress, extending from under the armpits to just above the knees. A white cloth around her right wrist looked out of place among the golden bangles. She was barefoot as was customary before a marriage. She stabbed Nasomi with her gaze.

Tambo, Kukalo, and Teeyana knelt before their father.

"Is this the girl, Tambo?" the chieftain asked.

"She's the one," Kukalo said when Tambo didn't respond.

The chieftain snorted. "Is this what has beguiled you? You have closed your eyes, shut your senses. Is this the woman who made you sneak out of the yard?"

Tambo didn't answer. He kept his face down, and Nasomi could see he made a fist that slightly trembled.

"Please, my love," the Bride said. "Tell me this is not true."

"Stand up!" Chieftain Go said his children. He pointed at Tambo. "You remain on your knees until you find your mouth." Kukalo and Teeyana stood and went to their father's side.

"You," the chieftain said to Nasomi's father. "Sapato is your name, is it not?"

"It is, My Chief," Father replied. He looked unsure of whether to kneel or remain standing.

"I make sure to find out things about people who vex me. First you take my land, and now you want to take my son."

"I would do no such thing, My Chief. I didn't know... It is not that way. It is only a misunderstanding."

"I was disturbed last night when I heard about it. The way I hear it, you offered her to fornicate with him while you used some of his workers to dig around your garden for you. You know it is against our deep traditions for a man to do this, especially before his marriage. The shame it has brought upon my house!"

Father gasped. "I would never lose my dignity in such a manner. What I have, I worked for with my own hands. Your son here is a good man, and he did what he did out of the kindness of his heart. My daughter would never do such as she is accused of. I have raised her in a proper way."

"Not proper enough from what I can see. The moment I saw you, I knew you were a man of trouble. This—" he waved in the air with both hands — "confirms it. I will tell you; I am a man of instinct, I follow it. I rise above my enemies because of it."

"Tambo, how could you?" the bride said. "It's not like you. I love you so much. Please tell me it's not true."

"It's not true, Reema," Tambo said. "Ask her. Nasomi, have I ever lain with you?"

"Not at all, My Chief."

"She might be lying," Kukalo said.

"Shut up!" Tambo said. He pointed at Kukalo. "You have a foul mouth, boy. I will get my retribution. Don't think I don't see your scheming."

"I will have no fighting amongst you," the Chieftain said.

"But you have been seeing her?" Reema asked. "Be truthful to me. My heart is not at peace here."

"Father," Tambo said. "Father, I will speak truly, and defend myself in this matter."

"I would expect nothing less. I am a man of discipline, and I require it of my children as of anybody else. Because I want you to see my fairness in this, and my arm of wrath on these people who have come to perturb our lives. I, Chieftain Shikepe Go, will not—"

"I cannot marry Reema."

His father choked and coughed. Reema screeched. She went to stand before him. "Tambo! The wedding is tomorrow night!" She grabbed him by his garment, shaking him. "What are you saying?"

"Silence, Reema!" Tambo shouted. The shock that broke her face was evidence that she wasn't accustomed to Tambo speaking in such a manner.

"What is the meaning of this?" Tambo's father demanded.

"You want the truth, Father, and I am done pretending. It is not Reema I want."

"You will throw your wife for this worm?"

"She is not a worm, Father," Tambo said.

"This can't be Tambo, my own son. Speak again, but watch what you say this time."

"I have always respected you, feared you. I have obeyed all your desires, fulfilled your wishes above my own. Your hand of discipline has been heavy on me, and I have done all I can to please you. But will you not understand this one desire of mine? It is customary among us for a man to seek his own wife."

"You want *her*? Has she bewitched you?"

"She is a witch!" Reema cried. "That's what she is. She must be taken to the streets and flogged! Stoned! She must vomit all the evil powers she has accrued. She must release my husband!"

"She is no witch!" Tambo snapped. "Keep your mouth shut and watch what you say. Don't deny you haven't understood how I feel about you."

"Tambo, you have loved me always." She fell to her knees, tugging at his garments, sobbing loudly. He wrenched her hands from him but she held him again. "That's all I know, that you have loved me. You have told me so."

"Get these filthy people out of my sight," Chieftain Go said. "See how they divide my family. No, take them to prison. I will speak to a Justice to grant a punishment so big—"

"Father, please—" Tambo said.

"No! You must see your folly in this. You might be my heir, but I will not fail to discipline you right. I am your father and you will listen to me."

"Father, listen—"

"Were we foolish in putting you together? Will you have not become heir to two inheritances? Will you throw it all for the dry bosom of a peasant? Your mother

and I were delighted when you fell in love with Reema.
We were happy with our arranging her for you. Your
mother mustn't return to this foolishness. You will cause
her only grief. This ends now."

"My heart is set; I will not marry Reema. We
have all known she is bad-tempered, lazy, and will not
make a good wife."

Reema wailed. She rolled onto the ground, soil-
ing her brideclothes.

The Chieftain shook with fury. "Your words,
son... I don't know you anymore. A few days have
changed you. I regret you are a son of mine."

"Because I want to choose my own wife?"

"Because you talk to me like I am a fool. Because
you defile our honor with your foolish escapades. If your
brother hadn't brought this to me, the whole city would
be whispering shame on my back. Because you dishonor
the name of Go by refusing the hand of a chief's daughter. Because you embarrass me before our servants, before a peasant farmer and his tramp daughter."

"Father, I am my own man now—"

"You think so, don't you?" The chieftain turned
around. "I will not have you as my heir, then. I denounce
you and replace you with your brother Kukalo."

Nasomi saw a glimmer in Kukalo's eyes.

"Father, this is harsh. And you have not taken
time to listen to me."

"You listen. Make your choice before the next
watch," his father replied without turning to face him.
"Marry your bride or forfeit your inheritance." He
walked away.

Tambo stood and went to Nasomi. He held out
his hand to her. "I choose you," he said. "If you will
choose me."

For a moment, it seemed there were only the two
of them there. The shouts and scuffle that arose, Kukalo
diving to the aid of the bride, the chieftain walking away
from all the trouble, Nasomi's father calling her name...
It all seemed to be in another palace, like a fading dream

upon waking. There was only Tambo and her. Fear, shame, regret weighed down heavily on her. But also, there was a sliver of certainty. She took his hand and let him pull her toward the gate.

She said to him, "I didn't mean for... I am so sorry... I didn't want this... I shouldn't have let you kiss me."

Tambo walked fast, pulling her to quicken her pace. "It only shows what is truly in his heart, what kind of man he is. I care not for the inheritance anymore."

"You do not?"

"No. Let them keep it, and may the depths swallow it all. Let them call us names if they want. We will live happily."

It was a strange moment to smile, but she did. They were outside the gate now. "Are you sure you know what you're doing?" she said.

He stopped and undid the cloth around his leg, tied it around her wrist. "On this day, Nasomi, daughter of Sapato, I bind myself to you until we are wed, and for all time till I die."

Nasomi took off her sandals. "Tomorrow I'll find me some brideclothes, and a white band for you."

CHAPTER 6
BECAUSE OF THE DREAMS

Tambo sold one of his rings, the one with the malachite gem, to a hard-bargaining merchant for ten copper coins. The coins were sufficient to purchase an abandoned shack in the shadow of the wall in Kowasa District, some timber, tar, stones, canvas, and the labor for the shack's repair. The four laborers, who comprised an elderly carpenter, two teenage boys, and one young woman, replaced much of the timber, roofing canvas, and floor stones and tarred the gaps by sunset in a single day.

The smell of rotten timber and moss lingered, and the young woman went and came back with bottles of opopanax and lavender. Nasomi sprinkled the perfumes with her fingers onto the floors and walls of the two rooms of the shack, and the result was something she could tolerate for a while.

The pit latrine outside was unusable. The carpenter said he would come back in two days with the boys to desludge it. Tambo made a disgusted face at the suggestion and opted to have it buried and covered up. He went to ask a neighbor, a short talkative man, if he and Nasomi could be using their latrine. The neighbor asked for money. Tambo promised to pay him three copper coins.

He sold his second ring, amethyst, to buy her better brideclothes, a thick straw mattress, two woolen blankets, a bundle of smaller stones to cover gaps on the floor, and a bundle of dry fish.

"You're not going to sell all your rings, are you?" Nasomi asked him.

"I'm not a lord anymore. We might as well use their value for what we need until we find some source of income."

"What if your father changes his mind and brings you back?"

"That man? Only if I grovel at his feet, roll on the floor a few times, shed gallons of tears. And I'm not going to do that."

He sold the tanzanite ring to have the clay oven and chimney repaired, to buy glazed clay pots, some clothes for himself, palm oil, and dry foods: sweet potatoes, biltong, yam, ground corn, beans. Enough to keep them for three months.

He didn't tell her what he did with the money from the sale of the fourth ring, the one with a lapis lazuli stone. He said, smiling, "It's a secret. For now. You will see it soon."

He used the coins from the fifth ring, of tourmaline, to "urge" a marriage priest to conduct the pre-wedding teachings and rituals. The priest was a spindly, large-nosed Indas man by the name of Gres. "This exceeds the customary price," Gres said when Tambo laid the coins before him, and he and Nasomi sat opposite the priest on low stools. "And it is customary for both of you to come with one or two family members."

Tambo replied, "We're just the two of us. No family."

"No one doesn't have a family. Even if you were a lonely flower, there must be some grass and other plants growing around you. Wise friends or any friends at all, if you're so desperate. Neighbors, maybe. Anyone who can speak well of you."

"We have no one," Tambo said. "Look..." He showed the priest the marks on his fingers where the rings had been and narrated his story. In the end, he said, "I have no family, no friends, no grass around me."

"I have heard of you," Gres said.

"You have?"

"It's not every day that fathers denounce their sons. People are talking about it, you being a lord's son." He looked at both of them for a long time, debating within himself. Finally, he picked up all the coins and flashed them a smile. "I always say love is incomplete without freedom. You have chosen freedom, love. I respect that. I will be your priest."

On their way home, Nasomi said she would go visit Naena, guessing that Father would not be home. Tambo went to finish up the small garden he had started.

As Nasomi entered the gateway, Naena ran up to her and gave her a tight embrace. "Somi! You look healthy."

Nasomi laughed. "Really? Not thinner? I've been struggling, you know."

"Come, sit with me. Talk to me." She offered Nasomi her favorite stool.

"I never thought I'd be a stranger in this home," Nasomi said.

"No, Somi. This is always your home. Wherever are you staying now?"

"A little house in Kowasa."

"Little?"

"Little. Tambo never went back to collect any clothes or money. His father was serious about cutting off ties with him."

"This is sad, Somi. I never imagined. I thought you would be in a mighty house right now, servants running around to your every whim."

"I can only wish so. But we're getting by. The wedding is in five days."

"I must come."

"Will Father let you? He must hate me now."

Naena patted Nasomi's hand. "He can never hate you. He is only disappointed, but he loves you. You should wait for him; I know he would love to see you."

"I don't know if I can face him today. I feel guilt the size of a cow in my belly. I know I betrayed him and all he ever taught me, but I also love Tambo so much. I don't know what to do now."

"He would understand."

"How is he taking it?"

"Coughing a lot. He hasn't talked about you since he came back with the news that you ran off with 'that boy'. But he talks to himself. He mentions your name, in his sleep also. He's become awfully quiet. He eats, works the farm, baths, sleeps, whispers to himself."

"Would you tell him how sorry I am? That I didn't mean for this to happen?"

"I'll try. But come and see him, too. Maybe some days after the wedding. The weight of it would have passed."

"I can only hope so."

"You're being too dark, Somi. It's just a tough moment. It will pass."

"I am afraid, Nae. So afraid."

"Of what?"

"Of Father never forgiving me. And of Tambo leaving me. He's been a noble all his life and all this is taking a toll on him. He tries to hide it, but I can see it. He's not used to hard work and little food. His hands blister easily, the food we eat makes him sick in the stomach. I am afraid he will get tired of suffering and go back to his father, and leave me alone. What would I do then?"

"He won't leave you Nasomi. He's sacrificed all that he had for you."

"I think I dreamed of his and my child. A girl."

"And it was one of those dreams?"

"Nae. It felt real." She wondered if she should also mention Father's death in the same dream, but it scared her; if the first part should be true, the second must as well. "The girl was as dark as him, and if I really think about it, she had his face."

"Then believe in that. He is your husband."

"What if he thinks I'm a witch?"

"Why would he think that?"

"Because of the dreams. They are getting real, Nae. I dream things and they happen. And don't say it's just my imagination. I know the difference between ordinary dreams and these... real ones. They come to tell me something."

"So, you're saying they're a sign from the *Mara*?"

"How am I supposed to know that? Last night I dreamed Tambo's mother was looking for him. And I can feel it is true. But how can I tell him without him thinking I am using divination?"

Naena stood and hugged her. "You weigh yourself down, Somi. Even when there are people about you, you think you are alone. Who you are, this kind and strong woman is what makes us love you, and if these tellings are part of who you are, they can't make us love you less. Only more. Tell him about them."

"Perhaps sometime after the wedding."

Naena escorted her partway home. "Do you want me to tell father about the dreams?"

Nasomi thought. "Maybe it's time he knew?"

"It is time he knew."

"Sometimes you know Father better than I do. Do you think he'll take it well?"

"You're just sad and guilty right now. You will see that his heart is still as big as before."

When she got back to the shack, Nasomi found Tambo kneeling on the ground, looking miffed. "My love!" she said, running to him. "Is anything the matter?"

"They took everything," he said, his voice cracking.

She saw that the door, rickety and full of holes to begin with, had been smashed in. "Who?"

"I don't know. They broke into our house when we were away. They took the rings, other things, everything..."

Nasomi dashed inside. Muddy footprints spread all over the floor where three or four people had rushed about the house. The beans, fish and sweet potatoes were entirely gone, as well as most of the biltong and yam. In the bedroom, the bed and beddings were intact but for a few mud splotches. The piece of cloth Tambo had wrapped the rings in and kept under the bed was missing. So was the wrapped bundle he thought he had hidden well, which was meant to be Nasomi's surprise gift.

"Who could have done this?" she shouted.

Tambo was still outside on his knees. He thumped the ground with his fist. "The little I had... This is unfair. The other rings would have paid for the wedding food."

Nasomi went to pull him up and together they went enquiring among the neighbors if anyone saw or heard the burglars. No one had, and the best comfort anyone could give was, "You have to be careful. There are thieves around here."

In the night, as they went to bed, Tambo seemed inconsolable and lay with his arms across his chest, scowling at the ceiling. Nasomi didn't know whether to touch him.

"My love," she said. "I am not a witch."

He turned to face her, his face shadowed, as the candle was on his side. But she could see his eyes. "Why would you say that?"

"Sometimes I have dreams, and they come true."

"Doesn't everybody?" He was still irritable.

"These are different. Exact. I dream of a cat passing by the gate, next day or another, I see it passing by the gate."

"Alright?"

"The night before Kukalo and Teeyana came to my home, I saw them in a dream, talking of coming to bring me to your father. I had never seen them before this, but it was true to every detail. I saw your home, the paintings on the walls. Had never been there before."

He propped himself up on his elbow. "How is this possible?"

"I don't know. I have no explanation for it."

"If this... It's a strange thing to have. It's like prophecy."

"Perhaps. I need to tell you this, my love. Last night I dreamed your mother is looking for you. And I think it's one of these dreams."

"My mother?"

"She has sent two men to search the city for you, to bring you to her. It could be this has already happened, but I think it is yet to. I saw the men moving about in the lower market of Kowasa. There was a procession of mourners carrying a body, so I'm guessing it will be on Burial day, late afternoon."

"The day after tomorrow?" He lay back down, looked at the ceiling for a long time. "We must go meet them," he said finally.

Come late afternoon of Burial day, Tambo and Nasomi moved about the lower market in Kowasa, scanning faces. A group of mourners passed, four of them carrying a wrapped body. The smell of the balsams clouded the air. The mourners sang a funeral song, and some wept. When they passed, two men approached.

"My chief!" one of them said.

"Wakani? Imazu?" Tambo said, recognizing the men. They touched their chests and dipped their heads, and he did the same.

"We're so glad to run into you here. Your mother sent us to look for you."

Tambo looked at Nasomi. "I know," he replied.

"We have been asking around, but couldn't find you. We thought we would start here, then onto Nkuku, then the Dragon, then—"

"Where's my mother?"

"She said to take the report to her at the palace gates every sunset."

"Sunset is nigh. Let us go."

The servants had come with horses, and they shared one on the way to the palace in Kwindi. Tambo and Nasomi shared the other. Tambo and Nasomi hid behind one of the trees lining the road near the gate as the two men went to report to his mother.

Tambo's mother was a tall woman with a heavy build, and a lovely smile. She held out a hand when Tambo knelt before her. He took her hand, stood up from his own effort. Nasomi touched her chest and curtsied. "My Chief."

The older woman embraced her, kissed her on the cheek. "I came home from a short visit and found I had no son. There is madness in this palace."

"Will he take me back?" Tambo asked. "Have you spoken to him?"

"He's a stubborn man. He won't change his mind. He says it's too late for you now."

"I don't need his wealth. I will make my own, and show him what I am capable of."

"You're just as stubborn as him."

"He's the one who kicked me out."

"How are you holding out?" She took Nasomi's hand. "Fear me not. I will welcome you as my daughter. All this madness will pass."

"Thank you, Mother."

"We have nothing, Mother," Tambo said. "The wedding is four days away and—"

"And I am finding out today?"

"It's not like Father would let you come."

"No, but I can send Yana over. She can bring some gifts, too. It's been a few days only, son, and you look so gaunt."

"I'll survive."

"No, you won't. You may not have a father anymore, but you still have a mother. I will not sit by as you drown in poverty. Wait here. Let Wakani bring you the deed to the house by the hill, and some wealth to keep you going."

"Oh, Mother," Tambo said, kneeling down. "I thank you so much."

"It's what I can do for now. Do yourselves a favor and sell the house, eh... your name, my daughter?"

"Nasomi."

"Beautiful name. Nasomi, Tambo, do yourselves a favor and sell the house soon enough. You know your brothers are spies for your father. They might want to give you trouble. Shift to the edge of Ninki Nanka maybe."

They thanked her some more and she went back in. Wakani came out a moment later with the said deed as well as a sack full of jewels and coins: copper, bronze, and gold.

CHAPTER 7

RETRIBUTION

The day of the wedding began with a promising breeze, birds tweeting in the scraggy trees outside, dozens of roosters trying to out-crow each other. Nasomi and Tambo woke up in each other's arms to a cool morning in the bigger, safer house. It was built from burned bricks, and it was so huge it was more like four rondavels connected together by covered passageways. The inside walls were plastered and painted with the Kepe symbols as in the palace, and had firestone torches hanging from hooks every few paces, which gave out a warm light in the night. The roof was high and thickly thatched; the floor compacted and smooth. The bed was exceedingly thick, comfortably wide and the right amount of soft.

Firestone was a precious black ore called *myama* by the people from who mined it on Mount Lupili a few miles north of Nari. Firestones caught flames easily from a single spark, and could hold a flame for years without getting consumed.

She went to the kitchen, to warm the leavings from last night's supper in the large clay oven whose inside was filled with some firestones and charcoal. She practiced her wedding dance as she waited. The kitchen was a large, round and roomy space. It had already been equipped with seasoned clay pots, and a good supply of wood and charcoal. She carried the food for Tambo who still lay in bed.

"I could smell it in my sleep," he said. He sat up and threw his feet onto the floor and accepted the tray she offered. She kissed him and said it was time to go and prepare.

"Today is our day," she said.

He smiled, took her hand. That sweet smile of his that proclaimed everything was well. "I could never regret loving you."

When she stepped outside, she was greeted by birdsong, the smell of the ground after last night's rain, and the sight of the lush green hill on which children were already romping, a maze of houses, and the hazy amphitheater towering over the view like a giant specter.

She walked the beaten red paths of upper Kwindi, which maintained their hardness and were untroubled by many puddles or much mud. The world seemed better with her good mood: green looked greener; every hue, on clothes or tree barks or on dogs, had mesmerizing depths to it. She basked in the glances of onlookers, quite certain they admired what a beautiful bride she was.

The wife and daughter to the marriage priest welcome her with song and ululation as she walked into their yard. They helped her prepare the food she would take for the groom: a whole chicken smoked over firewood, fried plantain, beans, goat meat stew, sweet fritters, and wheat beer.

Gres was in a restless mood. He bathed and donned his heavy white garment, draped with a red ruff, complete with bangles and neck chains of copper and bronze. He came often to where the women were cooking, making a comment on every food, saying it must be perfect.

"You remember the sequence of events? Repeat them to me," he said to Nasomi.

"I do. We will leave here at noon, walk to the groom's home. Along the way, people may give me gifts and wish me well. Those with me will accept the gifts on my behalf. When we reach the groom's place, the drummers — who have been playing all along the way — will start singing *The Sun Shines*, then I will dance through the door and find my groom sitting on the floor — and he shouldn't look at me till I kneel before him and touch his face."

"Good, good," the priest said, grinning. "You will do well. It is nigh noon."

Five people walked into Gres's yard: Nasomi's father, Naena, Teeyana and two young girls Nasomi guessed were Teeyana's handmaids. They bore gifts: clay pots brimming with goods, a mortar and pestle, gourds with their mouths covered with pieces of cloth, and little wooden bottles of perfumes and ointments.

Nasomi gave Naena a hug and did the same for Teeyana after a slight hesitation. She didn't know what to feel about Tambo's sister at first, but the girl whispered into her ear, "If Tambo can give up everything for you, you must be a wonderful person. Mother thinks so, too."

"Thank you..."

"Sister. You can call me sister."

Father put a hand on her shoulder. "My daughter, will you forgive me?"

"I am the one in need of forgiving."

"I made you feel like I didn't want to see you again. But this is your path. Everyone has a path. I want you to know that no matter what, I would never deny you as my daughter."

"I am so sorry for betraying your trust."

They embraced. There was an ululation and a *ting bang ting* from two drums being beaten as three women walked into the yard. Naena, Teeyana and the other ladies joined in the ululation.

"Ah! Let's get this young woman married!" Gres exclaimed, approaching to give Father a greeting. "A well-raised daughter you have here. Lead the way, Bride! This is your day."

The journey back to Kwindi was filled with laughter, drum beating, singing, and gifts. Nasomi walked ahead. Her father, Naena, Teeyana and her handmaids came immediately behind, accepting gifts from the random people who approached the procession. Some had only sweet words, some offered a piece of dance, some brought combs, spices, candles; there was a pair of new sandals in the mix, two dresses, a fleece blanket, and half a bag of corn. Gres, his wife, his daughter, and the drummers came behind, the priest shouting "A bride comes through, it's a day of joy!" and the others singing songs of love, growth, family.

Clouds blocked the sun, but the *Mara* were good to her today. Only a few drops of rain fell from the sky, little pieces of cold spattering Nasomi's face and arms. It was all wonderful for her.

Tambo was seated on the kitchen floor when she entered. He was dressed in a khaki robe, hemmed with deep brown leather. His chin was cleanly shaven and his hair cropped and combed. He smiled for her. "I knew it was you when I heard the music," he said in a loud whisper. He faced down and kept silent when Gres led the family members inside. They laid the gifts around Tambo.

"Begin," Gres said, and as though the drummers outside sensed it was time, they switched to *The Sun Shines*, called the "Bride's song" throughout Nari. It was a fast *pam pam pam pam* and a *bang bang bang*, mixed with various fast and slow timbres of the drums. Nasomi gyrated her waist as she slowly bent her knees to the ground when the women sang over and over again:

The sun shines
The sun shines today

And she waved her arms as her knees touched the ground, moving her hips still.

The sun shines
On this house today
The sun shines
Two people are become one

She moved on her knees toward Tambo, touched his face, and rolled up the hem of his robe till the white band tied to his shin was exposed. She unknotted it, showed it to Gres. "Say the words," the priest urged.

"Tambo, son of Chieftain Shikepe Go, I choose you as my husband on this day. Everything is yours, my care, my body, my love, and my future."

Tambo drew himself up to his knees. He undid the white band on her wrist. "On this day, Nasomi daughter of Sapato, I choose you as my wife. Everything is yours, my house, my body, my love, and my future." He smiled, added: "Even if a storm is raging outside, as long as I am marrying you, the sun shines upon us."

And thus, they were married. They stood and went into the living room, where the people who had remained outside, including some neighbors, came into the house. Much singing and dancing ensued, as well as drinking of wheat beer and eating of the wedding food. Nasomi and Tambo sat in the midst of all the celebration, holding hands. She loved the feeling as though everything else was distant and she was only with him in the entire house.

When the guests had their fill and the wheat beer was finished, they spoke their blessings upon the couple and began to leave. Tambo and Nasomi remained alone by evening. They wrapped each other in their arms and made passionate love, and fell asleep in exhaustion.

They were awake later in the night and talked as they lay snug in bed. "I did not imagine my life would turn out this way," he said.

"You mean you being a poor man?" she said.

He chortled. "That, but also very happy. You make me happy, Nasomi. My whole life has been about duty. Duty, duty, pleasing Father, behaving 'like an heir'. But with you, love and life flow—"

A bang interrupted him. It came again. The kitchen door was being bashed in. They jumped off the bed and covered their nakedness. As they rushed to the kitchen, Tambo picked up an ax. "Who—" Tambo started

to shout but the door cracked open. In walked Kukalo
bearing a cudgel, Reema, and a teenage boy that Nasomi
guessed was the younger brother Dembo. "What is the
meaning of this?" Tambo demanded.

"Retribution," Kukalo said. He pointed at Nasomi. "For her."

"You stole my husband, witch," Reema said to
Nasomi. "You will pay tonight."

"And freedom for you," Kukalo said to Tambo.

Dembo had in his hand a gourd. He lifted it to
show to Tambo.

"Whatever you want," Tambo said, brandishing
the ax, "you all need to get out of my house."

"The family house," Dembo said, rushing at
Tambo from the side. Nasomi couldn't warn him early
enough because Reema jumped her. Tambo's brothers
held him, grabbing the ax away from him. Reema
slapped Nasomi and pulled her hair. Nasomi threw a
punch at Reema's ribs, and she let go. Reema threw a
kick. Nasomi saw it coming. She grabbed the raised leg
and threw Reema onto the floor.

Tambo shouted. Kukalo had hit him in the belly
with the shaft of the cudgel.

"No, don't hurt him too much," Reema cried. She
stood and ran to him, but he pushed her away. "It is her
we must kill," she said, pointing at Nasomi.

"No," Tambo pleaded, wincing in pain. "Please.
Will my own brothers do this to me?"

"We're not killing anyone, Reema," Dembo said.

"Drink this!" Kukalo said, pressing his thumb
and finger on Tambo's cheek to open his mouth. Dembo
poured in the contents of the gourd. Tambo resisted, but
his brothers' grip on him was firm. They let him flop
down when he swallowed it all.

"Tell us now," Dembo said.

"Tell you what?" Tambo said, spitting and wiping
his mouth with the back of his hand. "What have you
made me drink?"

"What you have drunk is a potion from the mages," Kukalo said. "It wasn't easy to acquire. Ask Dembo how much I spent on this, and those mages are not easy to persuade. It's my brotherly sacrifice, to free you from the bondage of this witch. Now, Father will still not take you back as his firstborn son, but you will be free."

For a moment, Tambo was confused. Then he laughed. The laugh of a broken man who knew that even if they killed him, his devotion was true. "I am not beguiled, brothers!" He said "brothers" with spite. "My heart belongs to Nasomi."

Reema screamed out. "That can't be true. Give him some more."

"He drank it all!" Kukalo turned to her and tossed the gourd at her. "Do you know how much I spent to get this potion from the mages? Are you to tell me the mages are not powerful enough? No! Tambo is a foolish man, that I see, but he is not bewitched."

"I thought..." Reema said, her voice faltering. "It just had to be... It must be..."

"You thought wrong! You've made us waste money!"

Nasomi went to Tambo, caressed his shoulders. "Leave us now, all of you. You have had your answer."

"No one can bewitch me into loving them," Tambo declared. "Not ever."

"Please, Tambo," Reema said, tears coming down her face. "I only wanted to get you back, my love."

"I am your love now!" Kukalo said, grabbing Reema's arm as she approached Tambo. "He denied you and I took his place."

She yanked her hand from his grip. "I love him, and him alone."

"Swallow you, you serpent!" Kukalo slapped her across the cheek. "After all I am doing for you?"

"Ahh!" Reema held her cheek, glaring at Kukalo incredulously. "You slapped me!"

"And I won't hesit—"

Dembo touched Kukalo. "It's enough, brother. Let us leave. We've done our part."

Kukalo stormed out, shouting, "When I marry her, I will not fail to discipline her. She will know I am not as soft as Tambo. She will know! Bringing us all this way because she thinks she loves him. I'll show her love!"

"Sorry, brother," Dembo said to Tambo. He looked at Nasomi. "And sister." He grinned apologetically, grabbed Reema's hand and dragged her out. She was crying.

CHAPTER 8
THE GIRL IN THE DREAM

They all took to calling Nasomi's pregnancy "the Girl in the Dream": Tambo, Naena, Teeyana and Father, even the neighbor woman who came over once in a while to help out in the house for a few coins, though she didn't understand how the name came about.

"How's the Girl in the Dream?"

"She's kicking much in the night."

"When is the Girl in the Dream coming?"

"She's due for two more months."

Nasomi had told them about the dream and the little girl in it who had looked like Tambo. She left out the part about Father dying, because, given all the things that had happened, she suspected the dream to be a telling dream. Sometimes she felt like weeping, even though she had not dreamed it again for many months now. But how does one mourn for someone who has not died yet? Not knowing if there was anything she could do about it was what bothered her the most.

Perhaps cherishing her relationship with her father was the best she could do. When she was with him, she watched him with a deep fascination. How he spoke, moved his head, twiddled his hands. What a wonderful man he was.

She thought often: Everyone dies, and his time will come, one way or the other, whether as in the dream or not. To celebrate his life is the most important thing.

"I have a name already for her," Tambo had said. "But I will keep it till she's born." It was bad luck in Narite tradition to speak out loud a child's name before it was born, even if it was just a proposed one.

"I know it will be a good name," Nasomi replied. She didn't mind waiting. "But what if it's a boy?"

"I have a name prepared for him. But I believe it's a girl. Your dreams portray true things."

The only telling dream she'd had since that one was of a large wagon carrying stones down the road near the house. The wagon broke a wheel, tilted, and the stones tumbled off. Then rain poured down heavily, and the deep mud made it impossible to remove the wagon for five days.

When Teeyana visited one day and said a wagon blocked the road, Nasomi said, "It will rain today."

And it did a few hours later.

Teeyana visited often, bringing gossip and gifts. She would sit with Nasomi on a reed mat outside the house when it wasn't raining, and they would watch the birds fly into and out of the senegalia trees in the back, name shapes of clouds, and talk about daily goings-on. Teeyana was a sweet, modest girl, easy to talk to. Nasomi liked her much that it didn't long to tell her about the telling dreams.

"Did you have any more?" she would ask at her next visit.

"Not since the wagon one."

A few weeks after the wagon wreck was removed, Teeyana visited again, bringing with her a sack of onions and red beans imported from the kingdom of Wani. "I will not stay long," Teeyana said. "I must go supervise the sculpturing of a winged lion in Inkanyamba."

"The district or the King's Island?" Nasomi asked, receiving the gifts.

"King's. They want to adorn the entrance with a large sculpture from each of the eight clans. Father assigned me as his ambassador. Kukalo is unfit to do it."

"Unfit?"

Teeyana gritted her teeth into an apologetic grin. Nasomi knew that this had to be about Reema.

Nasomi was happy with her life, being married to Tambo, pregnant with his child. Deep down inside her, in the space of knowing, the place where she felt the *Mara* spoke to her through her dreams, she knew this was the life she was supposed to have. But sometimes the guilt of having robbed Reema of Tambo was heavy. She wished she could reach out to her, give her a hug or grovel for forgiveness, remind her she was beautiful, queenly and could have a wonderful life. Nasomi wished she could have a good telling dream for Reema, one about a good future.

But she might be the last person Reema would want to talk to. "It's well, Yana. You can tell me about it."

"She's gone."

Nasomi touched her heart.

"I mean she's left the city. Everyone thinks so. She snuck out of Kukalo's house two nights ago. Ran away with most of his wealth."

"You're telling me?"

"Copper, bronze and gold. She all but took everything. How she managed to do that without people in the house or in the entire palace knowing is... well, amazing. She's always been too clever for him."

"Kukalo used to beat her. Maybe she's had enough of that."

"Kukalo can be a brute sometimes. But Reema — she's hardheaded. She is clever. She can use any bad circumstance to her own advantage. Like a hyena, you see. You know that saying: Hyena will eat black and shit white? They quarreled much, those two, and he would say bad things to her, and she would accept it all without shedding a tear. Then she would tell him something that has the whole palace snickering behind his back, and in the morning she would cook him the best meal and tell him she loved him. He was smitten with her in such moments. He didn't see this coming."

"You think she was planning this?"

"No one knew, but it makes sense now, if you think about it. Nothing happens around Reema that she hasn't planned, or that she won't include into her plan."

"She probably has gone far enough."

"I think so. She wouldn't be foolish to still be in the city. Kukalo has sent spies around, but she went with four servants, three horses, and a wagon. I don't think he'll ever find her."

When Teeyana left, Nasomi tried to distract herself with chores, but she couldn't put Reema off her mind.

In the evening, Tambo arrived with the sweat and smile of a man satisfied with his work. He was getting darker from all the hard work in the sun. And slimmer. Farm work was not something he was used to, even after all these months, but he was a dedicated man. He tilled and weeded and scythed despite the toll it had on him. She knew he never wanted to show off any weakness. She loved him for that.

He set down a hoe and ax off his shoulders, came to give her a kiss on her forehead. "Almost done," he said. "We will finish the clearing tomorrow and we can start creating the mounds for planting."

She nodded, offering a smile. "Take a bath and I will serve you supper."

He stretched and cracked his neck and fingers. "Ooh, I'm exhausted. Some beer would do me some good too. I'm in the mood for singing."

Nasomi laughed. "What?"

"I want to drink and sing. For you and the Girl in the Dream. I can sing, you know."

"Well, if you call it singing... But I take what I am given."

He reached to pinch her and she dodged. "I'll show you how well I can sing, woman. But first I must be inebriated." He made gestures in the air. "That's when the voice comes out well."

"Ha! I am thinking to take some, too. For hearing well."

He laughed as he made his way to the bathroom.

"Yana came," she said, walking to the bathroom door to watch him undress. "She brought some onions and beans for us."

"I'm glad. She's always been a good sister. How is she? I have missed many of her visits."

"She's well. Busy with a project at the King's Palace."

"Mhmm. Good, good."

"She told me some news." As she relayed the news about Reema, Tambo listened with a mature attentiveness, lifting his hand to scratch at his head every few heartbeats.

When she was done, he came to her, held her on her shoulder and offered a wide smile. "Forget about her. It is good she has gone. We have our good life to live."

After supper and a generous amount of beer for him and a moderate amount for her, Tambo got to sing. He had hummed numerous times before and joined in a few choruses during New Year, the Burning, and whenever a Burial procession passed by near home. But now he was singing by himself. His voice was breathy, halting, and he struggled to inflect some parts, but he sang.

He bawled out parts of *The Crocodile ate the Lion,* switched to *Two Drunken Girls*, lingered on the chorus of *The Half-Man Fell in Love*, and stood and stomped his feet to *Village by the Hill*. Nasomi joined him, and she laughed so hard she had to hold her ribs. The baby kicked.

It was a beautiful night.

Two months later, the Girl in the Dream was born. Two elderly midwives knelt before Nasomi as she lay on a reed mat, drenched in sweat, washed in pain. They coaxed her to push, and Teeyana and Naena were her doulas, each holding a hand. Her abdomen was on fire, her back stung, her bladder pressed and she was afraid she would spray the midwives with a gush of urine.

Then the pain exploded, knocked hear near unconscious, whitening her vision. Her ears rang and her head pounded as she came to. She could feel the baby coming out, and relief shuddered through her every inch the baby moved.

"You can do it, Somi," Naena said, caressing her right hand. "It will pass. You will be happy in a moment."

Teeyana simply held her left hand tightly, saying nothing.

One of the midwives began to sing, while the other said, "Push, my daughter. Give us the child."

Nasomi did. A sharp wailing rang in the air, and there was a collective gasp of joy. Someone shouted, "It's a girl!"

Nasomi laid her head back on the mat, crying. So much joy welled up in her she didn't know what to do with it but cry.

They gave her the baby to feed after they cleaned it. Nothing in the world, in her life hitherto, could encompass the pride, joy, and love she felt in that moment. Not the lingering pain, not the sweat, not the wetness. Not the scary uncertainty of life she'd often felt.

The others went about cleaning her and the vicinity. They helped her onto the bed, covered her, returned the baby to suck her breast.

When all was ready, Father and Tambo were let in. Tambo knelt beside her, stroked the baby. He smiled so wide one would think he would rend his lips. "She's beautiful. Just like the mother. I am so happy."

"What's her name?" Father asked.

Tambo didn't speak for a while, leaving everyone in anticipation. "Her name is Ramona. Ramona Mwanakepe Go."

"I love it!" Teeyana said.

"Lovely name," said Naena.

"Good name," Father said. "It means *whom the Mara watch over.*"

Nasomi said, "I couldn't think of a more glorious name. Our Ramona. Our daughter. I can't contain my happiness, Tambo."

"Neither can I." He held her hand. "We've made one beautiful baby."

When everyone but Tambo and Naena left, Nasomi fell asleep to the sound of rolling thunder in the sky. She had a telling dream. She knew it was a telling because she *knew* she was dreaming. She was aware of her body on the bed. She could feel her mind whipping away from it, making sense of what she saw:

She was a ghostly awareness upon a grassy plain, with a grey mountain on the horizon. She could float anywhere, into anything. She felt the rumble of the earth when she became a rock, the sucking up of moisture from the ground when she became a little green plant. She turned and twirled with the breeze. She matched with a thousand ants in file.

Someone was coming down a path. It was herself, older, looking like she carried the weight of the world. She had a staff in her hand, using it as a casual walking stick, and a large frayed cloak bellowed at her back.

From the opposite direction, two people ran to meet the older Nasomi. The first was a girl about fifteen years old, the second a boy of about twelve. The girl rushed and embraced her. "I knew you'd come back, Mother."

"I told you I would. You're so grown up so big, Mona." She lifted her off the ground, twirled her around, laughing. "And heavy."

The boy held back, looking down. He wore all black: from his tunic to his heavily-soled boots.

"Meron," she called to the boy. "Come to your mother."

He only looked at her. "You came to me, in my dreams."

"It was truly me. I saw all that happened, but it's now over. Come hug your mother." He came and she pulled him into a tight embrace. "Everything will be fine now."

"Where's Father?" Ramona asked.

"He and Djina are waiting for Mdua. I thought to come ahead. I saw you coming."

"Who are Djina and Mdua?" Meron asked.

"One is a girl. The other is a dragon."

When the Nasomi dreaming floated into the Nasomi in the dream, the world warped away. She was trapped in a smaller darker place, and she thought she could see grass threads in the dark, forming a piece of tapestry. She smelled sweat, felt a cold prickle on her arm.

It took a while for her to realize she was awake, lying uncovered on the feather bed. Tambo snored softly next to her. She jerked up to see baby Ramona sleeping soundly. She watched the tiny chest heave and fall. Heave and fall.

She smiled.

CHAPTER 9
A LIFE LIVED WELL

Nasomi's premonition of a dream to be fulfilled became stronger with Ramona's growth into a jumpy curious girl. Father got sick after Ramona turned three. He coughed much and had trouble breathing. When he didn't have the strength to go to his fields anymore, Nasomi went to look after him. She made Ramona stay with Tambo, but the girl cried so much he had to bring her to Nasomi.

"Mona, it is important that you stay with your father," Nasomi told her. "Your grandfather is sick, and I need to take care of him."

Ramona wailed and refused to go. "I want to see grandfather," she insisted.

Nasomi was furious. "Mona! You will go with your father or you won't like what I'll do to you!"

The girl hid behind Naena's skirt.

"Let her be, Somi," Naena said. "Father feels better when she's around."

"You don't understand, Nae. She can't be here."

Tambo held her on the shoulder and took her aside. "The field is too hot and boring for her. And she's crying all the time. She's better here."

Nasomi sighed. "I guess there's nothing I can do."

"She needs time with her grandfather. Even in his worst moments."

"You're right."

He waved at Ramona as he went away. Nasomi went back to apologize to Ramona. "I'm sorry for shouting at you. You can stay all you want."

The girl grinned and ran to her grandfather's bedroom, and he told her the stories he used to tell Nasomi. Ramona didn't seem bothered when bouts of coughing interrupted his narration. She sat on a stool or on the bed, entranced in the telling.

"She's just like you when you were small," Father said when Nasomi brought him his medicine and found Ramona asleep. "Do you remember?"

"I remember some."

"It feels like it's you all over again. All the questions... and she tells stories of her own, you know that?"

"I do, Father. She's quite imaginative."

"Nurture that in her. Never let her lose that innocence."

She didn't know if that was a jab at her or just an expression of nostalgia. Nasomi picked up Ramona, took her to her former room and placed her on the bed. She distracted herself from thinking by keeping busy: cooking, washing, mixing Father's medicines; but she often caught herself wiping off a tear.

Naena moved about the city, from one medicine man or -woman to another, buying various remedies. They all seemed to offer similar mixtures of herbs, with yellow justicia and gum acacia as the main ingredients. But she always went to look for more, just in case she found something different.

Whenever she returned home, she and Nasomi bathed Father, kept him warm, dabbed him with a wet cloth when he had a fever, cooked for him all his favorite foods, took him for short walks, nagged him to take his medicines. In the kitchen, they held hands as they whispered prayers to the *Mara* for his healing. Nasomi still could not find the courage to tell Naena about the dream.

The next day, Father insisted on seeing his field. Nasomi went to find a cart to take him there. The work went on well without him; Gani and Nas weeded and patrolled the field faithfully, and brought home the coins from the sale of the crops. Father remained in the shade of the cart, glad to be out of the house. He told Ramona of a story of beings who created an invisible city with magic.

"What is magic?" the girl asked.

"Magic.... Mhmm. Magic is doing something that is beyond what is normal for humans to do. If you could fly, that would be magic. Or if a horse could talk."

"I want a talking horse."

He laughed. "That would be scary."

"The mages can do magic."

"Oh, yes they can. The mages used to be a group of people who lived in the caves of Mount Lupili. They discovered what magical properties *myama* had, and they isolated themselves in the caves, creating a language of magic and weapons of fire. They never let anyone know their secrets or learn their writing for hundreds of years. But Kanguya, the first king of Nari, managed to convince them and they fought with him in his battles. Their tribe has dwindled over the years and now there remains only two of them in the entire world."

"Are they nice?"

"Are they nice? Well, Ramona, I wouldn't know. I have not met them. They stay in King's Island, protecting the royal family and studying their magic. They rarely come out."

"Can they fly?"

"From what I hear, some."

On the way back home, Ramona slept in her grandfather's arms. Nasomi bit her nails till she couldn't contain what she was thinking anymore. "I would hate, after she's become so close to you, that you would..."

"Die? Nasomi, my daughter, I would hate that so much, too. I desire to see her grow up into a beautiful, intelligent woman."

"I don't want you to think I'm keeping her away from you. It's just that... that... I had a dream, Father."

"Tell me."

"I dreamed that you died from this."

He was quiet for a while. "Death comes for everybody."

"I dreamed this before I got married to Tambo. And it was so real, Father. Like the ones Naena has told you about."

"Like the ones you had as a little girl?"

"What?"

"You used to have nightmares, and they frightened you so much you were always afraid of going back to sleep. You would describe such strange things you saw in these dreams, and you thought they were real. I and your mother did all we could to explain that they were just dreams."

She thought deeply. "I don't know why I can't remember that."

"Well, you were young. And to be honest, some of the things you described were surprisingly accurate, but I put them off as coincidences, and... after a short while, they never bothered you again. So when Naena told me of your dreams, I knew they were back."

She took his hand. "Father, I don't want you to die. And I don't know what to do. I am scared."

"Would you let me?"

"Would I let you what?"

"Die. Look, my daughter. If this is my time to go, I'd be glad to. I would never have asked for a better life than this, neither of a better way to end it. I have seen you and Naena grow up to be strong, mature ladies. Nothing makes me happier. And to see you marry and have a child of your own, what a pretty girl she is, I know your future is a wonderful one."

"I would have never expected you to say that." She sniffled.

"If these dreams are part of who you are, embrace them. From my perspective, and I am quite sure others would say the same, your life is beautiful. You struggle with these little things like dreams. And yet there are so many wonderful things going on in your life."

"Nae told me something similar."

"You see? You know my life, Nasomi. I thought I would be a warrior, I wanted to be one. Then I saw myself being a rich merchant, the richest in Nari. When the Gold Road became a call to adventure for many youths in those days, that's where I wanted to go. But life stood in the way. Sickness, poverty, living from scraps and having to take care of my parents and siblings. I thought all that was in the way, but when I look back, it was all part of my way. My path. My gold road.

"When I met your mother, I found my happiness. I knew I would give up a thousand dreams just to be with her. Life opened up for me. Every morning — just waking up became an adventure for me because I got to see her face, and hear her speak. Then you came along, and we got Naena from your uncle, and my world was complete. I thought I wanted ten children." He laughed, coughed, took a deep breath. "I realized being your father was one of the greatest joys to me. I have wanted to raise you the best way I could.

"Should I be scared that I am going to die? Maybe, and my heart rips open to having to leave you children by yourselves. But you telling me your dream has given me a chance to see that I have done all I can as your father. I have made mistakes, said what I shouldn't have, lost my temper at inappropriate times. Yet, I have known joys and fulfillments kings and queens long for. Mine has been a life lived well."

Nasomi leaned on his shoulder and wept.

"I am going to be with your mother. I am excited to go be with her, and I am sorry this is the time I have to leave you. But I know I have left you with a small farm and some wisdom to carry you through. Nasomi, thank you for your dreams."

In the evening, when Naena returned, he called her to his bedside and said, "Naena, thank you so much for being who you are." Then he slept. He was so peaceful a storm wouldn't wake him up.

"What was that about?" Naena asked.

Nasomi hugged Naena. "Father being Father. I love you, sister."

Naena smiled. "I love you too, sister."

Over the next five days, they watched Father deteriorate in body but glow in spirit. He grew thin, his clothes hung heavy on him. He couldn't speak anymore, and Ramona cried for stories. He touched the girl's cheeks and smiled for her. There was a glimmer in his eyes.

He died on a cool night, wrapped snugly in a woolen blanket, a hint of a smile on his lips. Nasomi sat at the edge of his bed, Ramona sat on her favorite stool in rapt attention, as though her grandfather were still telling stories, and Naena stood by the doorway shedding silent tears.

Even though Nasomi had known this day was coming, it was not any less painful. Her heart felt as though it would rip out of her chest, her throat was as heavy as a stone, and she couldn't cry it out enough.

He was buried with three others in the grave dug for that week. It was a small Burial as far as they went. But it was the worst Burial for Nasomi. She had not cried as much for Mother as she did for Father, not had as much emptiness as she felt now. Perhaps because this was like a finality, like now she was truly set to face the world by herself. Rely on her own knowledge, judge by her own wisdom. Even though she was a woman grown, with her own family, she felt like a child who lost her parents in a throng at night. And will never see them again.

Teeyana, Dembo and their mother showed up. They comforted her and Naena, offered gifts and prayers.

When they returned home after the Burial, Naena said she would be fine alone at Father's house. She said she needed time to find strength in prayer. Tambo, Nasomi, and Ramona went to their home in Kwindi. The house felt hemmed in, and even though nothing actually moved, it felt like the walls were closing in and would squash Nasomi. She couldn't breathe.

"I need some air outside," she said. "Hold Ramona, will you?"

Ramona rushed to find her sandals. "Ma, take me," she babbled.

"No, baby, stay. I will not be long."

The girl covered her eyes with the back of her hands and started crying. Tambo picked her up, shushing and rocking her. "Mother will be back, Mona. Come I tell you a story."

Nasomi went to kneel under one of the senegalia trees at the back of the house. She couldn't pray, she couldn't wish for anything. The scent in the air was a medley of rosemary from the bush nearby, gardenia flowers, and smoked chicken coming from a neighbor behind the line of trees.

Above her, a bird tooted and trilled. A nightingale. She was mesmerized by the many ranges of its song, like it was really singing or telling her a tale. Of a brave man who walked his road and married a beautiful woman and had a daughter who could dream things.

She cared for nothing, desired nothing but to listen to this song forever.

She felt a knowing sensation well up in her. The best way she could think of it was: a light tug deep in her belly, calling her to experience something new, to listen deeply, to understand more. That and the sweet aromas and the nightingale's song brought her great peace, and she was ready to go back into the house.

The tugging feeling stayed with her for a week. She came to understand that it foreshadowed a telling dream. The dream that came one night was of Reema.

CHAPTER 10

THE KWINDI AFFAIR

Reema sat on the floor of a rotting decrepit hut. She was covered in thick clothes but she still shivered from the cold. There was a swirling fire floating above, but it gave only light and not heat. The cold had power here. The cold here was more than a lack of heat; it was an eldritch force gnawing at any feeling of optimism, happiness, joy. Nasomi was a formless ghost, but she felt this insatiable sucking power.

Large vines had broken through the floor at numerous spots, some creeping up and cracking the walls, threatening to break the hut apart.

Opposite Reema sat two old men, pallid skin so wrinkled they seemed to be like melting wax. They sat cross-legged, the ground having swallowed their bodies an inch deep. Nasomi wondered how long it had been since they ever got up. Their garments were sparse, tattered and so brittle that when one of them lifted a hand ever so slowly, a piece of his cloth broke off and drifted to the floor.

"This is everything I have," Reema said. She gripped the bound mouth of the heavy burlap sack beside her, pulling it closer to herself. "I have traveled so far."

As Nasomi watched Reema, she was drawn into her, became her. She could read her memory: she saw the desolate road, winding through creepy places, stretching for lonesome miles. Reema's companions had died along the way: one to a terrible fever, another to a jackal pack attack. Reema had paid much of the gold and copper she had come with from Nari to sorcerers for protection. But she still lost the other two servants to bandits and the consequences of performing unskilled witchcraft. Bandits took her horses, the timber from the cart was all now strewn ashes from fires she had made to keep herself warm.

"We know," one of the sorcerers hissed. "Not many have the courage to take that road."

Reema's fury was red hot. Nasomi could feel it. "I am tired of losing. She has taken everything from me. I need to know you will deal with her." Nasomi could tell that Reema was thinking about her.

Nasomi found herself ejected from Reema's body, and she was once again an unseen presence hovering above the other three.

"We will," the twin sorcerers said in unison. "Have Gweuka and Loshui ever failed?"

"All I have are stories to go with. People have told me you're the best, and I know I have tried to find help from others. They've all been worthless, thieving bastards."

"We do not fail," the two said. "We will do as you desire. And more. Give us the price."

Reema didn't.

"We know what you seek," one of the sorcerers said.

"Do you, now?"

"Your own power, your own magic, death to your enemy."

"Anyone can guess that."

"And only we can give that to you. Because we know that when you're happy with us, you will come back."

"Come back all this way? With what I've been through? I don't think so. If you can just kill her, I'll be glad to give this entire sack to you."

"Don't doubt Gweuka and Loshui. Here is our gift to you."

A vine moved. It elongated to Reema, crept up her thigh. Then it shriveled and broke apart into dry flakes. Reema gasped. "I can feel it! What is it?"

"Your own magic to command."

"Is that possible? You don't want to lie to me, I dislike people who lie to me."

"Try it. You can make yourself warm, cast a hedge of protection about yourself, know if a witch is stalking you, and not die from poisons."

Reema stood up. "The cold, it's gone. And I can fly!" She rose two inches into the air.

"It's more like carrying yourself lightly than flying," the sorcerers said. "Don't use too much of the power on one thing. May we have the bag now?"

"Take it!"

The burlap sack slid magically toward the sorcerers, and they giggled like children. The sack got swallowed into the floor, and a blue-green vine crept up from where it sank in.

"Well?" Reema asked. "What about her?"

"We will make her suffer. This very night," the sorcerers said in unison.

Reema's triumphant laugh jolted Nasomi awake.

She could still hear it fade away as she gasped and panted. She shook Tambo. "She's going to kill me! She's going to kill me!"

"Calm down, calm down." Tambo held her. "What is it?"

"My dream... Oh, Tambo..." Nasomi shook. "I saw her, Reema, in my dream. She has consulted with powerful sorcerers and has paid to have me killed."

"It was just a bad dream, my love. Reema is gone."

"Tambo, this was a telling dream!"

"Are you certain?"

"Something will happen tonight. I don't know wha—"

There was a staccato of knocks on the wall from outside. "What is that?" Tambo said.

Tambo and Nasomi jumped from the bed. She pulled a cloth around her body as he struck a piece of firestone against the clay wall. It budded a small light which he applied to a lamp that was on the floor.

Something fell from the thatched roof. A small white rat.

Another came down. Five more.

Nasomi screamed and stomped at one that scurried at her. It was quick: it jumped onto her leg. Her skin crawled. Tambo gave her the lamp after he slapped the rat away from her. He picked a rug from the floor, rolled it and used it to hit at the rats.

When Ramona screamed in her room, Nasomi rushed there. Ramona was standing on her bed, screaming and pointing at the wall. Through a hole at one corner, white rats squeezed into the room.

As she lifted Ramona and ran out of the house, the rodents jumped at Nasomi's feet, sinking their tiny teeth into her. She kicked them away, but they were deft little scoundrels.

Tambo came outside, hitting at the rats with the harvesting stick as they flooded out through the door, through holes in the wall, off the roof, and through the garden at the back. There were hundreds of them.

"*Mara* help us!" Tambo shouted. "This is Reema's doing?"

He urged Nasomi to keep running as he continued to hit at the little creatures, killing several. Like a little army, they bunched together, following after Nasomi. She was the target, after all. She ran faster, Ramona in her arms screaming, "Ma! Ma!"

When she looked back, Tambo was covered in rats. He had trouble shaking them off.

"No, run, leave me!" he shouted when Nasomi stopped.

But she put Ramona down. "Go, baby, run to Aunty Naena," Nasomi said, as a river of rats flowed toward her.

"It's far!" Ramona began to cry.

"Just go, baby. We will find you there."

As the little girl ran through the night, Nasomi faced the rats. She kicked and stepped on the little beasts, making her way toward Tambo. They scurried up her legs, scratching and biting into her skin, tearing through her wrapping cloth. She lost balance and fell.

She shut her eyes, and resigned herself to death, as she felt her warm blood flowing out of the many wounds on her body. Still, the rats bit relentlessly. She screamed. Tambo was shouting curses.

The attack stopped, and the rats scampered from her. She thought she was dead, afraid to open her eyes. Something — a hand — touched and shook her.

"Nasomi?"

She opened her eyes. Tambo, kneeling beside her, took a breath. "I thought you were dead." He took off his robe, tearing it into three pieces, tying them around her left thigh and right forearm and neck, where her wounds were deep.

"How did...?" she said, testing her voice to see if she was truly alive. "They stopped. How did they stop?'

"I think it's the dawn."

The sky hinted the gray of a new morning. Shudders ran through Nasomi as she tried to compose herself. She looked at the house. Part of the roof had fallen in, and the lower part of the wall was riddled with holes. Something inside fell and made a cracking sound. Tambo indicated for her to stay as he went to check.

Dozens of dead rats lay on the ground; these were the ones she had squashed through her squirming and rolling. The rest were as gone as though they had never existed.

"They are gone," Tambo said when he came back outside. "Our house... It's marred... Can you stand?"

She tried. She was too weak and she slumped down.

He picked her up. He winced. He had more bite marks than she did, and he limped when he took a step.

"Your leg." Speaking was labor. She was losing strength to stay awake.

"It will be alright," he promised, though he winced again. "I'm taking you to a medicine man." She put her arms around his neck, and he limped away in nothing but his undergarment.

She saw neighbors appearing among the trees. They stood and watched from a distance. None of them stepped forward to help. It was the last thing she saw before she became unconscious or slept, she couldn't tell.

When she awoke, she was looking at a low thatch roof. She was lying on a mat, her neck and back stiff. Outside, two people were speaking.

"I am just a simple medicine man," one voice said. "Only the mages can deal with this."

"It will be impossible to get to them," the other replied. Nasomi recognized Tambo's voice. "Especially now that I am no longer a nobleman."

Nasomi sat up. "Tambo," she called.

He rushed in. He was dressed in a new robe, bandages on his neck and arms and a wide smile. "Nasomi! How are you feeling?"

She inspected herself. She was bandaged in a few places, and her wounds were dry and there was some balm on most of them. "I am well."

"Thank the *Mara*!"

The medicine man came in too. He knelt before her. "It is good you are well," he said, giving her a wooden cup. "Drink this."

It was a thick bitter liquid but she drained the cup. "Tambo, we must go and see the mages," she said. "What if more come? I think Reema will only be satisfied when I am dead."

"So, you heard us speaking." He wiped his face with a palm. "You know how impossible that is. Who are we to go to the King's Island and demand assistance of his mages?"

"We must find a way."

CHAPTER 11

TWO KINDS OF MAGIC

Ramona was astride Nasomi's neck, clutching at her mother's forehead with her tiny hands. "Ma, what is that?" The little girl let go with one hand, and Nasomi lifted her eyes to see where the girl was pointing.

"That, baby, is the King's Island."

Ahead, at the end of the wide road cobbled with white stones, a crystalline moat surrounded King's Island, separating it from the rest of Inkanyamba District. Across a wooden bridge, two guard posts stood at the head of a path leading to an affluent scene of high stone buildings half-hidden by lines of verdure.

"That's where we are going?" Ramona asked. "To see the king?"

"Yes, Mona. To see the king. And the queen."

"I don't know how you put up with her," Teeyana said, laughing. She walked beside Nasomi. "She's been asking questions the whole journey."

"With a lot of patience. With a lot of patience."

Tambo was not far behind. He guided two donkeys pulling a cart brimming with crops. He had all but cleared his fields of the pumpkins, corn, and sweet potatoes. When Nasomi suggested he leave some to sell, he said, "We need to catch the king's attention with this gift. Then he will help us. We will plant some more."

A shirtless, burly, ax-wielding sentry approached them as they crossed the bridge. He said, "My Chief" to Teeyana, touching his chest and dipping his head. "I am not aware you were coming to visit."

"I did not send word. I come upon urgency. We would see the king."

The sentry eyed Nasomi, Ramona, and Tambo who pulled up.

Teeyana spoke. "This is Tambo, my brother, and his wife. I assume you have heard of him."

"That's not necessary, Yana," Tambo said embarrassingly.

The sentry scratched the back of his head. "I may have heard a rumor or two, My Chief... Eh, you will pardon me, I will have to detain you here and send word to the palace. I just can't let you..."

"We understand," Teeyana said. "Make sure to emphasize we have brought a gift."

"*Ela!*" the sentry called to the younger sentry who watched from his post. "Cas! Come here." The younger sentry was prompt on his feet. He was thin but he carried himself heavily, trying to show off his manliness and flaunt his budding muscles. "Cas, tell the palace we have visitors. Two tribal lords who seek an audience with the king. They bring with them gifts piled up to the size of a mountain, to honor the birth of the prince."

As Cas ran to the palace, the older sentry introduced himself as Afiwe. He ushered them to his guard booth; he brought out folding stools for them to sit upon. As soon as Nasomi put Ramona down, the girl dashed to the edge of the moat. "Mona! Come back."

"I just want to see," the girl said.

"I will watch her," Afiwe said. "Nothing defeats the curiosity of children, eh?"

Ramona picked a pebble, threw it into the water. She grinned back at the grownups as though she'd just discovered the secret to happiness. She picked another one, threw it in. Nasomi found herself smiling. If only she could be as carefree.

"The queen has a child?" Tambo asked.

"Born yesterday," Afiwe said. "A big bright boy, I hear. It's about time we got an heir."

Cas returned as quick as he went. "You may come through," he breathed. He helped Tambo lead the donkeys. Teeyana took Ramona by the hand. Afiwe waved, and the girl waved back.

Birds flitted and chirped about the lively orchard on the left of the wide paved path. Butterflies fluttered over violets and roses and dandelions. On the right, set about thirty paces apart, stood a series of statues three times the size of a human.

"What is that?" Ramona asked.

"That is a golden warrior queen," Teeyana answered. "A symbol of the Ula tribe. The Ula clan are the smallest tribe in Nari, smaller than clans of other tribes, yet they are the most powerful. They are the ruling dynasty. The king and queen, and most of the rich people in Nari, are Ula."

Ramona nodded her head as though she understood. "What is that?" She pointed at a jagged pyramid.

"A mountain," Nasomi answered. "It is the symbol of the First Naki clan, my clan. Your grandfather's clan. Every child becomes part of their father's clan and tribe. So you are Kepe, just like your aunty Yana."

The girl made a happy gasp. "I like being Kepe. What is that?"

"A tower. Symbol of the Jaad clan of the Indas tribe. They like to think they are knowledgeable people."

"And they like strange names like Baan, Haan," Teeyana added.

As they approached the palace of white walls, tall columns, hundreds of windows, a wide and high staircase, and gilded embellishments, two figures in thick hooded grey robes came their way. One held out a wrinkled hand to signal them to stop. Ramona clutched and hid behind Teeyana's dress.

The other mage took off his hood and smiled, but it didn't make him less scary. His skin was drooping and pale, his eyes near to shutting, his hair was wild grizzled tufts. He reminded Nasomi of the twin sorcerers in the dream, although he was sprucer by comparison.

Nasomi had heard plenty of things about the mages, bordering on the legendary: They could fly, move things with their minds, sleep underwater for hours, summon the rains, be in four places at the same time; they ate fire for breakfast, they could see your soul, they were reborn after they died. At a younger age, she had imagined them tall, slender and sinewy, with white eyes and skin the color of charcoal. When she saw them for the first time as a teenager at the amphitheater, she saw only old shrouded men. But there was still an air of mystery about them: they moved with an agility that belied their age, carried themselves like they owned the world.

"Step away from the cart," the one with a raised hand said. He was taller than the other, and he kept his hood on. When Tambo and Cas moved, both mages walked around the cart like it was a rabid animal about to attack. From their pockets, they took out a pinch of black dust. They sprinkled it onto the cart, and Nasomi caught a glimpse of their strange tongue. It was whispered rather than spoken, sibilant, and it touched something deep inside her. So this is the language of magic, she thought.

The black dust they cast onto the cart and ground began to vanish in sparks of gold, till nothing remained. "Come with us," the hooded mage announced, turning to walk toward the palace.

The other one flashed a smile to indicate everything was alright. He beckoned at them. "Leave the cart. Someone will come around to pick it. The king will see you now."

The mages led them up the stairs, through a door two carts could enter abreast, through wide and long corridors bustling with servants and warriors. Nasomi gazed about, admiring things, taking note of anything set right. She walked into Tambo's outstretched arm, and she noticed he, Teeyana and the mages had stopped.

A woman was coming ahead, breastfeeding a baby as she ambled. She was in a flowing black dress with gold trimmings. Her thick braids were wound into a bun at the top of her head, making her hair look like a crown.

"Kaan, Thorro," she said. "Who are these?"

Nasomi and the others knelt.

"They came to consult with the king," the shorter one said. "He has welcomed them."

She indicated for them to stand. "Teeyana Mwanakepe," she said, looking at Teeyana. "How are your parents?"

"Quite well, My Queen," Teeyana replied. "They send their greetings. This is my brother, his wife, and his daughter."

"Brother? How has he no... Oh, the one who...? I did not recognize you." She touched Tambo on the shoulder. "You should wear your rings and some good clothes. How will people tell you're noble?"

"But I am not... anymore."

"Just because the man says he doesn't want to be your father doesn't mean he stops being your father. It is nonsense. If you had come earlier to me, I would have resolved it."

Tambo gave a short self-abasing laugh. "I feel silly for being so unwise."

"Come back when all this" — she made a sweeping gesture — "is done with. I will appoint you to a guild or find something befitting."

Tambo knelt and clasped his palms. "I am so grateful, My Queen. This is more than we came to ask for." She asked him to stand. "We are happy to hear of the birth of the new prince."

The queen sighed, an expression of exhaustion mixed with satisfaction. She should be in bed resting, Nasomi thought. She saw the queen's eyes drooped, her skin was pale, her movements languid.

"I want to hold the baby," Ramona said, stretching her hands to receive.

This brought laughter to the queen. She knelt down and let Ramona touch the child. "His name is Keyula, next ruler of all Nari. What is your name?"

"Ramona. I am a Kepe."

The queen smiled. "Ramona the Kepe. The prince will need you to be his friend and protector. Can you do that for him?"

The girl nodded.

"Good. You should visit often, bring him gifts and say nice things to other people about him. And he will do the same for you." The queen stood, looking in need of much rest. "He's out by the gardens," she said, waving for them to go.

The mages led the way through another door, and they came to a courtyard garden. It was like stepping into another world from the one Nasomi knew. Everything here was perfect: the rows of flowers, the hedges trimmed to precision, potted flowers lining the ochre cobbled paths. A fountain of a golden lion spewed water from its mouth.

The king was short and fat, with a dense beard. He sat on a large chair made of weaved reeds, alternating glances from a vellum tome in his hands to two young men uprooting a small tree. When he saw them coming, he beckoned to them. They all knelt before him, even Ramona. The king raised a slightly amused eyebrow. Bringing Ramona along had been a good notion; she softened everyone's hearts.

"Have you checked them?" the king asked.

"No spells on the gifts, My King," the taller mage said.

"Have you frisked them for knives, anything sharp?"

The mage hesitated. "Uh... yes. They are safe."

"Good," said the king, indicating for them to stand. He relaxed in his chair. "I hear you brought me a mountain of crops," he said. "It is strange that you would already bring gifts for the prince when the news is hardly sent out. How did you know?"

"We didn't," Teeyana said. "It is a coincidence. We came to seek your assistance."

"You have my attention."

Nasomi narrated her story, careful to leave out the part of her dreams. She didn't want to raise questions she couldn't answer. As she talked of the rats and how she suspected it was Reema who did it, she saw the king shudder and widen his eyes.

He stood up. "How can this be happening in my city when I have mages?" He pointed at the two mages, one after the other.

"We cannot be in two places at the same time, My King," the taller mage said defensively. There goes one legend, Nasomi mused.

"No, no, Thorro," the king said. "I know what you want to say. I will not grant the Mage Council to grow. There is already too much magic going on in the city."

"You promised, My King," Thorro said. Nasomi could tell Thorro was holding back fury. "Then we can be able to handle such matters throughout the city."

"It is not the right time," the king said, flopping back to his seat. "People will start getting the wrong ideas. But you can get behind this problem here. Find whoever is behind these rats. Hang her at the north gate. Let the whole kingdom see that no dark magic is to be meddled with, or there will be consequences. Say you agree with me."

"We are with you," Thorro said.

"We are," Kaan dittoed.

"I want you to be with me. I do. My hand of judgment will not relent on this. Go now, deal with this today. We have a celebration to prepare for. I don't want the citizens shaking in fear when they should be drinking beer."

The king provided a horse carriage. Nasomi, Tambo, Teeyana, and Ramona had to ride with the mages, and it was mostly a journey of thick silence and averted gazes. Kaan was smiling silly, trying to lighten the situation, but it made him look like a corpse grinning at a haunted victim. Ramona clutched Teeyana throughout the way. Thorro kept his hood up all the way, and

Nasomi caught glimpses of dark eyes accustomed to hate.

"What the king said," Tambo said. "About too much magic in the city. Is it true?"

Kaan laughed. "Are you afraid?"

"I am frightened of it."

Kaan grinned again like a daemon. "See," he said. "Despite all superstition, there's no such thing as dark magic. Strictly speaking, though, it's not the magic at fault. It's the intent that's dark. Can you say how the sun rises and sets? That's magic that we don't yet understand. Or when you take some herbs and are healed of a fever. We call it medicine, but it's a magic we have come to take granted of. It's all around us. The king is afraid of the use of it through divination."

Nasomi saw Thorro elbow Kaan. But Kaan scooted an inch away, continued talking: "Magic given by the *Mara* is sometimes beyond our comprehension, although we study it. There are a few people gifted with this understanding... and there are some people with a command to it; born with extraordinary abilities, you can say. For them, their power requires no external cost, like the way we do with *myama*. Or as in witchcraft, which demands the use of unspeakable things. The Ntwenu people are a good example of extraordinary magic. They can move through shadows, or change shape or run faster than the wind... without the need to throw gold or *myama* dust onto the ground."

"How about someone who can see things in their dreams?" Tambo asked.

"Ah, a Seer. Yes, I would say they are gifted. Prophetic priests, too."

"What of your magic?"

Kaan held out his hand to Ramona. "Give me the pebble, little girl."

At Nasomi's nod, Ramona unfurled her hand and let a pebble fall to the floor. "I want it to rise," Kaan said. He spoke a phrase in that strange language, and everyone watched the pebble. Nothing happened.

He laughed. "Majen is what we call our practice. It is never used for evil, but for the understanding of the world, the revelation and guarding of secrets, the protection of good people. It has been used for thousands of years and it is superior to witchcraft, spiritual healing, sorcery, medicine, fortune-telling, divination... anything that demands an exchange of something physical or metaphysical for a benefit. But Majen demands a price. Nothing evil, though. Only gold, or *myama*."

He reached into his pocket, brought out some black dust and let it sprinkle to the floor. "Watch. *Zhef'mi pami. Ima.*"

The pebble rattled on the wooden floor, then floated into the air.

CHAPTER 12
LOST TRAILS

Kaan and Thorro set to work immediately the carriage arrived at the falling house. They walked among the dead rats, sprinkling the black dust, muttering in Majen. Nasomi caught a few phrases: *Zhef'mi pami, dham'ni vhii eft'an, vha ao ahn.* The black dust turned into golden sparkles as it touched the ground, swirled and shot northward, fading like trails of shooting stars.

Nasomi saw a rat twitch. Kaan saw it too, and he bent to pick it up. He sprinkled dust onto it, demanded something in Majen. The dust gilded, fogged, and flew away through the backyard, between the trees and bushes. One of the rat's legs twitched, and Kaan leaned his ear to it as though it were telling him a secret.

Nasomi thought she could almost hear a whisper whenever the mages threw their black dust and spoke their language. The trailing gold dust was saying something. Pointing the way. Perhaps repeating to the mages what she had seen in the dream.

"Do you hear that?" she whispered to Tambo and Teeyana when another trail of gold burst forth and dissolved away.

"What?"

"A faint sound, like a distant beautiful voice singing?"

"No," said Tambo. "There's no sound besides the irritating words of the mages."

Teeyana shook her head.

The rat in Kaan's hand was now stiff, unresponsive to his Majen. He threw it away.

The black dust ceased to respond. The mages were all but shouting: *"Zhef'mi pami! Fumakwi? Vhaaoahn!"* Kaan wiped sweat from his brow, and Thorro yanked back his hood. He was skeletal. High cheekbones, round eyes, and a scowl that could kill.

Nothing was happening anymore. Kaan turned to say something to Nasomi and the others, but Thorro caught him in the robe and pulled him toward the carriage.

As they passed by, they looked exhausted. Thorro said, "Our task here is done."

Tambo followed after them. "How can you say you're done when you haven't explained to us what you have found?"

The mages climbed onto the carriage. Kaan, looking guilty, said, "Let me assure them at least, Thorro." He turned to Tambo as Nasomi and Teeyana came closer. Ramona stayed back, poking at a dead rat with a stick.

"You have to fear nothing," Kaan said. "By all indications, the ones who sent the rodents are dead. Or dying."

The carriage driver whipped the horses into action, but Tambo jumped in front of them. Nasomi had seen him angry before, but this was something new. Courageous indignation. He stammered as he spoke. "S-s-stop! This is madness. Y-y-you can't say you're going. You haven't sho-shown us how to protect ourselves. I demand you tell us now!"

Thorro stepped down and bounded to Tambo with a raised fist. "Listen here, you worm of a man." He grabbed Tambo in the shirt. "Do you know the things I can—"

"Enough of this!" Kaan said.

Ramona, who had drawn nearer, started crying. Teeyana lifted her up and walked away. "Let's go away from the bad man," she said. "It's well, it is well. Hush."

Kaan pulled Thorro away from Tambo. "You're scaring them!"

"We can't waste time explaining high truth to simple people. We have work to do."

Nasomi went to Tambo's side. "Why do you hate us?" she demanded of Thorro.

The question caught him by surprise. "Hate? I don't hate you. How would I even... I have things to do."

"The king said to help us."

He didn't like her response. "And that is exactly what we've done! Tell me right now what you would have us do."

"They want to know they can trust us," Kaan said. "We are the Mage Council. We will protect the people of Nari from its enemies. I will explain a few things to placate their hearts." He turned to the others without waiting for a response. Thorro didn't seem to like it, but he kept his mouth shut.

"Sorcerers often make use of familiars in their nefarious business," Kaan said. "The common animals chosen have, over the times, come to mean particular things. And in many ways, magic works differently based on the animal's characteristics. A tortoise is a sign that the sorcerer is patient with whoever has aggrieved him, giving them a chance to apologize or repay a wrong. A crow is death on wings, a rage that gives no time for discussions. If one has no protection, she or her family member may die a terrible death."

He paused to check he had their attention. "Then there is the hyena, considered the most dangerous in the witching circles. Only a powerful sorcerer can control a hyena, or even yet turn into one. It symbolizes domination, ultimate power, death and suffering to anyone the sorcerer considers an enemy." He smiled. "But all that means nothing to Majen. We can crush a sorcerer like a snail. Now we come to the kwindi, the white rat here. Like the tortoise, the kwindi is a messenger familiar. It is an announcement. Of a new beginning, of something following after. Usually something not good."

"You're saying this was a message?" Nasomi said. "We would have been killed! She wants me dead."

"Then you are not done!" Tambo said. "You must help us. How can we face what is coming if this was only the beginning?"

"The kwindi is not an easy animal to control, despite its smallness. Only the overconfident sorcerer would use it. Hundreds of them came by your home, I wondered what hefty price was paid for such a stunt."

All her wealth, Nasomi thought but didn't say. She was now debating within herself whether she should tell them about the dreams.

"You were not the targets of this," Kaan said reassuringly. "Your house was only in their way. That's our judgment. This jealous woman you talk about, she couldn't have done this. It's magic beyond ordinary people. If she paid much gold to someone to do it... Well, what kind of idiots would be willing to throw their lives in this reckless stunt?"

"She would do that," Nasomi insisted. "She is that kind of woman."

"You're telling me she traveled from here all the way to Arwomba—?"

"Arwomba!" Tambo exclaimed. "That's where she went?"

A heaviness dropped in Nasomi's gut. The place in her dreams. With the vines and cold and rottenness. Reema went that far, literally and figuratively, to exact revenge on Nasomi. Terrible things were said about Arwomba: it was a dark place, hidden from the sun, full of strange creatures and evil sorcerers. Monsters there romped like pets and children were born with one eye and a dead man was king.

"I can't imagine Reema would go there," Tambo said. "It makes no sense."

"Exactly," Kaan said.

"If it happens again?" Nasomi said. "More kwindi? Dogs even?"

"It won't. We have queried the remnant magic here. Two sorcerers, acting as one. A difficult task to accomplish, I'll admit. But they could command so many kwindi." It was almost as if Kaan was admiring that. "They sent the kwindi to other kingdoms as well: Aiyo, Shodishu, Kon's Brother, Sipo... My guess is they were announcing their ascendance among the witch folk. Like the way messengers are sent to proclaim the arrival of a king." He stood affectedly, lifted his head, mimicking an announcer: "'Make way! Make way, you damn peasants! Here come the sorcerer-kings!' But like I said, an over-confident stunt."

"What do you mean?" Tambo asked.

"Because they are dead. Or dying. This cost them all the power they had. Our task now is to search Nari for the witches to whom this message was meant for. You're not witches. We checked you." Kaan turned and went to the carriage. He and Thorro got in and the carriage drove away.

"They don't know what I saw," Nasomi said. "Even if they are right about the sorcerers, what if Reema tries to find another way?"

Tambo squeezed her on the shoulder. "We will be alert, my love. We can now run to the king anytime and he can make the mages sort it out."

Teeyana came back with Ramona and helped Tambo and Nasomi to repair their home. The work took them four days. Some neighbors came to help after they heard the mages had come by and declared the place free of witchcraft. They brought foodstuffs, new timber, and thatch for the roof.

As the city became filled with much drumming and singing to celebrate Prince Keyula's birth, Nasomi was troubled by a continual trepidation. She started at every shadow, every dog and cat that came her way, every noise in the night that sounded unnatural.

Tambo seemed satisfied at the mages' judgment. But there was a fear constantly in Nasomi's mind. She was in need of a telling dream. She needed to know, to rest her mind. But none came.

She performed many chores one after the other and jogged down a street to the edge of the district and back home every evening. All to tire herself out so that she could sleep. Otherwise, she would blink in the gloom all night. And when she did sleep, her dreams were ordinary. Some were nightmares about kwindi, bony mages, and a vengeful Reema, but none of them were telling dreams. She knew the difference.

After supper, she would go to the backyard to kneel under a senegalia tree. She would close her eyes, try to clear her mind as she focused on the scents of the rosemary, the gardenia, the falling leaves. She listened to nightingales, insects, owls, distant human voices. She longed for the tugging sensation in her gut.

On the seventh night, as she whispered pleas to the *Mara* to send a telling, and felt a fever coming on and didn't mind that a stone was grinding on her left knee, a sharp snap of a twig behind her snatched her from her reverie. She turned to find Ramona standing there.

"Mona? You scared me."

"I wanted to see you."

"I have told you I don't want to be disturbed when I am here. Go back inside. You will catch a cold."

"Can I kneel with you?"

"Mona, please! I need to be alone. Go back inside."

The girl shrugged her shoulders in refusal. Nasomi picked up a stick and whipped the ground. "Go back inside or I will whip you with this!"

The girl cried and ran to the house. A moment later, Tambo came out. "Nasomi. Please come inside."

Nasomi arose and followed him into the house. It was warm and she was glad for it.

"It is time you let this go," he said. "I don't like how it is affecting you."

She nodded. "I don't either. I am so sorry. I need answers so that you and I and our daughter are safe."

"We are safe, Nasomi. We have a life to build. We can't let Reema be between us all the time. She is gone.

She is not our problem anymore. You must free yourself from her."

She sighed. "You're right. I am free of her now." She picked Ramona up. "Sorry for being harsh on you, little queen."

Ramona pouted. When she looked up and saw her mother smile, a smile caught on her own lips.

"You can come to me anytime you need to."

"Yes, Ma."

"I have some news," Tambo said. "The queen is putting me in charge of the smithing guild."

"You went to see her? I am so happy for you!"

"She sent word. I will go see her tomorrow. This is our win, Nasomi. I have proved my father wrong." He paced. "He must see that I don't need to depend on him. He must see that I am my own man now."

"You already did that."

"But he must see! You know what I'll do? I'll send Mother a gift. A big gift. I'll send it over by a wagon, accompanied by a minstrel to sing her a dozen songs. And nothing for him. Maybe a chest of garments. Some furniture. A load of curios..."

He listed a number of things but Nasomi wasn't listening anymore. She looked around. "Let us move to a new house," she said.

"You want to move? But... But you love this place."

"Yes."

"The trees, the smell of things... We are about to extend it and make the walls stronger, make the thatch fence thicker. And I was thinking of building a rondavel at the back."

"I just want to move... It is time to start new things."

CHAPTER 13

THE SORCERER KINGS

The spark to the next telling dream came seven months later, when she was heavy with her next child. Tambo brought her a gift. It was a cloak. Long, orange-brown, trimmed with fur in the collar, two leather straps for fastening at the neck. The moment he unfurled it and showed it to her, she got a sharp feeling in her gut.

"It was meant to be your wedding gift," he said, smiling. "The first one, I mean. It was among the stolen things back in Kowasa, and I've been looking for the merchant who sold it to me. I finally found him."

She got it from him, held it up. It had a good heft to it, tiny intricate weaves, a smell of newness. And the unseen threat of a telling dream come true.

"You don't like it?"

"I love it, my husband. Thank you so much."

"You don't seem happy about it. Is it the color? I can get a white one, green."

She could tell him to do that, but he'd feel bad about it. And just like when she'd tried to separate Ramona from her grandfather, somehow she felt that no matter what she did, this cloak would always end up with her. "The color is good; it fits well with my skin tone. Here, put it on me."

He fastened the leather straps at her neck, turned her around by the hand to admire her. "It looks good on you. But if you really don't like it, I can have it changed for something else."

"I really like it. It is just strange to see it is real."

"See it's..?" His mouth remained open for the rest of the incomplete statement. "You dreamed of this?"

"Of it. In the future, when it is frayed a bit. I don't know how many years from now that will be, but I have it on as I walk through some grass. I remember a mountain in the dream. You and I had traveled somewhere... will travel somewhere, and will return to meet the children on this grass field."

"Children? Are you telling me that you know...?" He pointed at her belly.

"It's a boy."

He touched the back of his head, amazed. "Why didn't you tell me this? You already know his name, don't you?"

"I do. I can never be sure about these tellings, to be honest."

"I have been mulling over names for all these months, for both girls and boys. So, the name I will come up with is one you already know?" He paced about. "Well, you can't tell me, it is bad luck. I have to be the one who says it upon his birth. There's a name heavy on my mind. It could be the one in the dream. What if I changed it? If I chose another name instead, would that mean I have changed the future? Or the name I pronounce at his birth will actually be the name in the dream, no matter how I come up with it?"

"I can't say. It confuses me."

That night, she had a telling dream.

Reema. Angry. Standing akimbo before the fading sorcerers in their falling shack. They were neck-deep into the ground now, the vines around them were thicker, looking more like human limbs than plants.

At the end of two vines were egg-shaped bulbs, pulsating sickeningly, as if about to bloom gigantic flowers. They hadn't been there before, and Nasomi guessed they had grown over the years as the sorcerers were gradually sucked into the ground.

"Why is she not dead?" Reema shouted. "I have given you everything!"

"One. More. Thing." They spoke in unison, their voices whispery and struggling.

"Get rid of her, that's what I asked, and I gave all my wealth for that. What more do you want?"

"Come. Look. Into. This. Bowl."

A cracked bowl sprouted from the ground. Water filled it but didn't leak out. Reema, and Nasomi's ghost in her, moved closer and looked into it. Reema saw a reflection of herself. Happier, and wealthier, with Tambo next to her, kissing her cheek.

"Put. Your. Hand. Bowl."

Reema brought down her hand but retracted it. "I will not until you give me what I want!"

"Good. Things. Your. Desires. In Bowl. We dying. Need no wealth. You. Do."

A sack of gold and shiny gems sprouted out of the ground, sliding toward Reema. She touched it to check if it was real.

"All. Yours. Our gift. To. Bride."

Reema touched the water with a finger, then all the fingers. The bowl didn't seem to have a bottom. When her hand was submerged up to her wrist, something in the water pulled.

But not at her hand. At something else inside her. At her life, at her breath deep inside. She felt her joy was being sucked into the bowl.

Nasomi was no longer Reema, but a floating awareness looking down at the scene. Reema was screaming, trying to pull her hand out of the bowl, which did not move from its spot. She was changing. Wrinkling. Withering like a plant scorched by a searing sun.

Nasomi was now inside the sorcerers, both of them at the same time. She felt their sense of triumph, their success at having secured the final ingredient to another phase of their transcendence. This was what they had wanted all along: Reema's essence, the part of her that gave her beauty, happiness, and meaning.

Reema was the ultimate prey, the one in whom they found all the jealousy, hate, desperation and wealth to unlock their power.

Nasomi felt the sorcerers' power changing. Taking new form. One of the bulbs cracked and broke in a spray of black goo. A creature rose from the mess. A hyena.

The other bulb broke and a second hyena emerged. From the final thoughts of the sorcerers, Nasomi understood why they spent their entire witching lives for this one moment: hyenas can eat anything. Flesh and bones. And ethereal substances: magic, and the essence of people. Villages, cities, and kingdoms would be at the mercy of their power. They would be kings among the sorcerers.

But something was wrong. Incomplete. The Bride was not dead yet. She was fighting.

Nasomi was omniscient again, looking at the entire room. Then she became Reema. There were other things down the bottomless bowl. Something slithered by her hand. She touched hair and rock and what felt like warm oil. Felt a wind. Then a piece of metal, a large coin. She grabbed at it. And that seemed to give her part of her will back.

With a cry, Reema pulled her hand out of the bowl and sprawled backward. The anguish affected Nasomi as well, hurling her out of Reema's body. Reema looked old and ugly, thin, nigh dead. Her beauty was gone. "You tricked me!" she yelled. She got up, with much effort. "You tricked me, you bastards! Look what you've done to me!"

The sorcerers' human heads cracked and dissolved into dust. The hyenas walked to each other, faced Reema. "How did she resist it?" one hyena said, its voice raspy.

"How did she remove her hand?" the other yelled.

"It will all be for nothing if she isn't drained," the other said.

They stalked toward Reema, chuckling. She backed away until her back hit a vined wall. She sidled and her hand came to the curtain on the door.

"Let's suck it from her corpse!"

"Give us the rest of your essence, Bride!"

The hyenas bound at Reema, but she was already out the door, running into the night. She ran through and over a field of creeping vines. She stumbled and the hyenas were upon her.

Nasomi was waking as Reema's scream rippled through the last vestiges of the dream.

"They killed her!" she shouted. "They have killed Reema!"

Tambo jumped off the bed. "Call me names if you want, old man!" he said, then looked to the left then the right. He ran halfway to the door, stopped and turned around. Embarrassed, he massaged his neck with both hands as he came back to the bed. "What was that you said, my love?"

"A dream. Another one. Reema! She went back to the sorcerers, and they killed her."

"Eh? Killed her?"

"How could this happen? Why did she go to them? Couldn't she tell how dangerous they were?"

Tambo held her. "If she could, she was blinded by her desire for revenge."

"It's all my fault." The room started closing in around her, and she had trouble breathing. She wheezed and pulled herself from his embrace. "It's all my fault!"

As she went out of the room, Tambo followed her saying, "It can't be your fault, Nasomi. She alone is to blame for this. That's the type of woman she is."

Nasomi ran down the corridor, trying to race against the shadowed walls getting smaller, trying to gnaw her. She needed to get outside, she needed to breathe. She unlocked the door.

Tambo was close behind. "Where are you going, Nasomi? Please, listen to me. It is not your fault."

She was outside before he could catch up. The air was sweet. It filled her lungs with some relief. "If it wasn't for me — if I hadn't come in between you — none of this would have happened. I feel like I am a bad person."

"You're not a bad person," he said, coming close but not touching her. "I loved you, and love you still. I would choose you a thousand times. We must feel bad for Reema's unfortunate end, but you must not blame yourself for it."

"I'm trying not to, but it's hard, Tambo. And the dreams... Why do I have to dream about these things? I want to be a normal woman!"

She wondered why this area was called a rich area when there were so little trees, hardly any bushes, so much stone, and paving everywhere. She missed kneeling beneath the senegalia trees at their previous home. She missed smelling the plants and listening to nightingale songs. Why did I suggest we move here? she thought.

"What can I do, my husband? Who will mourn her? Who will believe me when I tell my dream? Reema has died alone and afraid. She has no one to go to bring her body and bury her proper. And this will haunt me for the rest of my life. I don't know if I can bear it."

He embraced her. "Let's share that burden together. Like all life's challenges, you may not know what to do about this for now, but the answer will come. I'll be here by your side."

A sharp pain burned in her lower back, and her insides pulled and twisted. The cramps eased and came again. "Tambo. I think it's time. The baby is coming."

Tambo helped her inside. She could hardly walk by herself, and she was hot and sweating. Her vision was whitening. Tambo shouted something, but she couldn't distinguish the words over the pain that gripped her.

Presently, there were more hands touching and holding her, more voices telling her to be strong, it would be over soon; she saw faces: her handmaiden, her midwives, Naena. Naena was here! That thought comforted her.

There was excited frenzy all about her. They made her lie down, opened up her legs, and daubed the sweat off her forehead. *Bring warm water! Hold her hands! Where is that cloth! I thought I told you to prepare the cot! Did she eat?* The voices spoke all about her. She let herself be lost in them, let them wash away the strong guilt.

Like all life's challenges, you may not know what to do about this for now, but the answer will come. That's what her husband said. And she knew what to do now. She pushed and let the new life come out of her. She let go of the pain of Reema's death and reveled in the pain of her son's birth.

When he cried, tears filled her eyes and she laughed in joy.

"We'll call him Meron," Tambo said when they let him in.

"A nice name," Nasomi said, as the little boy sucked her nipple. She could think of nothing more beautiful than having brought forth life and seeing it depend on you.

"It's a name from the Binoan people of Kon. It means 'everlasting peace'". He stroked the little boy. "Is it the name in the dream?"

"Yes," Nasomi said.

He laughed. "I guess it was inevitable, even though I thought I tried to be clever by giving him a name outside Nari's walls. Welcome to our life, Meron."

CHAPTER 14
THE MEANING OF DREAMS

A year passed without a telling dream, and she no longer fretted at having another one. Two years passed, and her life was all about her family. Three years passed, she weaved baskets to sell in the markets and taught Ramona all about cultivation. Four years. Five. She all but forgot about the dreams until the first day of the year 371.

A Narite year was exactly three hundred and sixty days, making three seasons: Sun, Water and Wind, of four months each. A month had three weeks of ten days each. This meant that every last day of a year, the thirtieth day of the month of Tengo, would be a Burial Day. The Last Burial Day. People around the city held vigil, mourned out loud or in silence, for those that were buried on that day, for those that were buried throughout the year, and for the ending of the year.

The following sunrise, the first day of the month Ra, the beginning of the Sun Season and of the year, was imbued with song, laughter, indulgence. The women ululated over drumbeats; the girls danced in the markets. The young men colored their bodies in yellow streaks, stomping about the city, some of them in masks to scare and delight the children; and the older men gathered at corners to toast and chug thick mugs of wheat beer or corn beer or anything that could intoxicate them.

Nasomi had a lot of fun on that day. Eight-year-old Ramona came rushing to her as she dressed three chickens. "Mother, teach me how to dance like the people outside." She took her mother's hand and stubbornly tugged her outside the yard. A group of people, of all ages, were performing the Unification dance. It involved much stomping, the shaking of the shoulders and buttocks, moving about in loops.

Nasomi indulged Ramona, showing her the steps, encouraging her to express freely. She didn't know at what moment they became the center of attention. The circle of people cheered them on, and a drummer came forward to beat an accompaniment to the dance. She and Ramona were sweating by the time they were done, and laughing so hard.

Back home, Ramona helped her smoke the chickens. Naena came with spices and potatoes. Naena and Nasomi took turns telling Ramona their childhood memories. Teeyana showed up, too, bringing with her small sacks of beef and pork. The yard was soon filled with the smells of roasted meats, wheat beer and sweet juices for the young ones.

The feasting went well into the evening. Tambo bawled out a few songs and demanded each person do the same. They danced in alternating couples around a fire, let loose some live chickens to see who would catch one the quickest, and built towers of twigs to see who would build the tallest standing one.

When the children went to bed, the grownups watched the stars as they imbibed more wheat beer. Each said their New Year wishes, what they wanted to see happen in the year.

"I think I will marry this year," Naena said. "Ngabe has been throwing hints." The others clapped their palms to supplicate to the *Mara* the fulfillment of the person's wish.

"I wish to build a hundred houses for people," Teeyana said. *Clap clap clap.*

"I wish to receive a moonstone ring from the king," Tambo said. *Clap clap clap.*

Nasomi took a breath. What did she want? "I wish all the people in my life to be happy." Like an unwanted visitor, the familiar tugging sensation crept up within her, intensifying with each subsequent clap.

When she and Tambo went to bed, she had a telling dream: a young girl, with her back to Nasomi, standing still in a moving throng, sang *Going the Long Way*. Nasomi walked toward the girl, whose voice grew to drown out the rest of the crowd noises. The girl turned, stopped singing when she looked at Nasomi, but the song rang in the air. No, she wasn't looking at Nasomi. At someone who just walked by her. Nasomi awoke still hearing the words.

Her head spun; her body became heavy. But she didn't want to go back to sleep. She sat up, placing her feet on the floor. She took big breaths to calm herself, kept her gaze to the floor to avoid seeing the walls crushing towards her.

"Nasomi?" Tambo woke up, touched her back. "Is anything the matter?"

"Nothing is the matter. I couldn't sleep, that's all." She lay back in bed, facing him. She stroked his face until he closed his eyes and began to snore. She closed her eyes, too, promising herself that if she began to sleep, she would yank them open and stare at the ceiling.

But it was Meron who woke her up from a dreamless sleep in the morning. "We go! We go!" the boy yelled as he jumped up and down.

The sunlight was bright through the window, and dust motes danced in it. "Not until afternoon," she told him. "You have to bath first. Today you must keep clean all the time or else we will leave you."

"I'll be clean!" He ran out, and she heard him wake Ramona up. "We'll go see the kowasa, Mona! Wake up!"

In the afternoon, as the family neared the amphitheater, Meron got lost in the crowds. As Nasomi searched for him, she saw the girl from the dream. She drew closer, and the girl was singing *Going the Long*

Way. Nasomi came even closer. The girl turned and ran into the arms of a woman coming from the side.

"Nasomi?" It was Tambo. He'd found Meron. He held Ramona's arm as well. "Here he is."

After all this time, Nasomi thought. The dreams have returned. Why?

Tambo flashed his rings to push through the mass of people. He paid two copper coins at the entrance, led his family through a turning corridor, up a zigzagging stairway and onto the fourth row of spectators. It had a good view of the arena and the royal balcony, where they could make out the forms of the king, the queen, and the young prince. The few times Nasomi had been to this ceremony, she never had such a good view.

Ramona and Meron were here for their first time. They were anxious to see the actual kowasa creatures. On the arena, a group of mummers in kowasa costumes danced to a continuous beating of drums and sang shrilly choruses. Some of them were dressed as warriors, chasing after the kowasa costumes with fire torches and spears.

"I want to be a warrior," Meron said.

"You?" Ramona replied. "You can't even kill a beetle. What makes you think you can fight a kowasa?"

"I can!"

"Can't."

"I can! I can! I can! Ahhggh!" He scowled at her.

"I would rather you had a trade," Tambo said, picking Meron up putting him on his lap. "You're a son of nobles, you must aim for a noble pursuit. Like architecture, gemstone trading, or accounting for the city's treasury."

"I want to learn how to write and become a scribe," Ramona said. At eight, she was tall, dark and smooth, had Nasomi's hairline and body form, and Tambo's face and comportment. And her own sharp wit.

"That's good, Mona," Tambo said. "And you, Meron?"

"Treasure."

"You mean treasury?"

"Treasury."

"Good boy. Now, let me explain what is happening here. You see that one over there?" Tambo pointed to a tall dancer in the center of the arena. "That is Kanguya, the bravest of the warriors who had risen against the kowasa... Let me tell it from the beginning so you can understand:

"A long, long way south of here stretches a great desert that divides the continent. It is so vast we can place twenty thousand Naris there. It goes from east to west. Not all the way, mind you. In the west is a dense forest, and they say the great beasts, the inkanyamba, live there. The desert narrows somewhere in the middle, and people cross from here to Ao'Pan, and the Ao'Pan people come north. They call it the Gold Road. At the east end of the desert is a kingdom of mountains called God's Teeth. I have so much to tell you about these other places, but let start with God's Teeth..."

"I can tell him some," Ramona said.

"Oh, that's well. Go ahead, Ramona my princess. You're a good storyteller."

"Prepare to have bad dreams," the girl said to Meron, grinning impishly.

"Father, she's trying to scare me."

"Mona, don't scare your brother," Nasomi said.

Ramona said, "*I* had bad dreams. It's just the nature of these stories." She grinned again. "God's Teeth. It's from there that the kowasa came. Over three hundred years ago, for reasons we don't know. They emerged from the shadows of the mountains, flowing out in their thousands. They were headed here. They killed and destroyed whatever they could find in their way. Men, women." She brought her face toward Meron when she said, "Children." Meron flinched.

"Have you heard of the Kingdom of Bones?" Tambo cut in. "Even to this day, it lies desolate. The land is white with the crumbling bones of the people annihilated by the kowasa all those years ago. Micha, a neighbor to the Kingdom of Bones, has walls so high they reach the clouds, to shield its people from desert storms and from a possible kowasa return. The kowasa continued northwest, here. Many of our people died in the kowasa invasion. By then, we were scattered tribes feuding over little tufts of land, and we could hardly defend ourselves.

"Then a hero arose. Kanguya. A fearless warrior from the Baula tribe. He gave everyone courage when they saw how he fought against the kowasa. And you know, the kowasa in those days were big creatures. Taller than me, five or six times muscular. And a blue light flowed through their veins—"

Ramona cut in. "I can't imagine how these adorable creatures were that big. That's the part I fail to believe, because, you know, the telling of history tends to be exaggerated."

Tambo seemed nonplussed for a moment. "Well, that's how it is told, and the priests will swear by its truth and tell you that when the kowasa were defeated, they shrunk in size. Isn't that so, Mother?"

"That's what they say," Nasomi said.

"Now, Kanguya gathered the tribes together, the supreme chiefs and clan chieftains. He wanted to create a united kingdom to defeat the kowasa, who had started building a wall of stone right where this amphitheater stands. They killed anyone who came within three miles of it. Some tribes refused and chose to flee north and east and west." He nodded for Ramona to continue the tale.

"Only eight clans of four tribes chose to fight with him. Of the Somebo tribe were the Kepe, Ke'api, and Kara clans. The Indas were represented by the Madis and Jaad clans. Two Kaalko clans: Nyate and First Naki. First Naki is Mother's clan, and Father is Kepe. And finally, there was the Ula clan itself, Kanguya's people, as the rest of the bigger Baula tribe fled."

Meron squinted at her. "Is she telling the truth, Father?"

Tambo laughed. "She is. Kanguya also convinced the mages, who were hermits living in the caves of Mount Lupili. People marveled at his sweet tongue and courage to make the mages join in his fight. That is why we have the Mage Council now. Many good things turned into our favor, including the courage of the warriors, the mages' magic, and the abandonment of the former ineffectual gods to worship the *Mara*. The *Mara* are unknown in number or form. All we know is that they are many, they watch over us, they created everything, and they proclaim their presence and will through the stars that we see at night. That's why we have priests: to guide us in reading the stars and to tell us the meaning of things."

The meaning of things, Nasomi thought. She thought of the girl singing *Going the Long Way*. What do my dreams mean? she wondered.

"The kowasa were defeated, and the tribes came together as Nari, and we built this city," Tambo was saying. "The few kowasa that remained were caged, to be used as reminders of our victory. They are bred and kept beneath this amphitheater. Every second day of the year, the newly trained warriors are pitted against the kowasa. To remind us of our history, and to train the warriors into true courage."

The singing girl — was it a warning of something to come? Nasomi was deep in her thoughts even as the important event began on the arena: a score of young warriors ran onto the sand, cheered by the crowd.

The real kowasa were let loose upon the warriors. They looked less menacing than the actors in costumes. They were midnight-blue dwarf creatures that ambulated on all fours. Their front limbs were longer than their hind ones. Nasomi knew that they could stand on two limbs sometimes, and could swing their long-clawed front limbs dangerously. They possessed two thin tentacles on each side of their thick necks. The tentacles seemed to do nothing but wag in the air. Their heads were rather small, the shape of angry dogs. With large circular eyes the color of water, no visible ears, and thick nostrils.

The warriors speared and cut down the kowasa with little effort. Ramona groaned and placed her hands over her eyes. The kowasa organized themselves into curving rows of defense. In fives or sevens. They defended themselves well, even brought down two of the warriors. But they were all but helpless against the spears.

"Mother," Ramona said. "I don't want to see anymore. I want to go home."

"Me neither," Nasomi said.

"Why are we cruel to them?"

Tambo answered, "They look small and harmless right now, but they can be dangerous creatures."

"I don't think I will ever want to see that again. Can we go?"

"I'm hungry," Meron said.

They got up and made their way out of the amphitheater. As they rode home in a carriage, Nasomi said, "I will go and see Gres, our marriage priest."

"Indeed?" Tambo said. "That old man. It's been some years since we saw him. Why?"

"I must ask him a few questions. About dreams."

He looked at her. "You've had some?"

She shook her head. "A short one. I'm just curious to find out what he has to say."

"I'm coming along," Ramona said.

"Me, too," Meron said, not to be left behind.

"I'll prepare a great meal," Tambo said. "You must all come with your best hunger."

They dropped him at home, and Nasomi directed the carriage driver through the dusty, narrow streets of Kowasa District. Gres still lived at the same house where Nasomi had prepared for her wedding. He looked the same: a cheerful thin old man.

He held out both hands when he came to meet them. "I have conducted many marriages, and I've forgotten many faces. But yours I can never forget. Welcome, welcome." He lifted Meron, who stared at his large nose. "And what lovely children you have!"

"Thank you, Gres-wame. I came to seek your counsel."

"I am always here for you. I hope all is well in your marriage." He gestured her to a stool that seemed to have been there for such an occasion. A priest's home was open.

"Everything is fine. I came to ask about the meaning of dreams." She sat. Ramona and Meron explored the yard in search of play.

"Ah, dreams," Gres said. "Dreams are one way the *Mara* speak with us. It is through dreams they reveal their true nature, as well as our own. Like an astrolabe and a mirror in one. Did you know it was through dreams that priests over the years discovered the *Tumina*, who are the antithesis of the *Mara*? Some say they are stars that we cannot see either in day or night. While we think they try to undo the work of the *Mara*, when you learn deeply, you find they bring balance to everything. Like when something of equal weight would balance a scale. They try to hide what the *Mara* reveal, they take what the *Mara* give, they corrupt what the *Mara* bless. The *Tumina*—See now, I have digressed. What did you want to know about dreams?"

"I have been thinking about dreams. Some are forgotten upon waking; some linger with you a few moments after waking. Other dreams you cannot forget after many years. It's made me conclude that some dreams have meaning, some don't. Some are scary and are only there to wake you up screaming at night, but some — they tell us about what's coming ahead."

"I'm astounded. Not many people think about the subject of dreams. They leave the propounding of their mysteriousness to us priests. It is through dreams that we have discovered much truth over the years, for the *Mara* have given us the ability to dream, and also what to dream. In sleep, you are naked. Not in body, but in the soul. Bereft of all burdens of the mind, stripped of the story you tell yourself of who you are. Dreams will not hide the truth. You see the true colors of everything, hear the voices of the *Mara*, touch the fabric of the universe. You experience life with senses you tend to shut off when awake. Dreams remind us we are more than we like to believe."

"If I have a dream that shows what will happen two days or two years from now, does it mean that, no matter what, my life is already decided? That whether I try or not, things will happen exactly as revealed? That I have no self-will to change anything? That I can only wait for things to happen?"

Gres scratched his chin. "I know how many people would give anything for such an ability. To know what would happen tomorrow? It beats this plodding-about-the-mud of a life, not knowing what's coming."

"I think it would be scary to have such dreams."

"Do you have such dreams?"

"Sometimes."

He waited but she didn't give him any more details. "Say you had to travel through a jungle to get to the other side. What would you do?"

She thought for a moment. "Eh, I would... I think I would carry a few warm clothes, some food to eat on the journey, go with some friends?"

"Someone tells you there's a lion at some location on the journey, what would you do?"

"Travel with a warrior. Two warriors carrying spears. And with someone who knows the way."

"Yes. You see, your knowledge of what's ahead will help you prepare for it." He smiled.

"I never thought of it that way."

Nasomi thanked him, said she would come back for more counsel. On the way home, Ramona and Meron were arguing. Nasomi was deep in thought to bother about it until Ramona jumped over and sat at her right. "Mother likes me best," she said.

Meron came over to her left side. "No, she likes me best."

"Children, please. I like you both equally. There is no favorite."

"What if you have another child?" Ramona asked. "Who will you like better?"

Nasomi chuckled. "There won't be another child."

"Why?"

"Because..." Was she going to say because she didn't see any more children in her dreams? "Because I have only two hands. One for Ramona" — she put her right hand over Ramona and her left one over Meron — "and one for Meron."

CHAPTER 15

THE BRIDE'S RETURN

One night, Nasomi stretched her hand and discovered Tambo was not in bed with her. She was heavy with sleep, having been exhausted from the cooking and entertaining of guests on Meron's seventh birthday. She thought she might have overslept and it was morning, but when she blinked and squinted, she saw it was still dark.

She would have allowed herself to return to sleep, but uneasiness seized her. Something felt wrong. She jerked upright on the bed, listened. Nothing unusual. An owl hoot, the croon of a lonely cricket, the distant bark of a dog. Then... a short sound. It was quite far to tell what it was. Maybe it came from the kitchen.

She got off the bed, covered herself and raced out of the room. Ramona's door open and when she looked inside, her daughter was not in bed. She rushed to Meron's room. He was snoring heavily, both his firestone lamps still on. She ran down the corridor, shouting, "Tambo! Mona!"

She knocked into someone rushing out a door. A manservant. He yelped and scampered from her like she was fire, his eyes wide. "What is it, Bansi?" she demanded.

"Nhhhhhn!" He struggled to finds words. He ran past her, yelling along the corridor: "A witch, My Lady! Evil in the house! Witch!"

Nasomi ran to the kitchen. Tambo had his back to her. She would remember him like that in the coming years: an ax in his left hand, his veins bulging, the dull yellow light from the firestone lamps reflecting in streaks across his dark shirtless skin; he was in nothing but short breeches. He looked like how she would picture a legendary warrior up against a nightmarish beast.

Just as well. Opposite him, having come through the door, which was now cracked wide open, stood an old woman.

Nasomi recognized Reema immediately.

Reema's skin was grey and wrinkled. As if that wasn't enough ugly, she was wearing brideclothes, which were dirty and frayed. She was barefoot, and her feet were cracked. Behind her, two large hyenas walked through the door. They chuckled as they flanked Reema.

Reema saw Nasomi and smiled. "There she is, our beloved wife."

Tambo turned his head. "Nasomi, take the children, get out of here."

"Don't be rude, Tambo," Reema said. Her voice was still young and sweet. "I have some business with her as well."

"You... you died!" Nasomi said. "Those hyenas... they killed you."

"They almost did. I... How would you know this?" She made to take a step forward. Tambo shifted the ax to his other hand.

The hyenas pried Nasomi with their yellowish-brown eyes. Reema put her clasped hands to her mouth as she pondered and studied Nasomi.

"The mages found out everything and told us," Tambo said. He held the ax in both hands. "Nasomi, go. I will finish this." He charged, swinging his ax. Reema slapped away the ax like it was a twig in a child's hand. Tambo was sent against the wall.

"Stop it, my love!" Reema screamed as if shocked at her own power. "I didn't come to kill you."

Nasomi ran to him, but the hyenas bounded and blocked her way. She held back.

"Tonight, farm girl, I get what is mine... what you stole from me," Reema said. She knelt to touch Tambo.

He slapped her hand away. "He's always been mine," she said to Nasomi. "You came and ruined everything."

"You are evil!" Nasomi spat.

"Ha! If there's an evil person here, it is you!" She pointed a finger at Nasomi, and Nasomi felt a prick on her forehead as though Reema had actually poked her. "You husband snatcher, you! You are the evil one."

The hyenas stalked after Nasomi. She stumbled as she tried to back away, falling hard to the floor. One of them bit into her arm as she lifted it to shield herself. When her long screaming and squirming stopped, she saw none of them were eating her to death. There was a groan in the room that wasn't coming from her.

The hyena that had bitten her was in anguish. It coughed and jerked. Let out a pained groan. Reema stood like a statue, failing to believe what was going on.

Nasomi stood up. Tambo stood up. He shook his wrist as if to shake away the pain. He picked up the ax.

The suffering hyena gained its composure, and a deep silence fell into the room. They all stood where they were, looking at each other. A breeze wafted into the room, prickled at Nasomi's skin. But she was hot inside, hot with fury, and the blood trickling down her arm was warm. She wanted to grab the ax and hack Reema piece by bloody piece.

"What...?" said Reema, her voice steely. Nasomi could have sworn she saw Reema's shadow move even when Reema didn't. "What have I just seen, Gweuka?"

"She has power," the troubled hyena said.

"She is truly a witch then! All this time—"

"She's one of them!" the hyena said, retreating to Reema's side. The other followed suit. "The naturals. She has a sliver of the cosmos fabric in her."

"What? Her?" Reema laughed. "You're mistaken. She's a simple, ugly farm girl."

"I felt it!" the hyena turned at Reema, growled at her. "I know what I felt! She would have undone me!"

Reema slapped the hyena's head. "Don't you turn upon me like that, or I will be the one to undo you. I am your master."

They both slunk, subservient.

"You two are the most powerful wizards I know!" she yelled, irritated. "Or was I wrong?"

"We're powerful," the hyenas said together.

"Then kill her, whether she's a witch or not. Finish the task I had paid you to do."

The hyenas trembled, gaining their courage back. They snarled and giggled, looking at Nasomi like a piece of game to be eaten.

Tambo raised the ax at the distracted Reema. A tentacle from her shadow leaped at him. It elongated unnaturally, wrapping itself around his legs, slithering toward his torso. He dropped the ax as the shadow threw him down. He struggled against it.

The hyenas moved past the witch and bound toward Nasomi. She braced herself, but the hyenas stopped inches before her. They circled her, trying to decide whether to attack.

"You and I will be alone together finally," Reema said to Tambo. She straddled him as her shadow slipped back to its normal form. She produced a piece of white cloth. "I am so sorry it has to be this way, but this is to show you how much I love you."

"Get away from me," Tambo moaned.

"I will show you," Reema continued. "It had always been you and me, Tambo. You cannot imagine the things I have gone through just so I can have you back. But you will understand."

The hyenas snapped at Nasomi when she tried to move.

"Remember this cloth, my love?" Reema said. "The words you said to me as you put it around my wrist? 'To you I bind myself until we are wed'? Remember?"

"All I remember is I didn't want you anymore."

"I'm so sorry," she said. "Sorry that I wasn't good enough for you... but I am now... will be. Words have meaning, Tambo, and yours were all I clung to. I can still feel the words in this cloth. Your words." Tambo's own shadow lifted his arm toward Reema. She tied the cloth around his wrist. "And now, you're mine again. I have so much to tell you."

"Mother!"

Ramona came into view from behind a cabinet. She had a knife in her hand.

"Mona!" Nasomi screamed. "What are you doing here?"

The girl came forward. "I felt something coming. I hid to see."

"Mona, please, Nasomi, you need to go," Tambo begged. He was in anguish, sweat beaded his brow and chest.

"Not without you," Nasomi said.

"I can't move. She has done something to me."

Reema stood. "That should have been my daughter! We would have had these beautiful children together, my love." Reema moved with grace and dexterity that belied her aged looks. She came toward Nasomi, stroking the hyenas' necks. "I will go with him now, you witch. If you try to stop me, you will not blame me for what these two will do to you. Or your girl there."

She turned around. "Stand, Tambo. Time to go."

Tambo stood, but not from his own will. He fought whatever spell Reema put on him. He was not strong enough against it. Reema went to him, took him by the arm. As they went to the door, as the hyenas backed away with their teasing gazes still on Nasomi, tears were hot in Nasomi's eyes, anger was boiling in her heart.

She grabbed the knife from Ramona and charged at Reema. The hyenas parted from her and Reema turned to see the knife arc toward her face. Reema dodged, as quickly as lightning, and Nasomi stabbed into nothing. She lost balance, tumbled awkwardly forward.

Reema kicked her in the shin. The pain was searing. Nasomi heard Tambo plead, Ramona wail, the hyenas giggle. Reema kicked her again.

"Stop it Reema!" Tambo yelled.

"He's mine, you hear?" Reema screamed in Nasomi's face. "Mine! Mine! Mine!"

Nasomi saw a hyena dash past toward Ramona. Motherly instinct lifted Nasomi from the floor. She caught the hyena's tail as it toyed with and snarled at Ramona. She pulled hard, trying to hurl it.

The hyena yelped and distanced itself from her.

Reema's shadow began to expand toward Nasomi. "I do not want to harm you, but you are forcing me."

"Reema, stop," Tambo said. He was shaking. Nasomi saw that he was trying to move. "If you hurt her, I swear... I swear..."

"He's breaking it!" one hyena said, excitedly. They both watched Tambo with gleeful anticipation, as if rooting for him to break the spell.

"He'll be free," the other said.

"Stop that! I command you!" Reema shouted. Her shadow turned away from Nasomi and to the hyenas and Tambo. "You are bound to me and you will not break your bondage." She retrieved a large golden coin from her bosom. She tossed it down, and it began to glow. "You are bound to me," she croaked. "Come to me."

They obeyed and went to Reema. Tambo was shedding tears. "I can't do anything," he said to Nasomi. "She has put a spell on me."

"Out the door, all of you!" Reema demanded. She bent down to pick the golden coin. When Tambo and the hyenas were out the door, Reema said to Nasomi, "For his sake, I spare you. I can crush you like an insect upon my fancy. But I am only happy to know you will know hurt as I have. Suffer well."

She walked out the door. Nasomi was too weak to move, due to the loss of much blood. She fell to her knees, then to the floor, fought against the blackness that was trying to get her. She lost and was wrapped in it.

Ramona was bandaging her wound when she opened her eyes. She lay on the floor, face up.

"Mother, where has she taken him?"

Nasomi sat up. So forcefully she pushed Ramona away. She got up and ran out the door. It was cold outside. The moon was hidden by heavy clouds. A cold breeze pricked her face and skin, gnawing all the way to her bones. She didn't know where to begin. Reema and Tambo could have gone in any direction. It was as though this had been only a dream, as though she finally woke up to a reality where Reema, Tambo and the hyenas didn't exist. Or as though her story had reverted back to when Tambo belonged to Reema and she was only a sensitive, kind and naive daughter of a farmer.

She was vaguely aware of her daughter coming to stand beside her. This is real, she told herself. I have lost my husband.

"Mother, I am sorry I couldn't stop her."

"What? How can you say that? She is a powerful witch. There is nothing you could have done."

"I could have stabbed her long ago, but I was afraid. I had a bad feeling, and I went to see."

"You're safe, that's what matters."

Ramona, who asked so many questions, didn't ask who the witch was or why she had taken Father away. Nasomi was ready to tell her everything, from the beginning. To tell her that while Nasomi was shocked that Reema was still alive, she wasn't surprised Reema had spent the past eight years becoming a powerful witch just so she could take Tambo back.

"I need to find him, Mona. I need to bring him back."

"And then you will come to explain everything to me," Ramona said, hinting that she wouldn't bother her mother with the questions now. "I want to help. I have heard so many stories about witches and how to defeat them."

"You've not heard of Reema. In any case, I will not put you or your brother in danger. Let me be the one to do this."

Yet, her mind was as cloudy as the sky above. Where would she even start?

The mages. Of course.

CHAPTER 16

OF MAGIC AND NEW DREAMS

Naena listened with her fists pressed against her cheeks and tears in her eyes. "She deserves to die, Somi."

"I cannot believe I felt guilty about it all being my fault... Now... Now, I wish she had really died. I could have lived with the guilt. Nae, I need you to look after the children for me. Until I get back."

The children were inside Naena's house, eating a lunch of smoked fish, a vegetable salad, and mango juice.

"Anything for you, sister. I have enough activities and stories for them to last the afternoon."

"I mean for longer than that."

"What...?" Naena read Nasomi's face. "You mean you intend to pursue the witch yourself? I thought you said you will be going to the mages."

"Yes, I am, but I need only a certain potion from them, one that frees someone from a spell. And perhaps for them to point the direction Reema has gone. They have a way of determining that."

"You can't do that, Somi!"

"Why not? It has to be me."

"She's a witch."

"Whose hyenas, powerful as they are, are afraid of me."

"How is that?"

"I don't know Nae, but I mean to use it."

"But that might mean you'll be gone for more than two days."

"Yes, it might."

Naena picked up dirt from the ground, sprinkled it as she spoke without looking at Nasomi. "You know my wedding is the day after tomorrow, Somi. You know how important this is for me."

"I know."

"I'll be finally happy. I need my sister there."

"How would I celebrate knowing my husband is being tortured by a witch out there, all alone?"

"Let the mages find him, as you said."

"Look, Nae..." Nasomi leaned forward and took Naena's hands. "The mages — they can only point the way. I don't think the king would let them set a foot outside the city. It would have to be me to go."

"And if you die, Somi? What is going on is beyond you. It's magic and spells and witchcraft. You are just... just you."

"All I need is to get Tambo to drink the potion and he'll be free, then we can return and seek protection from the mages. If I can find him quickly, even by tonight, we can return in time for the wedding."

"That's you trying to convince me?"

"What do you mean?"

"Stop pretending, Somi. This is about your dreams. You knew about Father's death, didn't you?"

Nasomi opened her mouth but didn't speak.

"You must have known, Somi. I've thought about it and understand your behavior in those days. You had dreamed he would die and you didn't tell me about it."

"I was scared, Nae. I didn't want it to happen. I did all I could to make it not happen."

"You could have told me. I would have not wasted much time moving about the city, and spent more of his last moments with him."

"Nae, you have to understand."

Naena stood up, shook her head. "The only thing I understand is that you don't want to tell me things anymore. You won't be there for the wedding. Tell me that."

"Maybe not." Nasomi stood up, took Naena's hand. "I don't know, Nae, and that is the truth. I can't control these dreams. I hardly understand them. It's not like they tell me what to do."

"But you're coming back?"

"Why would you think...? Of course, I am coming back. I will bring Tambo with me."

"But you know when? How days, weeks?"

Nasomi closed her eyes, touched her face.

"Months?"

"Maybe."

"Somi!"

"I really don't know, Nae, but I will bring him back."

Naena stood up stormed toward the house.

"It has to be me," Nasomi said when Naena had one foot into the doorway. "It has to be me to go after him. That's the only way it can be."

Naena nodded, but not in affirmation. She saw she couldn't convince Nasomi. "I will take care of your children. It's my duty as your sister. I just pray you come back before they start calling me Mother."

Ramona and Meron squeezed their way between Naena and the doorway. A tear was falling down Nasomi's cheek and she quickly wiped it away.

Meron ran to her. "You're crying, Mother." He looked at Naena, squealed, "You made my mother cry!"

Nasomi turned his head to face her. "She didn't make me cry, my son. I just miss your father, and I must go find him." She beckoned Ramona close. "You're a big girl now. Wise beyond your years. I know I can trust you with taking care of your brother."

The girl nodded.

"I want to follow," Meron said, breaking into a cry. "Take me also."

"Stay with your aunt. I won't be long."

Ramona took Meron's hand. "I will do my best, Mother."

"I know you will. Whatever happens, I promise you this: your father and I will return. Your aunt here will keep you." She looked at Naena. "And she will take you once in a while to the Kepe palace, to see your grandparents. Won't you, Aunt?"

Naena nodded. She held out her hands. "Come now, children. Your mother must go."

Her heart broke as she was escorted by Meron's wail until he was out of earshot. Nasomi walked as calmly as she could muster, and when she was sure they couldn't see her anymore, she broke into a run.

Fortunately for her, she didn't need to go all the way to King's Island. As she passed through The Dragon on her way to Inkanyamba, she met a group of citizens fleeing in the opposite direction. She found out from them that some kowasa had escaped the dungeon. The mages were at the amphitheater trying to capture them. "It's better to be as far as possible, everyone within the vicinity has moved away," one man carrying a child said.

"I thank you," she replied, and left him with a cry of surprise when she dashed into the dreaded direction.

One entrance to the amphitheater was unlocked. The amphitheater seemed eerily quiet until she walked in. Two figures zoomed past her: a kowasa and a spear-wielding warrior. She walked through the cacophony of chasing warriors and fleeing kowasa until she found Thorro in a narrow hallway. He was uttering in Majen and two kowasa were magically dragged through the air toward him.

As he spoke, Nasomi had a growing tugging sensation within her. Maybe that's what I need, she thought. Majen can stir the dreams. She mimicked what she could hear in a whisper, gauging how it made her feel: "*Kwag fa pa'ni, pemsi asiene.*"

Thorro picked up a rope and bound the two kowasa. When he noticed her, he raised a brow. She sensed he recognized her.

"Most people would be shaking under a table, miles from here," he said.

"Because of these adorable creatures?"

"You're either stupid or you have never seen what these can do to a human."

"I need your help. She's back. The witch who had sent the kwindi. She's taken my husband."

"We are particularly busy, as you can see. And if there was any such powerful witch about, we would have detected her."

"Where is the other mage? You're rude."

"I am here," a voice behind her said. Kaan came leading four kowasa linked to each other by a rope around their necks. He bunched them with Thorro's two.

"She says a witch took her husband," Thorro said.

Kaan regarded her with some concern. "Is this true?"

"It is! The same witch who had sent the kwindi. She's a witch now, wasn't then. She defeated the sorcerers who had helped her at that time, I don't know how." She described how Reema looked, wrinkly in tattered brideclothes, and what she said about binding Tambo to her.

Kaan lifted an impatient hand. "She commands two hyenas? That would be nigh impossible, and it would raise magic alerts from the beacons we set around the city. Did you not imagine this? Maybe he ran away—"

"He did not run away! You must help me. If not, give me a potion that frees someone from the bondage of a spell."

Thorro stepped toward her. "Who are you to demand anything from us?"

"Are you not supposed to be protecting us from such things? What will the king say?"

"Get out of here, woman—"

Kaan stepped in between. "Let's do this right. Where is your home?"

"Second home around the bend by the hill at the eastern edge of Nkuku District. It is painted in red and white. You can't miss it."

Kaan held her shoulder. "I will personally come to your home, if the king permits me. We cannot stop what we're doing now, or else the kowasa will escape into the city. That would be a terrible situation."

"But... she could be too far by the time—"

Kaan noticed something behind her. He and Thorro rushed thither, after three kowasa that emerged from a door. The mages threw the black dust onto the ground. *"Zhef'mi pami! Khata!"* they screamed and the kowasa froze mid-stride and were dragged toward them. Nasomi felt a shiver move through her.

"Please!" Nasomi said, following them. "It has to be today. I'm afraid we'll miss them if we delay."

"Nothing is stronger than Majen," Kaan assured her. "If what you say is true, we'll catch your little witch."

Something moved at the edge of her vision. She turned her head and saw the outline of a kowasa in the shadow of a pillar. It looked at her with its deep blue eyes, like ponds of water reflecting a starry night. It slunk back in the shadow but she could still see it.

"Kowasa!" she said, turning to point in the opposite direction of the kowasa's hiding spot. She followed the mages when they dashed where she pointed, and when she looked back, she saw the little creature flit toward the other end.

"Where?" Thorro demanded.

"I saw one. I think it left through the corridor there."

The corridor led onto the arena, where scores of kowasa were bound together. The mages walked among them, trying to find any that were free.

"If you don't want to help me," Nasomi said, "give me some *myama* and teach me a few phrases. I will find her myself."

Thorro gave her a look as though she had just said the king was a dog.

Nasomi's Quest

Kaan was calmer: "Even if it were allowed, it takes years to master Majen."

Nasomi took a deep breath. "I have something to confess, that I have kept all this time. I am a seer — I see things in my dreams. Real things, and somehow your Majen strengthens my ability. If you could—"

Thorro was close to slapping her. "Do you realize you're saying you are a diviner? What would the king think of that?"

"It's true—"

"Stop wasting our time or you'll get in trouble for anything that comes out of that mouth. We are not children to be teased. We have a city to save. Get out!"

She hesitated, put her hands to her hips. "I am a good citizen of this city. If you cannot help me, what is the point of your existence?"

"You! Soldier!" Thorro called to a soldier who just walked in, leading five bound kowasa. "Come here. Take this woman and throw her out of this place. If she tries to return, I grant you permission to stab her."

Kaan shook his head in a resigned way when Nasomi looked to him for help. He turned away and continued looking for the supposed free kowasa. As the soldier led Nasomi out, she whispered Majen phrases to herself repeatedly to strengthen the strange sensation she was feeling. *"Zhef'mi pami. Khata. Kwag. Fa pa'ni. Pemsi asiene."*

The sensation tugged and swirled in her. It looped and danced all inside her body. She knew without a doubt that a telling dream was calling. It was all she had left.

CHAPTER 17

A QUEST BEGINS

Nasomi went to the Kepe palace in Kwindi to inform Tambo's parents. She tried to decide against it, but it was better they heard it from her than from rumor. And she knew the rumors would start soon. She was let through the gate with no trouble. Tambo's mother was on a reclining chair in the sun, hugging herself against the cold.

"*Ondi,*" Nasomi said, a term for asking permission to approach. She knelt. "How are you, Mother?"

"You're as rare as a good amount of heat in this Wind Season." She asked Nasomi to stand and sent someone to fetch a chair for her.

"This one is particularly windy and chilly," Nasomi said.

"How's the family?"

"Not good. It's why I came."

"I hope it's not too bad."

"It is. I just need to tell it straight... Reema. She came back. And she took Tambo with her."

Tambo's mother nearly fell off her seat. "How can that be? She's dead. Tambo had sent word that she died."

"That's what we all thought. But now— Mother, she's become a witch, a powerful one. She's put a spell on Tambo. He can't move of his own will and obeys everything she says."

Tambo's mother judged the seriousness of her words. When she saw Nasomi's expression didn't change — would Nasomi come all this way to make a jest? — she touched her heart. "*Mara twafe!* Come, daughter." She got up and pulled Nasomi toward the entrance of the first rondavel.

"Will I be welcome?" Nasomi said. "I wouldn't want to cause undue trouble."

"I am the one inviting you, and no one can chase you away. Yana's father needs to hear this."

Teeyana saw them as they passed through the long entrance corridor. "Nasomi!" she called, and came toward them when Nasomi waved. "You don't look okay. What is going on here?"

"Where is your father?" her mother asked.

"At the counting room."

Chieftain Shikepe Go had grown slender with age. His garment was oversized and heavy, having much length and many folds to it. His hair was grizzled and he was missing two front teeth. He still had his mean scowl, which he wore as he looked down at the majordomo who was helping him count coins, gemstones, and bits of gold. The scowl deepened when he recognized Nasomi.

"I am busy," he said, giving a dismissing wave, but he could tell this was serious. "What is it?"

"It's about your son, Tambo. He's been kidnapped by Reema!"

He coughed and sat down on a high stool. He dismissed the other man. "Isn't she dead?"

Nasomi explained everything, excluding the part of her dreams. When she was done, and he pondered on it a while, he said, "She's the woman he was meant to be with."

His wife gave him a slap on the hand. "Bitter old man! Is that what you can say? Your son is in trouble, and all you can think to say is that she's the woman he was—"

"What have I done for the *Tumina* to curse me and meddle in the life of my children? Tambo is bewitched, Dembo never married and has run off on dangerous journeys on his Gold Road, and Kukalo is a stupid boy when it comes to money, and to wives."

"I have never disappointed you, Father," Teeyana said.

"Who knows what will happen to you now?"

She gave him a scowl. "I am a respected woman in this city, and I make a difference." She turned to Nasomi. "You know what, take me with you. We will find him together."

"I forbid it," her mother said.

"I don't see anyone else helping."

"It's not your place to hunt down a witch. Neither is it Nasomi's. We'll ask the mages to help. The king is afraid of witches—"

"He's cautionary," the Chieftain corrected.

"The king is afraid of witches," the Lady repeated.

"I've already been to the mages," Nasomi said. "They have refused to help. They had me thrown away. Chased like an animal."

"I will go and see the king myself," the Chieftain said, looking at each of them as if he suspected they would be surprised he said that. "I will ask for some warriors, and add a few of my own."

"He's my husband," Nasomi said. "I must be the one to go and get him back."

"Nonsense," Mother-in-law said. "You will do no such thing. Let the strongest of warriors go and find Reema."

"But Mother—"

The older woman touched the side of Nasomi's head, stroked her temple and some of her hair. "I see you are agitated, child. But you cannot do anything by yourself. We're here for you."

"I cannot sit back and do nothing."

"You can intercede. You, me and Yana. Every day until Tambo is found. Find someone to look after your house. Come here with the children. Say you hear me."

"I hear you, Mother." Nasomi forced the words out of her mouth. Her heart was filling up with bitterness.

136

Kukalo appeared at the doorway, disheveled. He leaned against the doorframe to keep his balance, and he looked everyone over with dreary eyes. "I heard there was a meeting... What in the depths of death is she doing here?"

"Kukalo, mind your mouth," Mother-in-law berated. "Take a seat, we have an urgent matter."

"Tell me what it is. I like it right here." He grinned so wide he had to close his eyes. The stench of wheat beer inundated the room.

"Your brother has been taken by Reema. She came in the night, with two hyenas. We must find a way to bring him back."

He was quiet, as though pondering. Then his eyes went wide. After that, he shrugged and walked away.

"Kukalo!" the Chieftain shouted. "Come back right now, boy! Or you will know my wrath!"

The only reply that came was an incomprehensible mumble that faded.

"Ah," the Chieftain muttered. "See what the bad spirits throw upon me." He stood up, but his wife reached out to touch his arm. "Scold him later. Let us prepare to visit the Island." She turned to Nasomi. "Go with Wakani. You remember Wakani? He will help you put your house in order and bring you and the children here."

Wakani was one of the men who had come looking for Tambo back when the rings had been stolen. Nasomi recognized him as soon as he came. He was soft-spoken, kept his gaze down, a behavior which belied his muscular looks. In a few moments, Nasomi and Wakani were riding out the palace gate. She was on a red-brown mare, and he rode a dapple-grey stallion.

Rumor came rushing in the opposite way. "Have you heard? Have you heard?" a bony man said, coming in through the gate. He was laden with baskets of fruits and vegetables from the market. "Have you heard that Tambo was taken by a witch?"

Wakani beckoned to him and rebuked him. "We have heard, you fool. Stop boasting around with your big mouth and big eyes like this is good news. Shut up and do your work. This is not funny."

"I didn't say it's funny," the bony man replied, making a stance like he dared Wakani to get off the horse and fight him. "It's just the news in the city. Everybody deserves to know."

"Well, the Chieftain and Lady know, and that's enough. Shut your mouth and do your work. That's your place. Do you know who this is?" He indicated toward Nasomi.

The man shook his head and studied Nasomi, uncertainty and fear creeping on his face.

"Then shut up. Let us go, My Lady." As they rode away, he said, "I am sorry you had to hear that. Some people can be so insensitive."

"Thank you, Wakani. I was expecting such things, though. People will always talk."

"I say people should be minding their mouths."

The house was quiet and empty. Ghostly. The broken door swung in the light wind. All the servants had abandoned it. Narites were fearful of witchcraft and avoided places suspected of being visited by a sorcerer. Some were in the habit of going to medicine men and - women to bathe in herbs and have protective words chanted over them. Some kept talismans under their beds or tables.

Nasomi shook her head at the thought of her servants fearing to come back. She and Tambo would have to start all over again when this was over. Wakani looked around the house as he took a seat when Nasomi led him through the living room. If he was afraid, he did not show it.

She needed to dream. The feeling within her was strong. "Will you indulge me a little rest before we go?"

He nodded, keeping the questions he had to himself.

She went to her bedroom. She felt Tambo's absence, a palpable void he needed to fill. Silence was thick, her own breath was like the sound of a distant gale. She lay on the bed, wishing Tambo could walk right through the door and say, "I defeated her and came back to you."

But no one walked through the door. She stared at it for a long time. Sleep did not come. The door was made of teak, smooth, the deep brown grains of the wood wiggled along the surface like the door had flowed into shape from some thick liquid. It was Tambo's favorite door. He had loved it the moment he saw it at the marketplace and had insisted on installing it himself. It had taken him two sweet days, one to place each hinge perfectly, and another to set it into the frame.

She pounded her leg on the bed impatiently. This wasn't working; sleep wasn't forthcoming. She got up and returned to Wakani in the living room. He was going through a scroll on the history of the creation of the universe. She could tell from how he looked at it that he couldn't read. "Are you hungry?" she asked.

"Not particularly."

She boiled sweet potatoes, mixed them with pounded peanuts. As they ate, she asked Wakani to talk about himself. He was the third son of a drunkard stonemason and had helped his father in building a new part of the city's walls.

His father could drink beer like a thirsty horse, and though it never affected his skill, it affected his health. Wakani had vowed to never be like his father on that aspect, having seen him die a terrible death, but he valued the work ethic his father displayed. Wakani had worked throughout many households, many people had come to love him, and he was appreciated in the Go palace. He even had enough gathered wealth to start building his own home.

"That's good!" Nasomi said. "You're wise to think of the future."

"I won't be a servant forever. I want to be a rich merchant, have a big family of my own. Is there anything you need to pack? I can help."

"I will tell you, but I still need to take a short rest."

"Is there anything the matter, My Lady? You can rest at the palace."

"Just allow me one more rest in my home, to intercede for my husband."

He didn't question her anymore.

She showed him a guest bedroom and told him to feel free to eat anything if he got hungry.

When she lay on her bed again, sleep came quickly. And she had a telling dream. The telling dream she wanted:

Reema, the hyenas, and Tambo were hiding behind some bushes along a road. It was night. A group of carts passed by, laden with what looked like coal. Up where the road led, flickering light indicated village life. In the opposite direction, a black thing rose high into the sky, chewing off part of the world. A mountain.

"Let's go, you sluggards," Reema said, stepping onto the road. Tambo and the hyenas followed her, and they moved toward the village. Tambo shuffled his feet like he didn't want to walk.

Two men stumbled onto the road, singing a raunchy song. When they saw Reema and her group, they paused. Reema whistled and the hyenas sprang toward the men. The men screamed and ran off the road and in between some trees. Reema and the hyenas laughed.

"You should stop that," Tambo berated. "Stop scaring people."

"Oh, have a sense of humor. We will be together a long way."

"I want to go home!"

"I am your home now. You just haven't realized it."

Nasomi awoke and immediately got off the bed. She packed a few clothes in a leather bag with long straps. She threw in a handful of coins and a leather pouch for water. She threw on her cloak and gathered two more handfuls of coins from a chest.

She went to the kitchen. She got the knife Ramona had held, wrapped it in a cloth and placed it in the bag. She was fastening her sandals when Wakani came in.

He blinked from sleep and yawned. "I heard things, glad it's you. Did you sleep, My Lady?"

"Are you afraid of witches, Wakani?"

"Of witches, no." He raised a brow.

"I need your help, Wakani, because no one else will help me."

"Anything, My Lady."

"We must go after Reema, you and me."

He shook his head. "No, no, no, My Lady. I was instructed to bring you back to the palace, you and the children." He looked around, realizing the children were not here.

"They are with my sister, they will be fine," Nasomi said hurriedly. "We have no time for this. If you can't go with me, let me take the horse."

"The Chieftain is sending warriors after the witch... My Lady, I was told to bring you back."

She rushed outside and he followed. She reached the brown mare. "Wakani, I am taking this horse, and I am following after Reema. All these people whom you think will help – warriors, mages – they don't know what I know."

"What do you know, My Lady?"

She got up on the horse, and he looked like he was unsure whether he should force her to come with him, or let her be. "She went toward Mishi. Are you coming or not?"

He touched the back of his head. "What am I supposed to tell them? I need to take you to the palace. Please!"

She kicked the horse into a gallop. "It has to be me, Wakani!"

Wakani let out a shout of despair. "Eh, the trouble I will be in, My Lady!"

When she looked back, he was scrambling onto his horse.

CHAPTER 18
A FRIEND FROM GOD'S
TEETH

Wakani and Nasomi left Nari through the North Gate and crossed the wide bridge over the rushing Pana River. The bridge and river were reminiscent of the moat at King's Island, on a grander scale. A little way downriver, a gigantic wooden wheel spun from the current, scooping water and relaying it into suspended channels that fed the aqueducts of the city. It was not uncommon for a bridge crosser to pause and stare at the wheel, no matter how many times they had seen it. Nasomi mused that it contained so much timber that could build a house bigger than hers.

The road that led from the bridge came to a fork a quarter of a mile later. Mount Lupili rose up in front of them, looking as close as she could stretch her hand and touch it, and yet she knew it was a few miles away. They rode through a plain when they turned right, and though the grass was ankle-high, Nasomi recognized this place. She reined the horse and jumped down.

"Are you well?" Wakani asked.

"I am." Her voice caught and she cleared her throat. She was walking in her dream. The grass was much longer in the dream, but this was where she came to meet Meron and Ramona. On her way back from somewhere. She didn't want to admit to herself that she may return this way after a long while. Next Rain Season? After five years?

Her life was meant to be simple, happy, a clueless boring tale from birth to death. But now there was a powerful jealous witch in her life. And an ability to see the future in her dreams. She would have never thought of herself as the sort of person to have these things happen to her. She wasn't the sort of person who would leave the city to hunt down a monster. But now... Well, now she was. Now, she was to go the long way.

"Would you love to see a glimpse of your future?" she asked Wakani as they rode on. "Like if you could foretell what was coming ahead."

"I would. That would be nice."

"I think everyone would say that until they actually would."

"Wouldn't you, My Lady?"

She sighed. "I can, Wakani. And it's not nice." She told him about the dreams. She also had to distinguish between her gift and spell magic as used by Reema.

"Like an oracle," he said.

"What?"

"Like in the stories. There's always an oracle, living in a dark forest by herself, or on... on a mountain! She speaks to the gods and they give her visions of the future. Heroes come to her and she speaks in riddles, guiding them on their way to their destiny."

"Then who guides to her destiny? I am the daughter of a farmer, and a mother, and a wife. I want nothing more than that."

"In Ao'Pan, they call people like you transcendent. They don't believe in gods anymore, those people, My Lady. They think that humans are being transformed into immortal beings. You might think it's true; they have whole tribes that can dash like lightning or change shape. You'd like it there. You'd be worshiped."

Ao'Pan referred to both the region of the continent south of the great desert and the common language spoken there. Coincidentally, both halves of the continent shared the word "Ao". In her language, Ao'Mu, it meant "to speak" and she had learned that in the southern language, it had the connotation of "everything" or "every place". So "Ao'Pan" meant "language of the south" in Ao'Mu and "Ao'Mu" meant "the place north" in Ao'Pan.

The language Ao'Mu was originally called Shema as it spread hundreds of years ago due to trade and war, and some still referred to it as so. When the Gold Road opened, a treacherous route through the middle of the desert, where gold from the south was traded for wares from the north, "Ao'Mu" became the preferred term.

"There's a whole mess of transcendent people down there," Wakani said. "My favorite are the ones who can lift heavy objects six times their weight. What I'd give to have that ability."

They rode into Mishi about a watch before sunset. It was a sprawling village built from bamboo, wood, and stone. Nasomi asked the villagers if they had seen an old witch traveling with two hyenas and a bound man. They told her of the rumors they heard and directed her to a man who claimed to have seen the witch. Nasomi recognized him as one of the two who had encountered Reema in her dream.

"I thought we were too drunk, seeing things," the man said. He leaned unsteadily onto a post of a fence around a chicken pen. "But I saw her, if you say she came here. She scared me and my friend."

"Where do you think she went?"

"Toward Naki maybe." He burped and studied Nasomi. "It's on the east side of the mountain, if you don't know. If you ask my opinion, I hope she leaves those Naki people with boils all over their skins."

She chuckled. "They're not good people?"

"The worst of humankind. A pompous lot, they boast too much. Who is this witch?"

"She is to be brought to Nari for judgment."

"I'd leave her alone, if it were me."

Nasomi shrugged. "Direct me to your most skilled medicine man. I may need some potion or other."

"Medicine man..." He thought for a few heartbeats. "Ah, go to Mihide. He is no medicine man, but he knows things. We have a saying in this village: Mihide knows. Yes, just that. Mihide knows. He probably knows the name of the witch by now." He chuckled and gave her directions.

Mihide's house was long and wide, L-shaped and set on a foundation three feet above the ground. The wooden steps up to the door creaked as Nasomi climbed them. She rapped on the door and called, "*Ondi!*"

The door opened and a short elderly man stared at her. He had narrow eyes, full grey hair, and a tapering beard. "A Narite," he said, eyes widening, stroking his pointy beard. "You're welcome. How may I be of service?"

"I was hoping you might help us with a witch problem."

Mihide looked past her to Wakani on the horse. Wakani waved. "Might this be the same witch I heard passed by last night?"

"Yes. With a captive man and two hyenas."

Mihide tsk-tsked. "I don't know how I can help. Witchcraft and magic are beyond me."

"We were told if there was anyone who would know what to do, it would be you."

"Come in, then, you and your companion. Tell me all you know and I can think of a way to help you. You're in time for tea." He spoke calmly, with all the confidence of a man who supposedly knows everything.

As Wakani tethered the horses, three children came from behind the house and ran to him. A girl and two boys about Meron's age. Her heart stung at the thought of having left her children. Meron must be in tears right now, she thought, and Naena might be at a loss of what to do.

"Azuku," Mihide called to the children. "No playing rough. I don't want you mistreating those horses."

"Alright, Grandfather," one of the boys said. The three petted and admired the horses, speaking excitedly.

Mihide gestured Nasomi and Wakani inside. He gave them stools to sit upon and he went into another room. He returned with three wooden cups of steaming brew.

"Rooibos," he said as he gave each one a cup. "Good for your skin, and for long life." He sat cross-legged on a rug, sipped his tea. "I am listening."

"The man is my husband," Nasomi started.

"And the witch?"

"The woman he was supposed to marry, before he met me."

Mihide bent forward, interested. "Tell me more."

"I met him twelve years ago and we fell in love. I didn't know at the time he had a woman he was set to marry, but he chose me instead. She returned years later with magical powers and has put a spell on him to obey everything she says."

Mihide asked probing questions on Nasomi's narration, and she ended up telling him about the dreams. If he had been listening before, that aspect en-raptured his attention. He asked more, she told him about the deja vu, the first tellings. She cut herself short when she realized he was too good a listener and she might tell him about the itching pimple on her left side.

"I didn't come to talk about the dreams. I want to find my husband."

"Yes, indeed. I am sorry. It is rare for a witch that powerful to come by this little village, and even more intriguing that her pursuer is a gifted Dreamer. We are living in interesting times. Let me see how I can help."

He reached into his sleeve and retrieved a short rod. It had holes along its length. He set his mouth to one end of it and blew. A windy discordant sound ema-nated from it. Mihide might know things, but he was no musician; the sound was jarring to the ears. He set the flute back into his sleeve, smiled, waited. He gestured for them to finish up their beverages.

A moment later, the front door opened, and a man entered. He reminded Nasomi of Tambo: tall, dark, unkempt hair. He was slimmer than Tambo, moved more impatiently. And his eyes were watery; he wiped their edges with the back of his hand. But for the smile on his lips, he looked like he wept in perpetuity.

"This is my neighbor, Nin," Mihide said, as the man took a stool. "Nin, these two are after the witch who passed by yesterday."

Nin nodded. "I heard of the witch." He spoke softly.

"Nin, they want to know where the witch went."

"I would not know. My focus was elsewhere, on... that thing, Mihide."

"Yes, yes, I know. But you could have roamed hereabouts, just to check on things. You can never know what you find."

"I can't be everywhere, Mihide. A witch passing by is interesting, I daresay, but it wasn't a priority."

"It is now. Let's help in what way we can."

"And... the thing?"

"It is still our priority. Just find out where the witch is, see to it that she is bound. That will suffice, won't it?" he asked Nasomi.

"Yes." Nasomi was confused about what was going on, but if this man Nin could help subdue Reema as quick as possible, she welcomed the idea. "And could you also direct us to a medicine man who can give us a potion to free my husband from the witch's spell?"

Mihide thought. "Can Jiro make it?" he asked Nin.

"That fool? He might know a thing or two about warding off witchcraft. But I wouldn't put my trust in his knowledge."

"The mages have such a potion," Nasomi said. "My husband's brothers had acquired it some years ago, when they suspected he was bewitched. But the mages wouldn't help me."

"If the mages have it," Nin said, smiling, "then I can get it for you. If you can wait until tonight, I can—"

"Tonight? We cannot delay any longer, I am afraid. We need to get to her quickly. You don't understand."

"We do," Mihide said. "We want you to give us more time to find your witch and the potion."

"And how will you disempower a witch? Get a potion from the mages?"

Mihide smiled. "We have our ways. All I ask is for a little patience."

Nasomi saw that this was a waste of time. An old man and a weak-looking man could not help her. These two would blabber time away. It seemed to be what they enjoyed doing. She and Wakani had horses, they could get to the witch faster. Besides, Nasomi was getting more convinced that Reema was headed back to Ar-womba. Where else would she go?

"If you cannot tell me how you intend to help, I think it is time for us to go," she said. "We have miles to—"

There was a thump above. Something scuttled across the roof. Outside, a child screamed. Nasomi ran after Wakani, Nin, and Mihide outside. Between them and the children stood a kowasa. It faced the children, tentacles wagging in the air.

Nin produced a dagger Nasomi had not seen before. He dashed toward the creature, but the boy called Azuku shouted, "Stop, Nin! Don't kill him." The boy ran between Nin and the kowasa.

"Azuku, move!"

"No. He says he doesn't want to hurt anyone." The creature cowered behind the boy, its deep blue eyes swimming like a puppy's. Azuku cocked his ears as if listening. "He says he came looking for her." He pointed at Nasomi.

"Bring it in, quickly," Mihide said. "Before anyone else sees it."

They all went back inside, taking the kowasa with them. Mihide didn't want to cause alarm in the village. Nin and Wakani held weapons, one a dagger, the other an ax, in case the kowasa decided to become unfriendly.

"Can he really do that, talk to them?" Nasomi asked.

"He can," Mihide said. "His mother could, too. She died from a terrible infection, though, when he was but a baby."

"He can really talk to the kowasa?" Her mind was heavy with astonishment. "Do you know what this means? It means we can finally understand what they want."

"No, it doesn't," Mihide said, rather bitterly. "I would request that you keep this secret."

"For over three hundred years, we have been wondering what the kowasa sought when they came this way, why they ravaged whole kingdoms, why they became little and docile when defeated. And the most pressing concern: if another horde will return. If Azuku can talk to them, we will know the answers. Take him to Nari."

"I will do no such thing. Not yet, at least. It's not the time."

"If you solve this mystery for Nari, you will be rewarded."

"Ha! Is that so? You think your people are good people? No, I know your people. Keeping these so-called enemies of yours captive, making a sport of killing them, prying children from their mother's teats to train them as warriors. Preparing for a war that will never come. The mages, too. They do unspeakable things to humans. They practice dark things. No, I cannot trust Azuku to Nari."

Nasomi didn't have an answer to that. She turned to Azuku, who, with his friends, was petting the kowasa. "Ask him his name."

"He has no name," the boy said. "They don't have names."

"How do you know it's a he?"

Azuku shrugged. "He says he wants to follow you. He thanks you for saving him."

"You saved the thing?" Nin said. "So, it followed you here."

"I only stood in the way of the mages capturing it."

"Yes. They recognize kindness," Mihide said. "It has become indebted to you now. You must go with it."

"What? I can never do that."

The kowasa bounded toward her and attached itself to her leg. She all but screamed. Her skin crawled, as she remembered Reema's rats climbing all over her. The children burst into laughter.

"We can't keep it here," Mihide said. "It will cause us much trouble."

"I can't just go traipsing with it, either. What if it attacks me?"

"He says he will keep following you," Azuku said.

"You're the one who can talk to it. I wouldn't even know what to do with it. How to feed it. It doesn't even matter. I have an important mission."

"I can teach him a few things," Azuku said. The kowasa turned and went to him as if it had heard him calling it. They spent a moment silently staring at each other.

"They communicate with a language of the mind," Mihide explained. "It's like pictures in the head." When Nasomi looked at him, he added, "So the boy says."

Azuku beckoned to Nasomi. "We have made a language for you to understand. When he says yes, he will do this" — the kowasa wagged the topmost right tentacle — "and this when he says no." The left tentacle wagged, slower. "When he is happy" — all tentacles wagged. "When sad or angry" — the tentacles lowered, even the head.

Azuku grinned at Nasomi. She grinned back, rubbed his head. "You're such a clever boy."

Mihide was eager to get rid of them. He opened the door and gestured for them to leave, promising to send help along the way. When Nasomi asked how, he just continued shooing them off. The kowasa climbed to the roof and jumped into a tree next to the house.

"Please, not a word about the boy," Mihide said as Nasomi and Wakani mounted their horses.

"My Lady," Wakani said uneasily as they rode away. "Are we going to go a long way?"

A sudden realization came to Nasomi: Wakani was not with her in the dream of her return. "I will not hold it against you if you decide to go back at any moment, Wakani."

CHAPTER 19

THE REDLAND

The kowasa was out of sight for most of the way to Naki. Three times it disproved Nasomi's guess that it had finally left her alone. The first time, it jumped from behind a bush ahead of the riders, chasing after a rodent, disappeared again. When Nasomi and Wakani rode through an avenue of trees, the kowasa fell from a branch and offered her a dark purple fleshy fruit, fixing its gaze on her until she took a bite. Up it went into the trees, out of sight again, and Nasomi threw the fruit away. It had a sharp sour taste, and she wasn't in a mood for potential illness. As they went down a winding path overlooking a long bamboo fence, out the kowasa came again, all tentacles wagging and eyes wide in delight. It jumped onto Nasomi's horse and gave her a translucent stone with grimy blue grains inside it.

"Are you sure about this thing, My Lady?" Wakani asked. He still held the ax at the ready.

"He would have followed us anyway. It is good to know he's on our side."

"He?"

"I've decided it's a he. I want to give him a name. Maybe Kanguya."

"You want to call it Kanguya? The most celebrated name of our kingdom? The one who fought against the kowasa?"

"It's the only name I can think of."

"My Lady, anything but that. What will people think?"

"We're not in Nari." She said to the kowasa. It wagged its yes tentacle.

There was significant traffic of people going the other way by then, skin and clothes stained black from the *myama* ore they conveyed in their carts. They stared wide-eyed at the kowasa, pointing and whispering among themselves, and Nasomi was surprised when Kanguya didn't rush into hiding. He knows we're not in Nari, she thought.

The road forked left toward the mine, and further on to Naki village. At first glimpse, besides the bamboo fence, Nasomi could not tell this village apart from Mishi. The architecture was the same, a forest of houses built from bamboo. The people were not accommodating, though. Six men in dark grey robes rushed at them, bearing spears.

"State your business," one of them said, as a crowd gathered behind the soldiers.

"We want a woman who came by here, traveling with two hyenas and a man," Nasomi replied.

The crowd parted and a young beautiful woman in a brown and orange flowing gown rushed through. She had rings on all her fingers, and her hair flowed in thick long braids. "What do they want?" she demanded. Her bitterness belied her beauty.

"They want the Bride," the leading spearman replied.

"Well, she's not here!" the young woman. "What do you people want from us?"

"I don't understand your question. We are only passing through, trying to track—"

"First it was an ugly bride with hyenas, now you with a kowasa. We know strange when we see it. You won't find us to be docile people if you're bringing an army to attack us."

"I am Nasomi Sapato, from Nari, a First Naki by clan. I am your tribesmate—"

"Ha! You think that means anything here?"

"Just show us which way the Bride went, My Chief," Wakani cut in, "and we will leave you alone."

"It's My Queen for you. Strange and rude, all you from the city," the young woman said, folding her arms. She indicated east with her head. "She went that way, to the Redland. Off you go!"

The people cheered as Nasomi and Wakani went on.

"What a paranoid group of people," Wakani muttered. He put his ax away when Kanguya jumped down and dashed ahead until he was out of sight.

Nasomi expected to come into the Redland within a short time but they rode on and on through thin woods. At a creek, Wakani watered the horses and refilled his and Nasomi's water pouches. They circumvented a marsh. Wakani used twigs and the sun's position to keep them going in their intended direction.

It was nigh sunset when the land became rocky and ochre, with surprisingly verdure shrubs and bushes. Baobab trees, tall and wide and sagely white, scattered across the land. They spotted a hut next to a tree, headed toward it and found themselves moving through a dotted settlement. Some of the baobab trees had been hewn through to make dwellings.

"It will soon be dark," Nasomi said, "and I feel a dream coming. We must take a rest here."

Wakani sighed in relief. "I thought you would say to keep on riding."

Well, they just couldn't keep on going without the guidance of a telling dream. She had been whispering Majen phrases to herself throughout the journey and had a strong tugging sensation in her belly. They stopped by a homestead of four red huts, spoke to a man and his wife. Nasomi showed them two golden coins, saying she would pay for a night's accommodation.

"Silver and gold and copper mean little to us unless we have travelers passing by to buy things off from," the man said. He took the coins anyway.

A hut was offered. It was warm inside despite its shabby looks. She and Wakani were given shredded blankets to be used as bed and coverings. Wakani set his

as far from hers as the room could allow, looking un-
comfortable about the arrangement.

Nasomi laughed. "It is well, Wakani. At least
you're close enough to protect me if somebody thinks of
attacking me in the night."

He smiled shyly, placed his ax at the edge of his
sleeping spot. They were invited outside, around a fire-
light, to eat a supper of a hard cornmeal and a sour vegetable Nasomi had not eaten before.

"It's the leaves of the baobab tree," the woman of
the homestead said. The man asked for some stories
from Nari. Wakani obliged him, telling the tale of how
Kanguya the first king built the first curve of the wall
even as he fought a battle against the Sofaza people.

Nasomi asked if they had seen an old witch pass
by.

"She came here," the man said. "Her hyenas
scared the little children of the village. 'Who among you
is the most powerful wizard?' says she. And when
Aghere walks toward her, she says, 'Make me beautiful
again.' But Aghere shakes his head and says he's a powerful man, but not enough to grant her what she wants.
He points her to the mighty tree and says, 'There's your
most powerful wizard.' She gets all angry, and black
smoke is coming off her, and we start to run away from
her. 'Are you jesting with me?' she says.

"Aghere stands there and says he's no man to
mock anyone. He points to the tree, says, 'It will give you
all you desire. If you are worthy. If you are patient to
hear its whispers.' She walks to it, slow, slow. Like she's
putting her hand on fire, slow, slow, she touches the
tree. And we're all watching, craning our necks forward.
And then she touches it." He burst out laughing. "Nothing. Nothing happens. Her hand is there for a long time.
She turns around, angry she looks so ugly. Uglier than
before. I've never seen anyone so embarrassed. The
whole village laughs at her, even her manservant laughs
at her. And the hyenas. She shouts, 'You're worthless.

The whole lot of you!' and she storms away. That was how she went."

"So, there's nothing special about the tree?" Wakani asked.

"Every baobab tree is special. They are not called Trees of Life for nothing. For thousands of years, we have dwelled among them, and they give us food, water, shelter, medicine, rope. And they tell us everything we need to know about the world. When six leaves fell from this tree" — he pointed at a tree silhouetted in the moonlight — "I knew I would have six guests today. And there you came, you, your horses and the kowasa."

"Ha!" Wakani teased. "That makes only five."

"The trees don't lie. Women conceive when they drink of its waters, men grow the courage to face evil spirits when they eat of its fruit. When a leaf falls, we get a visitor, or someone somewhere learns a great lesson. When a tree falls, we know that an entire people have fallen. Maybe because they have refused to listen to wisdom, they have mistreated their women, they have become evil, or they have taken to fighting amongst themselves."

"Not that I don't want to believe you, but when was the last time a tree fell?" Wakani said.

"If you have time for a long detour, come with me tomorrow a few miles from here. We can be there by noon. There's a leaning tree, held by the last of its roots. I can tell you that in the next five new moons, it will be on the ground."

"We have no time for detours," Nasomi said. She yawned. "Excuse me, I am in need of much sleep."

She went to the hut, and she said a prayer for her husband and children as she lay on the hard floor. Sleep came easily, and she slipped into a telling dream:

She was in the kitchen of her house. It was quiet and empty. The door was wide open, broken at one hinge. A form appeared at the door: a hooded man. He stepped in, looked around, made a sound of deep thinking. Kaan, the mage, moved as though he floated rather

than walked. When she drew closer — and he didn't
show any signs of perceiving her — she heard him muttering strings of Majen.

He moved from room to room, having a quick
glance, touching nothing. Then he went back to the
kitchen. He knelt, sniffed, tossed some *myama* dust onto the floor, watched it burst into golden lines. He made
the same sound of thinking. "Mhmm."

Nasomi entered his mind. It was a realm of wonder. She had never really thought minds could be actual
disparate things, having been in the minds of others
through these dreams: Reema, the hyena sorcerers,
Tambo's mother. The mage's mind amazed her. It was
full of shapes she hadn't seen before but somehow could
recognize, sounds she had never put together but were
part of her daily life.

Kaan's mind was playful, yet mature, shaped by
years and years of dedication, of breaking apart every
truth and making new truths. When he stood and looked
around, he did it in noncommittal sweeps, yet the information he took in was vast: the layout of the furniture
and how it had determined the movements of the people
that lived here; the pattern of dust settlement, how air
moved through the house; he *saw* connections between
the dust and the dulling lights from the firestone lamps
on the walls. That was strange, how he made links between things that could never be more so different. He
saw and connected, judged, judged his judgments, made
guesses, stacked guesses in a part of his mind the way
Nasomi would stack folded clothes.

He saw traces of magic in the *myama* trails,
some sort of a reconstruction of the events that had tak-
en place here. "This is a magic not filled by hate," he said
to himself, drawing conclusions from stacks in other
parts of his mind. What passed into his memory were
hundreds of situations where people used spell magic
out of jealousy, fury, and hate. Those emotions gave the
magic they used evil twisted potent, and most times
were detrimental to the user as much as the victim.

"This is a magic fueled by love," he said to himself. "A love so deep. That is why we couldn't detect it." It surprised him, having never seen or heard the like before. It was something he needed to go and discuss with Thorro.

He walked out of the house, regretting that it was too late to help the woman who had come to the Mage Council for help.

Nasomi awoke, a tear flowing into her ear. She held back the weeping, fell into a normal sleep inundated by a series of dreams involving tall trees, blue monkeys and a young angry queen who axed down people she didn't like.

A shout woke her up. Someone was shaking her shoulders. She screamed when she saw a dark shape with red eyes above her. The thing pressed her down. She heard Wakani shout, "My Lady!" and something flew in the air. The ax passed right through the daemon without hurting it and embedded into the wall.

"Stop, stop! It's me!" cried the daemon. "It's me, Nin! From Mishi. Quit being so dramatic!"

"Nin?" shouted Wakani. "How is it you're here?"

Nasomi got used to the darkness and saw it was indeed Nin. No, it was more like Nin's form came together to show he was a man. His eyes were red like rubies, when before in Mishi, Nasomi could have sworn they had been a deep brown. He put something in her hand. "Here's the potion you wanted, from the mages." It was a leather pouch. "The witch is nearby, you must hurry."

Wakani came to touch Nin to make sure he was real.

"How did you get this?" Nasomi asked. Her heart had settled its thumping and she stood up.

"Will explain everything if we ever meet again. Arrrgh!" He touched his head.

"Why are your eyes red?" Wakani asked. "How did you get here?"

"I found her, your witch, tried to get close. But she felt me, Nasomi! She felt me, way before I was upon her. She did something to me, gave me a terrible head-ache. I would have died, I tell you, if I didn't sip some of the potion. I will be fine. Just need some time to heal."

He stood up. Wakani moved away from him, watching him with trepidation. "She's going to Mifir-hana, the witch. I couldn't subdue her. I can't help you anymore, she did something... she almost killed me. I wish you luck, Nasomi. I wish you luck."

"How did you find...?"

"You don't want to ask too many questions about me." He put his finger to his lips. "Not a word about this. Not a word." He parted the curtain at the door and stepped outside.

Nasomi and Wakani rushed out after him, but he was nowhere to be seen. The pouch was real in her hand, so all this had actually happened. But Nin had vanished.

Wakani touched the back of his head with both hands, shaking his head vigorously. "Just two days away from my usual life, and the world is a place of mystery and wonder."

CHAPTER 20

THE MADNESS

The moving was too slow for Nasomi. Every mile seemed to be an infinite distance. They pushed the horses as hard as they could. They rested little. They kept as straight a direction as terrain could allow. Wakani became glum. He brooded, didn't speak much, and often scratched the back of his head out of habit.

"I know this is beyond what I had intended," Nasomi said to him, seven days from the Redland. She'd seen his agitation, had overridden it with her hope of catching up to the Bride, had ignored it as she tried to ignore her own growing frustration.

He gave a weak smile, as if saying *It's well, My Lady*. He scratched the back of his head, didn't even look at her, as though the rolling hills ahead were a marvel to behold.

"Wakani, talk to me."

"The horses, my lady. They are thin, tired. We drive them hard through bad territory, they have nothing much to eat. What will My Chief say when I return them like this?"

"I will explain to him. And you? Tell me straight, how this is affecting you."

He scratched his head. "I... I will do as I am told."

"It's too much for you."

"I have a daughter, three years old now. Her birthday was yesterday. I thought we would be back by now. She must be wondering where I am."

"What is her name?"

That brought a smile to his face. "Khuya. Sweet little girl."

ENOCK I. SIMBAYA

Kanguya the kowasa appeared, dragging the carcass of a rabbit. Wakani jumped off his horse, picked up the rabbit where Kanguya dropped it. He skinned it with his ax. Nasomi got down her horse as well, went to sit under a tree. She drew up her knees and hugged herself. Her bones ached from the much traveling and sleeping on hard ground and on tree branches.

"I would have gathered three copper coins by now," Wakani went on. "I pray the house I promised to buy by end of Ra hasn't been bought yet."

"Take me up to Mifirhana," Nasomi said. "You can turn from there." Kanguya came by her side. She stroked his back. The kowasa wagged happily.

"I don't want you to think I would abandon you," Wakani said.

"Don't worry about me. Turn back from Mifirhana if you have to. I have Kanguya here." *And my dreams,* she didn't add, rubbing her belly as if she could reach the usual feeling inside.

The dreams. They were frequent, even without her whispering in Majen. And they frightened her. Among a few random ones of people and places she didn't recognize, there was a recurring dream of a boy held captive in an old well. His unending cries were unbearable to hear. He coughed and spat from the choking smells of rotten things down there, as well as his own urine and feces. Once every day, a silhouette opened the well cover, dropped food for the boy, closed the well again.

Then there were the dreams of Tambo and the Bride. Reema constantly professed her love for Tambo. He replied with scowls and the pouting of his lips. She bathed him, cropped his hair, shaved his beard, fed him. He could speak and think of his own will but was helpless when it came to the rest of his body. His hands and feet moved according to Reema's whims. He couldn't look away when she bathed or chose to disrobe whenever she desired. He couldn't refuse when she told him to build them a shelter when they stopped to rest. He couldn't stop walking even when his body ached because she said to walk.

When Wakani went off to gather firewood, there remained a lonesome milieu. Nasomi spoke to Kanguya, more to keep her tormenting thoughts at bay.

"I simply watch as everything I love is taken away from me. I feel everything, see everything. I see the hatred, the helplessness, the greed, the evil... I can do nothing about it, Kanguya. Nothing. No one hears me shout in a telling, I cannot touch or move nothing. I am not there inasmuch as I am *there*. I am more invisible than a ghost. I hate it."

Kanguya wagged his yes tentacle, curled up and fell asleep. Nasomi sighed. "It has to end." She fell asleep and in the ensuing dream, she watched Reema and company climb down a rocky hill, head toward a deep blue lake in the distance.

Nasomi and Wakani covered the rest of the way to Mifirhana in three weeks. Wakani suggested they cut through by going straight eastward, but thick vegetation forced them northward, and adjacent high hills constrained them to take a winding route. Nasomi almost screamed in delight when the lake, and the town Mifirhana by its edge, came into view.

Mifirhana was hot, humid and hilly. Dwellings had been built in such a way as to avoid cutting down too many trees; so Mifirhana was both a forest and a town, and Nasomi couldn't tell its extent.

They left the horses by an inn, walked to a more open marketplace. Nasomi was about to ask after the Bride, when, by happenstance, she was face to face with Reema and Tambo.

The two moved among the clustered stalls like a man with his aging mother. Reema carried a basket of what she'd picked out in her bag. When she saw Nasomi, her mouth went wide.

"You!"

"Nasomi?" Tambo said. His expression was a medley of surprise and delight.

ENOCK I. SIMBAYA

Nasomi reached into her bag, found the wrapped knife at the bottom. She shook off the wrapping cloth even as she charged at Reema, letting her bag fall off her shoulders. Reema said something to Tambo. He rushed toward Nasomi and caught her, squeezed her knife-holding hand.

"Let me go, Tambo! Let me kill her!"

"I am not doing this." He twisted her hand so hard some bones cracked. "Reema, make me stop! I am hurting her!"

"Wakani, get her!" Nasomi said. She kicked Tambo in the leg to set herself free, but his grip was firm on her.

Wakani had his ax in his hand. He didn't move, though. "The old lady? That's her?"

"That's her Wakani. Get her now."

He moved too late. The people around them closed in, placing their hands on Tambo, getting him away from Nasomi.

"What's going on here?" people demanded.

"You're hurting the woman!"

"Who is this man who hits a woman?"

"Let's beat him up."

They caught Wakani, too, divested him of his ax. There were calls for mob-dispensed justice:

"Sticks and stones!"

"Murderer, thief!"

"Off with his head!"

"He attacked an old lady!"

Nasomi heard thumps, saw fists and kicks flying at Tambo and Wakani. Some sensible people were calling for calm, for a chance to understand what was going on before resorting to violence.

In the midst of the various shouts, Reema's voice shouted, "Loshui! Gweuka!"

No one took her seriously as she continued calling for Loshui and Gweuka. Then there were cries of dismay and everyone was trampling and stampeding away. The hyenas came to Reema's side, snarling and snapping their teeth at those who hadn't run fast enough. The market was soon empty, except for a few brave ones who peeped from hiding spots.

Wakani found his ax. He picked it up and threw it at the Bride. One of the hyenas jumped and snatched it from the air in its mouth. The other charged at him. He turned to run, but it was too fast for him. It brought him down, and he was screaming as it dragged him by the leg.

"Bring him to me," Reema said. "I remember you. A servant in the Go palace. Let's see whom the ax will kill today." She snatched the weapon from the hyena's mouth.

Nasomi picked her bag, rifled for the leather pouch containing the potion. "Quick, drink this!" She untied the fastening and brought it to Tambo's mouth. "It will set you free."

"Tambo, shut your mouth!" Reema cried. She was now looking their way.

He shut his mouth so hard Nasomi heard his teeth snap together.

"Slap her."

The back of his hand came too quick for Nasomi's reaction. Her vision darkened; her ear rung. Her limbs became weak, she couldn't hold herself together. The world spun. She felt the back of her head hit the ground.

When she could see better, Reema was standing above her, looking down at her with a hatred that could roast a pig. She stroked the ax shaft as she spoke.

"He was mine and will always be. Should I prove it to you?"

She threw the ax away, picked up the potion pouch. Much of it had spilled out. She sniffed at it, made a disgusted face. "Here, Tambo, take it."

Tambo came close, received the pouch.

"Drink it," Reema said.

Tambo lifted it to his mouth.

"Wait, stop!"

He stopped.

"Spill it all to the ground."

Nasomi watched as all her hopes of freeing Tambo poured out of the pouch, seeped into the soil. She cursed, "Swallow you, Reema!" She got up and threw a slap at Reema. Reema caught her hand. And for a heartbeat, her hand felt warm where Reema held it. Reema let go quickly as though she'd just touched a hot cinder, then gave Nasomi a burning slap of her own.

"Mine, I have told you. He will love me, like he loved me before, and give me children. And you won't be there to ruin it. Tambo, my love, please bring me the knife."

As Tambo choicelessly picked up the knife, brought it to her, he said, "Please, Reema, don't do this. She's my wife, Reema."

"I am your wife now, Tambo. Where was she when we met, when we planned our future together? She destroyed all that. You have to see that."

He gave her the knife. "I will do anything you say, just don't hurt her. She will go back to Nari, and you can take me away. Please. Please."

Nasomi dashed for Wakani's ax, but a hyena jumped in her way, snapping its teeth and sending her back to Reema. Wakani was unconsciousness where he lay on the ground, his leg bleeding.

"I will make a small cut then," Reema said as she brought the knife toward Nasomi's neck. "A deep one. Something to remind her to never have come in between us again."

The hyenas blocked Nasomi's escape. Reema brought the knife closer, and Nasomi reached the limit she could crane her head away. The knife touched her neck.

Something jumped at Reema. She screamed like a scared little girl as she struggled against the kowasa on her back. She must have remembered she was a powerful witch, for she composed herself and a smoky hand from her body grabbed Kanguya and threw him off her.

166

"Bite her, Kanguya!" Nasomi yelled. "Bite the damned witch!"

The hyenas were upon Kanguya, and all three were rolling on the ground, biting and scratching and snarling at each other. Claws had protruded from Kanguya's paws, and they reaped deep gushes in the hyenas' hides. Reema turned back to Nasomi and kicked her in the belly. Nasomi bent, trying to breathe air that she seemed to be unable to find. Reema kicked her again when she fell to the ground.

Nasomi had no more fight left in her. She'd lost. It had all been for nothing. She let all her struggle go, didn't bother with the pain anymore. She let Reema have her way, only watched as the Bride administered blows and kicks. She saw Reema's shadow wave, form spikes that crawled toward her. Nasomi didn't move even as her mind screamed for her to. She didn't care anymore.

What happened next was something she only made sense of a few months later, when she recalled it. At that moment, her mind was not with her, but her eyes saw and her ears heard: the Bride stopped hitting her, was facing the kowasa in shock. Kanguya had glowing blue light waving on his skin; no, deep in his skin, veins of light; his claws were sharp and long, he thrust them repeatedly into a hyena. And was he slightly bigger in form? Had he just bulged twice his puny size in a matter of heartbeats?

Reema shouted something, her shadow turned toward Kanguya. It shoved the kowasa off the hyena, but it was too late for the hyena. It lay dead. It began to break apart in dry flakes, like ashes blown by the wind, until there was nothing left of it.

Reema screamed. Kanguya got up and came at her. Reema dashed away. So did the other hyena. And Tambo, too, at Reema's call. Nasomi was left alone, and nothing made sense anymore.

She didn't know how long it was before she was out of her stupor. All she realized was that she was standing. How she got up—she couldn't remember.

Reema, Tambo, Wakani, Kanguya, the hyenas. None of them were there, and in their place was a growing crowd of strangers. Men, women, children were staring at her, whispering, pointing at her.

She regained some senses, but she was not herself entirely.

"Where is she?" she demanded of the crowd. They gasped and pulled back a bit.

"The witch who took my husband, where is she?" She ran at them; they gave her way. She went to a stall, started pulling a plank out. "You know where she is. You're hiding her. Kanguya, bite this one."

She ran back and picked the knife from the ground. She yelled something she didn't know she could say. A string of mumbles and shrieks. A new language. She even smiled.

"She has run mad," someone said. "She needs help! Call the Daughters."

"Kanguya, you silly dog. Why are you not biting these people?" Nasomi laughed at herself. "You're not a dog. You're a... a blue thing. Where are you? Kill them, Kanguya! Like you did the hyena."

The world was an interesting place. It was a mat beneath her. She put her foot on Nari, watched it crumble into dust. She jumped into the Redland, frolicked among the trees. She kicked Mount Lupili from her way.

"I need her," she said to the people as she danced on Mishi, watching the tiny people vanish as Nin had. "I need to tell her I am sorry—Look!" she said as she jumped over the great desert into Ao'Pan. "Do you see that woman? They are drowning her son to punish her. But they don't know he's a god."

Two women came forward, each taking her by an arm. They carried her away. She spoke to them, in her mumbling language, wondering why no one had ever learned to speak it. It was the best language in the world.

They threw her into a dark room, and she was overwhelmed by fear. "Please!" she begged, banging on the walls of the room. "Please, the room will eat me! Get me out of here!"

The walls were closing in on her, and she screamed and cried. No one came for her. She cowered to a corner, even as the walls kept coming closer, threatening to crush her like a bug. She didn't know if she slept or imagined things, but she was in a telling.

She was in Reema's mind, which was full of pain and bitterness. Through Reema's eyes, she saw Tambo seated on a rock, morose. The remnant hyena was by her side, looking like a lost kitten.

"How?" Reema said out loud. "How was she able to find us?

Tambo looked away.

"You know, don't you?"

"I don't."

"Don't lie to me, Tambo, I am not in a good mood. Tell me. It's that natural magic of hers, isn't it?"

I worked so hard for this, Reema thought. It isn't fair that she has everything. She sweated not a drop for anything, but she gets a natural magic. Damn the *Mara*!

"Swallow you, Tambo! She killed Loshui!" She walked to him, grabbed his arm, made him feel pain. "How is she able to find us? How can she command a kowasa?"

He tried to be brave against the pain, but she kept squeezing.

"Tell me!"

"I will tell you! Get your hand off me!"

"Only when you tell me."

"She dreams things. Sees things in her dreams. The past, the future. Take your hand off me!"

She did. She turned from him. "You could have told me earlier. Now I have to do something about it."

"What can you possibly do?"

"Something to ensure she will never catch up to us."

CHAPTER 21

THE SEER

For a month, Nasomi blubbered and screamed in the tiny dark room. Someone brought her food three times a day, but she kicked the plates away. The pain of her failure and gloominess of the room oppressed her when she was awake. The telling dreams haunted her when she was asleep.

She dreamed of a war; arrows flying, spears stabbing into flesh, fires consuming homes and villages, turning to ash in heartbeats what had taken ages to build. A wall crushed down. A whole people left their ancient home. A young girl clutched a straw doll, eyes swollen from crying, as she moved among the dead bodies of her family, calling for her mother.

In another place, a teenage boy devastated by acne boiled with murderous thoughts at his friends who danced around a fire and didn't invite him. A starving mother received kicks and insults wholeheartedly in exchange for a morsel of bread for her baby. A pretty young lady packed a few belongings into a sack, not sure where she would go, as long as she got far away from her unfaithful husband, out to an adventure she'd been dreaming of.

And then, there was the boy in the well — she always dreamed of him. Alone in the dark, dank, stinking well. No one to hear him cry. No one to rescue him. Some light would enter when the stone covering the well would open, and a shadowy face of a man would look down on the boy. "Keep silent in there," the man would say in a gruff voice. "Or I will throw this stone to crush you." He would toss down a piece of bread, close the lid.

These were the dreams that dominated her madness: the sadness, the destruction, the hurt, the crushed dreams in the lives of people she didn't even know. Sometimes she woke up with a terrible hunger, and she would salvage what she'd kicked onto the floor. If the girl who checked up on her brought food at such a moment, Nasomi would snatch the plate and yell at the girl, banging the door shut and wolfing down the food.

One dawn, she woke up from a dream of a bleeding man who knelt down to accept his death from a spear wound to his shoulder. He shivered from the night wind, winced when his wounds throbbed; but when death didn't come, he stood up and went to look for his daughter. Nasomi was lying on the floor, and she watched the morning light through her tiny window. She had ripped the curtain off the previous night. She got up. The room didn't seem as dark as before. The walls remained solid and didn't close in on her.

The door opened and the girl quickly put the plate onto the floor.

"Thank you," Nasomi said. The girl's eyes went wide, she looked at Nasomi for a long time. "It smells good," Nasomi said.

"You're talking sense now, Esha," the girl said.

"Nasomi is my name."

"Esha is our term of respect for a woman. Musha is for men."

"I see." Nasomi sat on the bed. It was thick, soft, probably made of feathers. The floor was compacted clay; she counted four ruts upon it. She was in a thick seamless dress, and it stank of sweat. Her hair was a stiff mess; dandruff sprinkled out in copious amounts when she scratched it.

Nasomi went to pick up the plate, but when she sat down to eat, she fell into weeping. The girl came to sit next to her, put a hand around her.

"I'm so sorry," Nasomi said. "I feel ashamed."

"Do not be, Esha. You were not yourself."

"The way I treated you. It wasn't good of me. You've brought me food every day, sheltered me... I feel so bad."

"I understand. Don't be too harsh on yourself. You are well now. The elders insisted that you needed to face the pain in solitude."

Nasomi learned that she was under the care of a religious women's group called the Daughters of Mohale. They cared for the sick in body, mind, and soul, and offered spiritual guidance according to the precepts of their goddess.

The girl went to report Nasomi's recovery. Nasomi was moved to a bigger and airier room, with a view on the square where worshippers came to lay their gifts for the goddess. Nasomi said she wasn't quite ready to face the world, and the Daughters indulged her. Four women came, at random moments, to talk to her, and each proclaimed Nasomi had been cured of the madness.

She was surprised to learn that Wakani was still in Mifirhana. "I did not want you to think I'd abandon you, My Lady," he said when he came to visit her when the Daughters allowed her other visitors.

"But your family. Your daughter."

"I will go back to Nari tomorrow, My Lady. I just wanted to know you were well."

Wakani did not go. He brought her food, some of which he'd cooked himself, and attended to her. He told her about the goings-on in Mifirhana, as if he was now one of its people. The whole town, he said, was talking about the incident at the market, and the old Bride had run off eastward. Kanguya the kowasa romped about the town, making friends with children and dogs.

"The brown horse, My Lady," he said, touching his heart. "She was too sick. She died. The other one has adapted well to Mifirhana, and has grown healthy in the stable. He is fit to carry us both."

"Return with it to Nari. I will find a way."

"Do you mean to continue pursuing the witch?"

"I do. It's the only thing for me to do. You need to go back to Nari, Wakani."

"I will go tomorrow, My Lady."

But he didn't go. For another month and some days, Nasomi wept when she was left alone. Her dreams changed, too. In her sadness, she saw the shape of the world. She floated over the kingdom of mountains a thousand miles southeast of Mifirhana: a vast jagged land, black and grey, with splotches of thick forests. Some peaks were topped with white, some spewed columns of fire; red hot rivers flowed down into bright bubbling lakes. Leonine creatures roamed this land, with skin the color of the mountains, and long tails ending in stings.

North, south, east, and west her dreams took her. She saw Mishi, Nari, and Naki, knew how far each was from her position in her room in Mifirhana. She saw three frozen cities north of Arwomba, desolate and cold, preserved in an unchanging frigid era. She saw a great city of stone and fog, thousands of miles south, with buildings so tall they reached the clouds. Through the unending fog, humans with eyes the color of emerald hefted stones and sang echoing songs.

Seas, bays, plains, plateaus, vales, hills. The landforms of Ao filled her dreams. Sometimes, she went deep. Beneath the dark well where the boy was held captive, she saw fractures, felt the world groaning, saw red hot seas.

She had no dreams of Tambo or the Bride, no matter how much she focused and thought about them. She saw Meron and Ramona in Nari, him playing with some newfound friends, and her sitting on a stool, her hands on her cheeks in deep thought.

This is not right, she thought often. Nobody should be able to have this ability.

When she was ready to face life again, she went out to sit at the edge of a wide staircase and watch people go in and out to seek counsel from the Daughters.

Kanguya bounded out of nowhere, rushed to embrace her leg.

She smiled. "I missed you too, my friend. I see you've gotten to like it here."

He wagged all his tentacles, then dashed away to play with children. The town children had taken to the kowasa as well. They didn't fear him as children – or even adults – of Nari would. And it seemed he caused them no harm.

Wakani came, dressed in one of the unremarkable brown tunics of the men of Mifirhana. He washed Nasomi's hair and braided it into cornrows. Much hair remained, so he tied some of it into a bun at the top of Nasomi's head, and combed out the rest into a thick puff at the back. "This your look, Nasomi Esha," he said. "It fits you so well."

Nasomi looked at her reflection in a water basin.

"I love it. Thank you, Wakani. I didn't know you could dress hair so well."

He smiled. "I have a daughter. And wife. They let me mess with their hair the way I want. I have a gift for you." He presented a leather headband studded with cowries. He placed it on Nasomi's head as though placing a crown on her. It had four loops dangling from its bottom edge, two to go over the eyes and the other two over the ears. It was a common accessory for the women in Mifirhana.

"Now I look like one of them," Nasomi said. "Or should I say one of you. You seem to have fitted well here."

"They have given me a small cabin not far from here. I get to help them chop wood, or feed their horses. Do you know that in the entire Mifirhana, there is a total of only twelve horses? Of which one is ours."

She was quiet for a while. She was thinking about how she could dream again of Tambo. The Bride had done something to deter Nasomi from dreaming them. Wakani didn't disturb her silence until she said, "Is it always this hot in Mifirhana?"

"So they tell me. It's a wonderful place, and I admit I will be sad to leave. But I need to go home. You're something of a celebrity here, My Lady. The Mad Esha with a Pet Kowasa. That's what some call you."

Nasomi gritted her teeth. "Anything but that, surely. I hope I am not scaring people by being out here."

"Please don't worry. It is meant to be more humorous than insulting. There's nothing much in Mifirhana for people to talk about, so they're always obsessed with any unusual thing... Well, there's the missing prince now, so you're off the top of the list."

"Missing prince?"

"It's really strange how he disappeared. He went out playing with some of his young companions, never returned to the palace. If he's dead, or never found, his uncle Majiyo will become the ruler. The king and queen died four years ago, and they had no other children besides this one."

"You truly have become of these people." She chuckled. "How old is he? The prince."

"Seven. No, wait, eight."

Could it be? Nasomi wondered. "You said he's been missing for how long?"

"Six days now."

"I could be wrong, Wakani. But I know where he is."

"Eh? You do, My Lady? One of your visions?"

"In a well. An old well. He's trapped there – held captive."

"There are many old wells in Mifirhana."

Nasomi thought. She remembered that whenever the boy's captor opened the well cover...

"A guava tree! Next to the well, there's a guava tree, with a single branch over the well if you were looking at it from below."

Wakani stood up abruptly. "I'll be back, Esha. I must report this." He ran off.

Nasomi sat on the staircase for over a watch of the sun. Kanguya brought her five unique stones and went off to play again. She got tired and went inside to rest. She fought against sleep, desiring not to dream any more strange things.

Presently, before she could succumb to the power of sleep, there was a hubbub outside. She went to see what was happening. The whole town was running in one direction.

"He's been found!" they shouted. "Prince Tebula has been found!"

Nasomi went out to join them, breaking into a trot to get a good view. Ahead, someone was shouting, "Get out of the way! Out of the way!"

People stopped moving. Nasomi pushed herself through until she came to a gap in the bodies. The man shouting "Out of the way!" was carrying a boy in his arms. The boy was limp and pallid. His eyes were wide open but Nasomi could not tell whether he could see. Her heart went out to him.

She thought of her children, couldn't imagine what she would want to do to the person who would hurt them this way. And she was caught in a whirl of emotions. Pain at her failure to get Tambo back, sadness at having no dreams to guide her to him, shame for having left Ramona and Meron the way she did, frustration at not knowing what to do next. Her husband was bound by a spell somewhere in the east, her children were without their parents in the west, and here she was in the middle of goings-on she had no idea why she was part of.

Wakani came running toward her, excited. "Just like you said, My Lady! You were right."

Before long, Nasomi was the center of attention. Questions, exclamations, and even a few insults, flew her way, too many for her to grasp and answer. A woman of small stature, in a flowing white robe, came before her, and quietness more or less settled among the people. This is the prophetess, Nasomi guessed, the leader

among the Daughters of Mohale. From Wakani, Nasomi
had learned that the prophetess was addressed as the
Eyes and Ears of Mohale.

"The Goddess bless you," the small woman said.

Nasomi didn't know how to reply. Wakani stood
beside her and it was all the comfort she could wish for.
She was feeling as if the madness would overwhelm her
again.

"How did you know where to find the prince,
Esha?" the Eyes and Ears of Mohale asked Nasomi.

"I dreamed him."

"You dreamed him? We have searched for him
for many days. Just this evening we would have declared
him dead and began the mourning ceremonies. Thanks
to you, and to the Goddess, he has been saved."

"Finally, a true prophetess," someone said.

"Careful what you say," someone interjected.

The prophetess lifted a hand for calm as murmurs spread. If she was insulted by the comment, she
didn't show it. "Nasomi Esha," she said. "Tell us how you
were able to dream this."

"I just did," Nasomi replied, not sure how to answer the question.

"Do you have such dreams then?"

"Quite often."

"And whoever tried to harm him, would you
please tell us who they are?"

"I am afraid I cannot. I did not see him clearly."

"She knows nothing!" a cry came.

"Isn't she the mad Esha? Why should we believe
what she says?"

"She had a hand in this."

Wakani shouted, "Don't you say bad things about
My Lady. She was in a care room for two months! She's
done a good thing for you ungrateful people."

There was a general murmur of agreement. The
prophetess extended a hand toward Nasomi. "It is the
Goddess who led you to us, in our time of need. Come,
have supper with me, and tell me of your dreams."

ENOCK I. SIMBAYA

"A Seer!" someone said, and some people took up to chanting: "A true Seer! The Goddess is good to us!"

CHAPTER 22
THE CONSPIRATORS

Without a telling of Tambo and the Bride, Nasomi was lost for what to do. Among all the strange and
scary dreams she had, there was emptiness where she
sought for them. She knelt in her room whenever she
was alone, trying to force up the familiar feeling of a telling, focusing her mind on Tambo or on Reema, but
nothing of them came when she slept.

The prophetess implored her to stay a few days
in Mifirhana, and pestered her about whether she had
any dream of whoever put the prince in the well. Nasomi
had none, got tired of explaining to the Eyes and Ears
about the haphazardness of the tellings, kept reminding
those who fawned on her that she was no special seer, or
any seer for that matter. She stayed, though, because she
was waiting for a dream to guide her to Tambo.

As days went by, she was faced with only one
choice: to return to Nari. There was a pit in her belly,
and it dug deeper whenever she thought she had to give
up Tambo. She cried over it, made her peace with it,
cried over it again. It meant letting go of the dream she
had had about returning with Tambo, letting go of the
conviction that it had to be her to get him back, letting
go of the promise she had made to Ramona. Her children would have to grow up without a father. She would
say he was dead, and she would mourn with them.

Reema had won. She was the victor in this. She'd
broken a home, taken a husband and father. Driven Nasomi mad, and was gone beyond where Nasomi could
reach her. On the night before she could depart, Nasomi
failed to sleep, fighting within herself over the two

choices. Returning home seemed the wise thing to do, but was she to give Tambo up just like that?

The next morning, as Nasomi was preparing herself, Wakani knocked on her door. "It is I," he said. "May I enter?"

She said to come in. He was dressed in the clothes he came with from Nari, had a good smile on his face and Nasomi could tell he was trying to conceal how truly excited he was about finally going home.

"I thought you might need these back." He had in her hands Nasomi's folded cloak, the leather bag and something else wrapped in a cloth. Nasomi looked into the bag. There was the water pouch, a piece of cloth, and her coins.

Delight and hurt sprung in her heart when she took the cloak. "I thought someone had stolen these."

"I kept them in my room."

The wrapped item was the kitchen knife with a white handle.

"You kept this?" Nasomi asked.

"Yes, My Lady. It looked important."

"It's... not. But I'll take it. I guess I cannot leave it here. I will discard it on our way. Is everything ready?"

"Yes, My Lady. Though the prince has requested your presence. He awaits you at the palace."

"Me? Why?"

"You told them where he was. You saved his life. I think he means to thank you. I came to escort you there."

An idea came to Nasomi: Maybe I should ask him for a horse. She rewrapped the knife and tossed it onto her bed. Maybe, she thought, maybe I can even go to look for Tambo, even without the dreams. Either way, a horse would serve me well. Wakani and I could go our separate ways. "Help me with my hair," she said to Wakani.

The palace of Mifirhana wasn't as grand as any in Nari were, but it was majestic in its own way. It was set atop a hill, hewn stairs leading up to it. Around the four buildings that made the royal dwellings were well-maintained lawns and flower gardens. Guards stood vigil at a number of spots about the hill. Wakani led her by the arm all the way to the Meeting Hut. Kanguya came along.

"Go in there, kneel, and the rest you will be told what to do," Wakani said. "I will wait for you here."

Nasomi entered. The Meeting Hut was as wide as it was long. It had a dais in front upon which the young prince sat in a chair and on a larger chair sat a man Nasomi guessed was the uncle, Majiyo. She walked in between rows of filled benches, a score pair of eyes upon her and the kowasa slinking beside her.

Nasomi knelt when she was near the dais.

"Rise and come closer," the boy said. She could tell he was trying to be confident, to show manliness in the presence of his representatives. She took as much information as she could in a non-offending glance at him: a slender boy, wide eyes, a large shaved head. He wore no shirt but a deep brown sash across his bony chest, and a leopard-skin skirt up to the knees. His feet were shod in sandals with short thongs fastened about the ankles. He looked to be about ten years old.

Meron is nigh eight, Nasomi realized. And as motherless and fatherless as this prince was. I should go back to Nari.

"I want to relay my gratitude to you," the prince said. For finding me," the boy said. "I called for you to show you that..." He was remembering rehearsed words. "Tha... to show you how delighted and grateful I am."

"Had it not been for you," the uncle said — his gaze was penetrating, as though he was taking her apart — "Who knows what would have happened? This ability of yours, surely it comes only from the Goddess."

"Perhaps," Nasomi replied. "I, too, am delighted I was of help, My Prince. When I had the vision, I didn't know what it was about, or whom I saw."

"These visions of yours," Majiyo said. "Explain to us how they work."

"In truth? I don't know. I don't choose them, or understand them. They just come to me through my dreams."

"You said you saw Prince Tebula in the dream when he was in the well."

"Yes."

"And you did not see who did it? The evil one who put his dirty hands upon the ruler of Mifirhana?"

"I did not."

As the people looked at and nudged at each other, Nasomi noticed the prince shivered slightly. Her heart went out to him, and she couldn't keep back the mother in her.

"Are you well, My Prince? You were in that dark smelly well a long time, with little room to move."

"I was scared," the prince said. Majiyo gave him a sharp look and the boy kept quiet.

"The prince is recovered," Majiyo said. "He is strong now. Only some pain in his legs, but it will heal. If no one has anything to say...." He gestured to the seated council of the four elder Daughters in the front, and older leaders immediately behind the Daughters.

They all shook their heads.

Nasomi spoke again, to the prince. "I know what it means to be alone and afraid. It is scary. All you think is how it is the end of you. I have felt it many times. But there's something that happens to help. Often, if not always. Sometimes it's other people, sometimes it's the mysterious goings-on in the world, the workings of the *Ma*— of the Goddess. I felt your pain, My Prince. I know what you experienced. I was there with you. You did not see me, did not feel me, but I was there, and I understood your suffering. You were not alone."

The prince jumped off his chair and ran to hug Nasomi. The gesture surprised many, shocked some, left Majiyo with a stupid face. An atmosphere of loving peace settled in the room. Nasomi saw someone wipe a tear; grins and smiles flashed all around, and a few touched their hearts.

"Thank you, Esha," the boy said fervently. "Thank you."

Nasomi returned the embrace, unable to contain the mirth that came bursting out. Kanguya did not want to be left out. He bounded forward and hugged the prince. Tebula seemed to love it. He let go of Nasomi and hugged the kowasa back. The room was filled with laughter and happy chatter. Majiyo stayed still in his chair.

The prince dashed to get a basket next to his seat, presented it to Nasomi. "For you. A small token of appreciation."

"Thank you, My Prince." She retrieved from the basket a long supple dress adorned with ruby gems and gold trimmings. Her mouth went wide. "I thank you for this, My Prince!"

"Can I play with him?" Tebula indicated the kowasa.

"You can. His name is Kanguya. He likes to pick up shiny stones."

"Even me! Come, Kanguya, let's go outside." He ran outside and Kanguya followed.

"Prince Tebula!" Majiyo called, clearly miffed. But the boy did not return. Majiyo pointed to a spear-wielding warrior. "See that he is safe."

Everyone else took it upon themselves to shuffle out of the room, and Nasomi could see that it irked Majiyo.

An elderly woman put her arm around Nasomi. "You're a gift to us, Esha. You brought happiness to him."

"The first ever council meeting full of happiness," another one said.

Nasomi turned to go outside, but Majiyo called, "Nasomi Esha? Would you linger a moment?"

The prophetess and the other three Daughters of Mohale and two elders lingered, too. Two warriors wet to stand by Majiyo's sides.

"Here," Majiyo said, making a sweeping motion with one hand, "in the presence of the few most trusted people in Mifirhana, you may divulge the truth."

Nasomi was confused. "I don't understand what you mean, Musha."

"*Mushae* is how you address me. Your visions, your dreams. I need you to tell us who you think the evil people who did this are."

"I spoke the truth. I know nothing more. The dreams can take a long time to reveal things."

He leaned back in his seat. Was that satisfaction she saw on his face? Nasomi looked at the people around her. They hate him, she thought. They might even suspect he was involved in the prince's abduction, but they fear him and cannot say anything.

"Is there anything then, we can do for you, Esha?" he asked.

"A horse," she said.

"Granted."

The prophetess stood and came to stand beside Nasomi. "Truly, Mushae Majiyo, she can stay in Mifirhana a few more days. Her presence is a joy to the prince, and he will heal better." She squeezed Nasomi's hand and looked at her, her eyes pleading.

"Eyes and Ears, we cannot detain her if she has an urgent need to go," Majiyo said. "She is a foreigner, one who has caused quite an unpleasant stir in our community."

"She found the prince."

"And we are full of gratitude. But it is up to us now, or our people will think we cannot lead. If there are any visions needed – you are the Eyes and Ears, are you not?"

The prophetess looked offended. Nasomi turned to her. "I am sorry. I have no more dreams to help."

"May you go well," Majiyo said. "The Goddess protect you, and help you find this Bride you are looking for." He indicated the warrior on his right. "Adomo here will take you to the stables and give you the best horse."

The one called Adomo nodded and came toward Nasomi. He gestured toward another door and he walked after her. Outside, Nasomi stopped. I should find Wakani, she thought.

Adomo gave Nasomi the lightest shove with his spear. She scowled at him, warning him not to do it again. He smirked and shrugged, pointed the way to the stable.

The stable was a shelter made from knobby poles and thatch. It was small by any standards, a single undivided structure with all of twelve horses in it. The entire Mifirhana had only a dozen horses. She found the gate and opened it. The stench of horse dung burned the insides of her nose.

She was immediately attracted to a sleek black stallion, smooth in looks as in movement. While the others moved away from her, the black one stood proud and lowered his head to let her pet him.

"That one," said Adomo, "is for the Guardian of the throne."

She turned to face him, horror-stricken. His voice! It was the same gruff one as the prince's captor in the dream. "It's you!" she blurted.

"It's me what?"

But he knew what she was talking about. It showed on his face. Adomo shifted his spear, not directly pointed at her, but tilted forward enough to make her know he was threatening her.

"Esha, take the black horse if you want it. Just leave."

There was a bundle of blankets and reins at one end of the stable. All she had to do was pick what she needed and ride away from Mifirhana.

And let them kill a young boy, she thought.

With a good look at Adomo, she took a few steps toward the bundle, then dashed aside and ran for the gate. Adomo shouted, and something hit her at the back of her head. She fell to the ground. Her head felt like it was on fire.

She rolled to face upward – No, it was Adomo who rolled her over with his foot. Her vision was blurry, but she could tell that it was the butt of a spear that came down at her face.

The world turned black.

When she came to, she was moving. Being dragged on the ground. Adomo set her down, and she tried to get up.

He pushed her down with his foot. "No noise, Esha. Don't make me stab you. I will know what to answer to people if you force me to kill you. I let you have the Mushae's horse! The one he rides to in battle. You're a stubborn woman."

The man shoved a piece of cloth into Nasomi's mouth, while holding her head to the floor. When she struggled, he punched her in her belly. He picked up some rope and tied her hands behind her back, as well as her feet. He dragged her to the further wall.

She was in a room she didn't recognize, mud walls and thatch roof. It stunk of urine and the only light came through a small square window. The gag was choking her and she breathed in heavy dust from the floor. She sneezed and tried to cough out the gag. Adomo kicked her.

"I said no noise."

Wakani, she thought. I should have gone to find him.

Adomo walked to the wall and hit his face in it. He winced, touched his bleeding nose. He seemed satisfied and came to drag her to the edge of the hut. He turned her face down, and she heard him walk out of the door. It banged shut, and she heard him close a latch.

Outside, Adomo began shouting. "Mad again. The Esha has gone mad again! She hit me!" His voice faded as he repeatedly shouted that Nasomi was mad again and had attacked him.

A gloom enwrapped Nasomi. She wriggled and squirmed. Her hands and feet chafed; her shoulders hurt. No position – sideways, on her back – eased her suffering. She gave in to tears, to despair.

With great effort, she spat out the gag with the help of her tongue and a wild shaking of her head. She wheezed a number of breaths in, coughed. When she was young, she could get her clasped hands over her shoulders. But now, her shoulders threatened to tear off.

The gloom thickened. As the walls seemed to close in on her and she thought she might lose her mind again, she scrunched her eyes shut. It was coming upon her, the madness, breaking the walls of her mind, shattering her soul.

She heaved herself into a kneeling position, forehead to the floor. She was breathing hard, fighting the fear, battling the insanity. "No!" she declared. "Not again!"

Her body shuddered terribly, and a warm sensation rode inside her belly toward her throat. She lifted her head and let out a cry. For the first time while awake, Nasomi was thrust into a telling.

She knew it was one because she was both a bound woman in a hut in the small kingdom of Mifirhana and a lithe boy bounding from tree to tree in a dense forest somewhere far east of where she was.

Then she was the boy entirely, and she wondered if her body in the hut fell to the floor or remained kneeling.

The boy climbed skillfully up a gigantic tree, gazed east when he was near the top. Nothing but the forest canopy that stretched to the horizon was in sight, but he gazed dreamily as though he could peer at something hidden by the trees. An uninhabited city that was supposed to be his home.

He had never been there, having been born by the ocean shore. And this spot was beyond the permitted limits. His father would throw a fit. But for now, the boy was here and he needed to be about his daydreaming. There in the west was the abandoned holy city of Dunia. The home of his ancestors, awaiting the return of its people. He hoped the Return would be within his life-time. He always dreamed of it, making up scenarios of him leading the exodus as a mighty warrior. He pictured entering one of the mighty stone temples to worship at the statues of the old gods.

He could almost hear the scolding he would receive from his father when he got back. He let go of the trunk, dove down. His belly fluttered and panic burst through him as he plummeted. He caught a branch deftly, spun around it and let go to land on another.

He hopped from branch to branch, tree to tree. He dove down, somersaulted to land on his feet on the ground. He ran in between thick trees, came to an opening that ended abruptly in a cliff overlooking an ocean. He had done this many times to know when to stop before falling over the cliff.

Nasomi would have gasped if she had come here in physical form. The ocean was vast and blue. At the horizon, it was so one with the heavens that she couldn't tell where the water ended and the sky began. The air was filled with the smell of the salty water and roasted fish. She smelled it through the boy's nose.

On the beach was spread a habitat of dwellings made from timber, stretching for miles below the plateau. The people moving about down there were strange to Nasomi: gaunt, livid and tall, with so little flesh that she could make out their skeletons. They were the boy's people, for he was equally emaciated.

He was relieved he couldn't see his father. He leaped down the cliff, bounding from rock to rock like a cricket.

The telling shifted.

CHAPTER 23

THE HEART OF MOHALE

She was back to herself, but not really. She saw her body lying on the ground, all tied up, face mashed against the dirt floor.

Like a specter, she went through the wall. Something outside was whispering to her, an anguish, a cry for help. She floated over the stable, up the hill, over the palace. It was awfully quiet, not a single person in it. She went toward the marketplace, and as she lingered over the spot where she fought the Bride, a group of four men ran past and through her.

She followed them. They talked quickly, excitedly. She understood the gist of what they were saying: The Mad Esha had lost her mind again and had attacked Adomo. Somehow, she'd abducted the prince and taken him toward the lake. It seemed the whole Mifirhana was gathering there, looking for her. Some took boats and launched out onto the water, and the rest either gossiped or searched through bushes.

The call of anguish came stronger upon her and she whipped about in search of its source. She knew that cry, had heard it many times in her bad dreams during the madness. It called her in the other direction of where the crowd was, in the outskirts of the town.

There were Majiyo and Adomo, traipsing in the thick of some woods. In between them, they carried a bound Prince Tebula, squirming to free himself. They threw him onto the ground, and from a belt on his waist, Adomo retrieved a familiar wrapped item. Nasomi's knife.

He unwrapped it, its blade glinting in the dimming sun as dusk was approaching, extended it to Majiyo. Majiyo grabbed it, knelt down by the boy, and sighed.

"It has to be this way, Tebula," he said. "The throne was meant to be mine before disputes made your father be king. You know the history, but it doesn't matter now. Your father is dead because he was weak against a simple illness. And you're a boy, you cannot rule."

"His ghost," Adomo said, great concern on his face. "What if the Eyes divines him and he tells it was us?"

"I tell you again, Adomo: She won't. They'll be ripping the Mad Esha apart, the prophetess won't even think of it."

"I do everything you tell me, Mushae."

"Are you doubting me now, Adomo?"

"I am not, forgive me."

"We have come this far."

"But something always gets in the way. If we—"

There was a rustling. Majiyo put a finger to his lip. He stood to check if anyone was coming. A mole flitted by, got lost into a bunch of leaves. He turned to Adomo, whispering, "Lift him up."

They took the prince deeper into the woods. The boy squirmed, his screams muffled by the gag in his mouth.

As Nasomi whipped back toward herself, she came across Kanguya. The kowasa was sniffing the ground and air, bounding in the direction of the prince. He cocked his head up, as though sensing Nasomi.

Nasomi said, *Kanguya? I am here!* No sound came from her. Kanguya sniffed the air again, then the ground, and bound away.

Kanguya! she called again.

He stopped, came back to where her awareness floated, wagged a reluctant tentacle.

You can hear me? Come to me, Kanguya!

The kowasa was now jumping up and down, wagging all his tentacles. It was strange, but he could feel her. Without knowing how she did it, Nasomi transmitted into Kanguya's mind the image of where she lay bound on the floor.

Kanguya sprung, headed in her direction. There was a fury in him. She could sense it. It bloomed and burned hot even as he came galloping toward the hut. It was doing something to his body: he began to glow and grow. Blue luminescence waved through his veins, visible through his hide. His limbs bulged to grotesque proportions, the rest of his features elongating.

Ramona would be fascinated to see this, Nasomi thought. History was right, after all. This was the true form of the kowasa. He wasn't as big as in the stories, but the creature coming after her was a menacing beast, not the same tiny thing that loved to romp and pick up shiny rocks.

"Kanguya?"

Wakani was among a dozen people that were headed to the palace when he saw Kanguya dashing by. The kowasa didn't stop or slow down his charge. Wakani ran after him, and a few others followed.

Kanguya crushed through the hut's wall as Nasomi returned to her body. He lifted her off the ground and bit off the ropes binding her, set her down.

She rubbed her wrists, wincing at the pain in her shoulders. "Thank you, Kanguya."

She stretched out a hand to touch him. He stood to the height of her chest, his tough skin rippling with a blue glow. "I have so much to know about you and your kind. Come, the prince is in danger."

Adomo had left his spear leaning on the wall next to the door. She picked it up as she stepped out to meet with Wakani and the other people. He gasped in delight and ran to her. "My Lady! I have been searching for you. The things they are saying—"

One of the others stepped forward. "Where is the prince, Esha?" He looked apprehensively at Kanguya, who stood by Nasomi's side.

"I am not the killer you want," Nasomi said. "We must hurry before Majiyo kills the prince."

A collective gasp. A woman said, "What vile ac-cu—"

Nasomi dashed forward and they moved out of their way. "Are you coming?" she shouted back at them. She and Kanguya ran to the stable, and the others followed.

She threw a blanket onto the black stallion as Wakani and others came in. They got their own blankets and chose their rides.

"I knew you couldn't have done those things," Wakani said, as his horse caught up to Nasomi's. "'Not my Esha,' I said to them, and they told me to shut up or they'll think I helped you."

Kanguya took over the lead, faster now than any of the horses were. When they arrived at the spot she had dreamed, there was no one there.

The others began to doubt. Wakani stood between her and them as they looked ready to apprehend her. Nasomi hoped to the Mara that she was not too late. "I saw them in my vision," Nasomi said, trying to sound convincing. "They have the prince, him and Adomo.

Nasomi jumped off her horse and followed Kanguya as he sniffed the ground and air. He dashed into some bushes and there came a human cry.

"Get away from me, beast!" Majiyo shouted as he emerged from hiding, propelling himself backward with his hands.

Kanguya emerged with Tebula in his hands and unbound him as he had Nasomi. The boy was wailing, trembling, and the kowasa embraced him.

There was a rustle from the bush and the warrior called Adomo jumped out and ran. Someone on horseback pursued after him.

Majiyo stood up, dusted himself. He stood tall and proud even when Nasomi and the others half-surrounded him. "I see you have found her," he said. "Bind her and bring her to trial."

The others exchanged confounded looks.

"Mushae," said a man, who was reverent enough to dip his head and doubtful enough to remain standing. "What are you doing here with the prince?"

"You will ask me that question? You? To the Guardian of the throne? I came to save the prince from where this foreign woman hid him to kill him."

Nasomi pointed the spear at him. In fury, he reached out to grab it, but she pulled it out of his reach, stepped aside and pointed it at him again. "You have been exposed, Mushae. Confess your crimes."

"You all stand by while this woman accuses your ruler? You shall all be put to the spear. I will cut your heads off and hang them in the trees for all to see." He tried again to grab the spear from Nasomi. She dodged, pointed it back at him. "And you, Mad Esha! You will know suffering to no end."

No one moved.

"If you won't believe me, ask the prince."

He beckoned to Tebula, who was embracing the shrinking kowasa. Kanguya's glow was fading and he was reverting to his smaller size.

"Tell them, Prince Tebula. Did I try to kill you?"

The prince looked at Majiyo with eyes wide and lips quivering. This was a scared boy, a boy who wouldn't dare speak against his uncle.

"Tell them, I say! Am I a bad person? Wasn't it the Mad Esha who tried to kill you? Tell them, tell them now!"

"Don't be afraid, My Prince," Nasomi said. "I am here, and so is Kanguya, and these your people. He cannot hurt you. Speak the truth."

The boy pointed a trembling finger at Majiyo. "He wanted to kill me. He tied me up and said the throne is his. And Adomo... Adomo..."

"You can tell it all, My Prince."

"Adomo captured me and threw me into the well. Mushae told me if I told anyone, he would burn the whole palace."

"Ha!" Majiyo said defiantly. "You are a little traitor, Tebula. It matters not. I am the true king of Mifirhana, and there's no one here who can defy me. Who among you dares to face me, Majiyo Etungu, the great pillar of Mifirhana, the warrior who killed a hundred men with his bare hands?"

No one moved.

"Then bow to your king, fools." Nasomi saw too late his raised leg. He kicked her in the belly, grabbed the spear from her hand as she fell.

Wakani rushed at Majiyo, tried to wrench the spear off his hands. Majiyo threw him off, began to laugh as he raised the spear to stab him. "Foreigners, you both! You're the ones trying to destroy our kingdom."

Another man dove at Majiyo and threw him down. "I stand against you, Mushae," the man said.

Blows and kicks were exchanged. The others joined in until Majiyo was overpowered and pinned down. The ropes that had been on Tebula were joined and used to bind him.

Tebula embraced Nasomi. "It's all over, My Prince," she said, patting him on the back. "You're safe now."

A flurry of voices announced the rest of the town's arrival. They came, loud and furious, demanding to know what was happening. Those who tied Majiyo explained. There was doubt at first, but when Majiyo refused to defend himself, looking away in shame and defiance, there was a general outburst of delight.

The people shouted, "Nasomi Esha!" They lifted her off the ground and sung songs meant to celebrate warriors. When they set her down, and she was laughing, she stood facing the prophetess.

Eyes and Ears raised a hand and the people gave her their attention. "We have finally learned the truth here," she said. "And we've always known it in our hearts. But today, the Goddess has opened our eyes."

Outcries of "Yes!", "Mohale is with us!", "We're blessed!" and "We knew it!" burst forth from the people.

"The Goddess saw it fit to bring Nasomi Esha in our land. We acknowledge you, Nasomi."

Murmurs of agreement.

"And we acknowledge your gift. It can only come from the Goddess. It is my pleasure to declare you a true Seer of the Goddess. More than an Eyes and Ears, or a Mind. But a Heart! Come." She extended a hand and Nasomi took it. The prophetess made her turn to face the people. "Here before you, good people of Mifirhana, stands Nasomi Esha the Seer, the Heart of Mohale."

As she was overwhelmed by the joyous noise that emanated, the sight of people jumping and dancing about and the prince standing next to Kanguya and smiling, Nasomi felt a gush of the familiar tugging feeling within her. It washed all over her, enveloped her, wrapped her like a mother wrapped a child in a blanket.

CHAPTER 24
BIG STORY, SMALL STORY

The feeling lingered, as thick and real as the new supple, glowing gown the prince gifted to her. She was constantly aware of it even as she walked, with as much grace as she could portray, through a throng of admiring people. She smiled and said "I thank you" to anyone who passed a compliment. She felt it bubbling in her belly as she went to the spot for the important people of Mifirhana.

Several mats had been laid side by side to form a large one. Upon it were pots, trays, and plates brimming with foods, and more were being set down by young men and women who came and went like a bunch of ants. Nasomi sat on a stool in between the prophetess and an empty stool, whose owner, the prince, was entertaining a group of inquisitive children. He turned to Kanguya who stood by his side, and gave the kowasa something from his pocket. It was small, and it glinted in the light of a nearby fire. Kanguya romped up and down when he took the shiny stone. What a pair these two make, Nasomi thought. When the prince saw her, he waved enthusiastically. She waved back.

"You look radiant tonight, My Heart," the prophetess said.

"I thank you, My Eyes and Ears. You are dressed finely yourself."

The prophetess was in a fine brown dress dyed with red floral patterns. She had white bangles on her wrists and ankles, her hair combed out into a puffy cloud. On her forehead, half-hidden by hair, was a cowry band similar to the one Wakani gave Nasomi. She smelled good too, like the leaves of red ivory wood. The most beautiful thing on her was her smile.

"It has been a while since we had a feast here," the prophetess said. "Ever since the king and queen died, there has been a gloom that settled in the whole kingdom, and Majiyo wasn't helping things."

"What will happen to him?"

"Exiled, perhaps executed. It will be the prince's decision, with guidance from the Daughters and the Elders. It's a tedious ritual—the execution, if it comes to that, and I know the prince will be loath to demand it."

"Any child would be."

"But he has to think of the people. Majiyo will come back, more vengeful, if he's allowed to live." She touched Nasomi's hand. "Talk to the prince. He adores you and will listen to you."

Nasomi saw Tebula and Kanguya displaying shiny stones to an intrigued audience, saw him give one to a demure girl. "I cannot do that, Eyes and Ears. I cannot be involved in this."

"You already are, My Heart, can't you see? All this celebration wouldn't be possible without you. You're the Heart of Mohale now, her judgment shines through you. If you pronounce that Majiyo should be killed, everyone will judge you wise. The prince will know it is the right thing to do."

A heaviness fell upon Nasomi, but also the feeling of the tellings grew warmer. She needed to trust that feeling, else she would be drowned in politics she couldn't handle. "I cannot bear that burden, Eyes and Ears. It wasn't *me* who caused all this. It was the dreams – say it's the Goddess if you want, or the stars."

The prophetess looked disappointed. "You are needed here, My Heart. With you, Mifirhana is a happy place. You came to us at the moment we needed you most, even if we didn't know it yet. You are a force to reckon with, a power, a queen."

Nasomi gave her a sharp look. "Don't say things like that. People are hearing."

"I say what I see. You think yourself small, but My Heart, you are a thing closer to a goddess. I have been imagining a big story with you as our Guardian Queen. I know the prince would choose you. Your visions will be good for us, showing us the rise of our enemies, and we can thwart them down should they arise. Mifirhana would prosper, maybe even start mining copper, build bigger iron kilns, and send our own people to walk the Gold Road. We would build high walls, annex some other tribes for labor and grow a large army."

Nasomi opened her mouth to speak but the prophetess touched her lips. "You are about to mention your children, your husband. Listen to me first. We can even send for your children to come and live here, and we would create a palace for you. You can send warriors after the Bride to retrieve your husband. You will be a happy family here, in your own grand palace, in a happy, peaceful Mifirhana. And when the prince is of age and he takes up the throne, he will protect and cherish you and ensure that you are fulfilled all the days of your life."

Nasomi sighed. "You have thought of everything, haven't you? But I must tell you I'm not what you make of me. Not a seer, nor the Heart of Mohale. I am just me. A mother. A wife. That's my story. I cannot be anything more."

"What about the prince? He would be the most heartbroken. What would he do without you?"

"He has you, he has the Elders. Please don't ask of me what I cannot give."

There was a long exchange of looks between them, Nasomi's irritated glare and the prophetess' disappointed glower.

Nasomi was rescued by a call from Wakani, who came bounding to her. "Nasomi Esha! I mean My Heart, My Lady. Come dance with us."

Nasomi took the man's offered hand, stood and went with him to a group of people holding up fire torches. They surrounded her, and her heart leaped for a moment. But they began to dance, and she was in the midst of a frenzy of torches as more people joined in. There was a rhythm to the stomp of their feet. *Stomp, pause, stomp, pause, stomp stomp stomp.*

Someone began to sing, a sharp voice raised above the din. The whole throng joined in at the same time. Their voices blended into one mighty consort, with no voice of the many out of place.

She caught some of the words, of a deep-chested tongue that wasn't Ao'Mu:

*Tsuyugarakaitero
Karanayoaruteyo...*

The chorus went on for a while, and the words were having an effect on her as Majen did back in Nari: touching a deep place in her soul. The singing suddenly stopped. The silence was piercing, and the fire of her tellings burned hot. Then when a new chorus began, she was drunk with the feeling.

*Keira ozotakutotera
Weka ozotsuyugara*

She'd never heard anything so beautiful. She'd never seen such synchronized glorious madness. Someone grabbed her hand. It was Wakani. "Just do like me," he said.

He moved like he'd known the dance all his life. The dance was easy to follow. A few stomps later, she was one with the people in dance, and mirth was bubbling up inside her, and she let it out.

When it was all over and the eating began, Nasomi felt she couldn't contain the feeling inside her anymore. She knew that a telling dream, or dreams, was coming. With power. Something big was going to happen.

"What do the words of the songs mean?" she asked the prophetess.

"It's the language our people used to speak before Ao'Mu," Eyes and Ears replied, after a moment of deciding she wanted to talk to Nasomi. "Very few elderly people still know how to say some things. From what I know, the songs are talking about how the world was created from music and colors."

"It's a beautiful language."

"It is being forgotten, alas!" She chuckled, became silent. "My Heart, I am sorry about trying to force you to stay."

"It is well. I would want to be here all my life, if I could. But you must understand. I must go where my dreams lead me."

When Nasomi went to bed later, she didn't take long to fall asleep, and she was in a telling. Her awareness flew eastward over Mifirhana, over a vast forest, over a stone city overtaken by nature. Miles upon miles over a changing landscape: settlements, rivers and lakes, hills, a green basin, bare lands, a swamp, and then she stopped over a winding vale traversed by a river. As she floated down, she felt something break. Something opened, a barrier was removed. On the ground, under the shelter of a tree, sat Tambo, Reema, and the hyena.

Reema finished saying something, and Tambo laughed. His good happy laughter that Nasomi adored. The way he laughed when he was without a single worry. He was thinner than the last time she saw him, burned by the sun, withered by time. He also looked... happy.

Reema cut off her laughing, stood and looked up. As though she could sense Nasomi. Reema had the look of realizing that someone else was here.

"It is time to go," she said.

"We just sat down right now!" Tambo complained. "My feet are killing me."

"Don't argue with me. Stand up, you two. Off we go. The cave is nearby."

In her soundless voice, Nasomi shouted, *I'm coming for you, Reema! I'll get you!*

As they moved, Reema looked back over her shoulder. She swept her hand in the air, and Nasomi felt the barrier close again. She couldn't see them anymore.

The telling took her further southward, to a wall five hundred feet high. The wall stretched for miles, made Nari look like a chicken pen in comparison. She passed through the wall, flew over a kingdom of stone and fire, came into the chamber of the grand palace. What drew her here, she didn't know.

She met a sleepless king seated on his bed. In his mind, he was worried over an impending civil war. His people wanted him out, and he was determined to thwart the rebellion. His door banged open, and someone rushed in with a dagger. Outside, weapons clashed, and blood flowed. Nasomi knew, without even seeing it, that somewhere in the Redland, a baobab tree had fallen.

She awoke.

Why do I see all these things? She wondered. All I want is to get Tambo and go home.

She wouldn't let the matters of the world distract her from Tambo. Good thing she was still heavy with need for sleep, and the feeling inside her was strong. She was determined to break Reema's barrier once again.

CHAPTER 25
IN THE KINGDOM OF BONES

When the barrier shattered, Nasomi found Reema, Tambo, and the hyena moving through a foggy, soggy forest. It was daylight but the canopies of the tall, moss-covered trees were so thick they blocked the sunlight. Cicadas skirled in the trees; frogs croaked beneath. A cave appeared at the end of the path, as though it came to them rather than them to it.

Reema sniffed. She smiled. "This is the place. Can you smell that, Gweuka?"

"I can," croaked the hyena. "Magic. Centuries of witching work."

The form of a man appeared at the cave mouth.

"I saw you coming," he said, his deep voice emanating from the ground as well as his mouth. He was muscular, should have been a wrestler instead of a sorcerer. He wore chains and bungles made from bones and teeth, and his eyes were white as though he were blind.

"I was told you are the most powerful man in this area," Reema said, stepping forward.

"You are no hag," the man said. He drew closer. "You're a girl, with so much desire. I see it on you. And you..." He examined Tambo. "You are not a free man. I see your bonds. For a sacrifice, I can free you."

"I am the one with a request," Reema said. "Get your face away from him."

He went to the hyena, and his eyes went wide. "A wizard, most powerful. How did you come to be...?" He turned to look at Reema warily, as if realizing he'd underestimated her. "What do you want that you possibly can't get yourself?"

"Beauty. Youth."

The man sneered. "Then you shouldn't have become a witch. The nature of magic is to take away, not to give."

"As you said, I am no hag. I am young and beautiful beneath this sheath of ugliness. I only wish for my true form to be restored. It is possible, I have heard stories."

"In that case, I have something for you. But it will cost you. Give me your familiar." He grinned, teeth yellow as corn kernels.

He sensed, too late, the presence of Reema's shadow rise behind him. It towered over him, and when he turned, it sprung arms to grasp him.

"I can feel what you have in there," Reema said. "I will take it myself."

The man showed fear, which quickly morphed into fury. "Let me go, silly girl. I am Ituntulu, the devourer of corpses, the ruler of the sorcerers, conqueror of—"

Reema didn't let him finish. Her shadow hurled him against the rock of the cave. He coughed blood. The shadow picked him up like he was a piece of sweet potato, thrust him to the ground. "Eat him, quickly," Reema said to Gweuka. "Devour his power before he can resist."

The hyena was upon the sorcerer, ripping off his flesh even as he screamed. Tambo vomited as he turned to look away.

"Reema, you promised you wouldn't do such," he groaned.

"He had to be subdued, my love," she said, full of remorse. "Don't think I enjoy this. If this is what we've been looking for, it will stop today. I will give it all up, that is still my promise."

Gweuka's body was expanding as he devoured the flesh and power of Ituntulu. Reema stared at her palms and flexed her fingers, feeling her own magic be-coming stronger. She walked into the cave.

It was lit by a crude fire torch pinned in the ground. The cave floor was rough, uneven. Skeletons hang from the walls, the bones clinking in the breeze that wafted in. In the darker part of the cave was a mat upon which were a miscellany of gourds, charms, bones.

Reema picked up each, felt their weight, and sniffed at them. She tossed those she deemed worthless, gave to Tambo those she wanted to keep.

"This can poison entire villages." She threw it away. "This one can heal deep wounds; we might need it." She gave it to him. "This one can bind other people, but not as powerful as what I can do. Useless. This one chases away bad dreams. This one... this one does not reveal itself to me. It might be what we're looking for." She kept it herself, thrusting it in her bosom.

"This one can take away wrinkles. Interesting." She gave it to Tambo. She went through all the items and they came out with a dozen.

Outside the cave, something was amiss. The ci-cadas and frogs were silent, and the fog was thinning away. Shapes started to appear: human and animal. They came through the fog, or jumped down from the trees, or rose up from the ground.

"Run!" Reema said, and was the first to dash away.

They ran in between the trees, beside a rocky hill, ducking and going around overreaching and thick bush-es. When the pursuers proved to be equally agile, com-ing at them from all directions, Reema commanded Gweuka to crouch. She and Tambo got onto his back. The hyena was big enough to carry them now. He was fast, too. He was soon way beyond the reach of their pursuers.

When they were far and safe, Reema said they could stop and rest. They made beds of thick leaves, re-clined on them. The moon was full and bright, casting its beautiful light upon a fertile land. Nasomi saw among the wild plants numerous rows of corn stalks that looked to be untouched for many years. There were trees all around, tall and short, bearing all types of fruit, none of which had been picked. Many had rotted and fallen, some sprouting saplings.

White things, entangled in the vegetation, gleamed in the moonlight. Bones of people and animals, dead for years. Nasomi looked about, saw skulls peeking in mounds of sands, hand bones and leg bones lying far from skulls, perhaps dragged and half-eaten by animals. Somehow she could see the deeply buried bones too, as if they were calling to her, crying in anguish for her to listen to the tragic end of their lives. These were the bones of the people who had tried to return and rebuild the kingdom, but death reigned here, and only sorcerers could flourish in such a place.

Nasomi shook their lure off, focused on the group she had followed. She watched Tambo and Gweu-ka fall asleep. Reema didn't sleep. She had a look of worry on her face.

Seeing that the other two were asleep, Reema retrieved the mysterious charm from her bosom. She closed her eyes, whispered something. The night seemed to get darker. Wisps of thin dark smoke broke out from Reema's body. She took in a long anticipatory breath and opened her eyes. She waited.

She stared at the charm in her hand. Then she threw it away. Reema turned about, staring at the space Nasomi was occupying. "It's you," she said, taking a breath. "You scared me."

Tambo spoke as he walked through Nasomi's apparition, "Is that supposed to be a joke? I've got one for you: I see the charm didn't work." He grinned, a hint of tiredness on his face.

"No matter. We still go on."

"Why can't you give up, Reema? Mhmm? Nothing you ever do works. I can't take this anymore."

"Tambo, Tambo, my love." She touched his face. "We have traveled too far to stop now. I have so much to prove to you. Just wait and see."

He shrugged, throwing up his hands in exaggeration. "I will watch you die, you know that? Someone powerful enough is going to kill you. And then I'll be free to go back home. That's all I look forward to now."

She gave a short mirthless laughter. "After all that you've seen me done, you think I'm easy to kill? And what I have gained here is beyond what many gain in a lifetime."

His voice was higher now: "I thought all you wanted was to restore your beauty!"

She shook her head. "Of course. But I will not let anyone think weak of me again once I have my smooth skin back. I can't let myself be an ordinary woman."

"You want to be a witch forever?"

"I didn't say 'witch'. But 'powerful' is what I mean. There's a difference. I know you don't believe me, but I don't want to be killing people. I want their respect, admiration. They'll write about me on slates, talk about me in the histories."

He pulled his own ear toward her, mocking her that he was listening.

"Tambo, this will end soon. You know I love you. We needn't fight each other anymore. I want you by my side, to build with me something amazing."

"All I have seen you do—"

She touched his cheek. He didn't seem to have the will to move his face away. "I can't be the Bride anymore. I hate that name. It makes me the person who could never be her own woman, who could never stand on her own feet. I must give myself a new name. I am thinking Reema the Beauty, Reema the All-Powerful."

"Oh, oh, oh!" Tambo said, slapping his forehead. "I understand you now."

A smile disappeared as quick as it appeared on her face, and she squinted at him to see whether he was joking or not. "You do?"

"Yes! You are a child! Oh, *Mara* help me, you are a child who doesn't yet understand how the world works! You think this is some bedtime story, about a princess who was cursed with ugliness and she went on a quest to find her beauty back and defeat all her enemies. And she got her beauty back and became so powerful the whole world bowed before her. And the man who said bad things about her — a man she kept under a spell if we have to mention all the details – this man will realize his mistake, he's been cruel to her, mocked her. Then he will bow before her in all her glory and take her hand, show her affection, say he was blind to have not seen she was all he needed. Because you'll be the all-powerful, glorious one. Right? Right?"

"Tambo, where is all this coming from?" She was shaking her head repeatedly as though he were the child. "Go back to sleep, I need time to think."

"We are going to finish this here and now! I am not going to let—"

"I said go sleep!" Tendrils of shadow wafted from her back.

He shut up, turned obediently and walked away. Reema clenched her fists and let out an angry cry. Nasomi drew closer and Reema jumped back. "Who is there?" she demanded. She threshed her hands about as though she were chasing away flies.

Something pushed Nasomi backward. Reema laughed. "It is only you, dream witch. I see you've broken the veil again." Reema spoke to the air: "I am glad you can see this, dream witch. I want you to see."

Nasomi came at Reema from behind, and Reema turned sharply. She waved her hands and an invisible force fought against Nasomi. Nasomi tried to say something, like how she spoke to Kanguya.

Reema? Hear me, you witch.

But Nasomi was still just a perception with no actual voice to communicate with.

"Watch all you want, dream witch!" Reema said. Watch me win while you fail. This is all your fault, farm girl. But watch me rise from the dirt you threw me onto. Watch me reclaim everything you took from me. Watch me become the queen of the world while you sit there, wherever you are, sobbing at your unremarkable life. Nobody brings Reema down. Nobody!"

She threw her hands wide apart, and the barrier shut again. Nasomi was pushed up and away from Reema. Nasomi tried to return, but the veil was strong.

A cacophony of voices and sounds of wild animals caught her attention. She swooped down and came near to the cave where Reema killed Ituntulu. She found herself in the midst of a council of sorcerers. It comprised a jackal, two lynxes, an old man, two younger women, and what looked like a big-headed toddler. They didn't seem to sense her.

The jackal was speaking. "She can't be that powerful," it said. "Ituntulu was caught unaware. That is all."

"We cannot think of her as weak, either," the old man said. "If she could catch Ituntulu unaware, she is someone to reckon with."

"And we'll reckon!" the jackal said. "Don't be too soft, old man. We must avenge our master. We cannot let the witch who killed Ituntulu go away."

"Of course, Chonse. But first, we must choose who will be our new leader and replenish our power."

The jackal scoffed as though the answer was obvious.

One of the young ladies lifted her hand. "I propose Chonse the jackal." The other lady said the same.

"We choose Malwi," said both lynxes in unison.

"I choose myself," the jackal said, glaring at the old man.

"I choose myself," Malwi said.

"That makes three each," one of the women said. They looked alike, these two. Twins. Nasomi remembered Reema's hyenas had also been twins. "Now, Kamo must break the decision."

They all looked at the toddler, who was enchanted in chewing a finger. They all leaned toward him, anticipating his vote. He opened his mouth... and sneezed. Then he returned to chewing his finger and dozing.

One of the young women gave him a slap on the back, too hard for a baby but it didn't seem to bother this one. "Kamo, you must choose."

He removed his finger from his mouth and pointed at the jackal.

The jackal whooped. "Yes! Kamo knows what I am made of! Now, listen here all of you. As your new leader, this is my decision: we will all go hunting down this witch. We go hunting her tonight."

CHAPTER 26

DREAMWALKING

The entire kingdom escorted Nasomi from the palace hill. A mile after that, less than half were still with her. They had brought her gifts, but she declined most of them, bequeathing them to Tebula instead. She accepted what she could carry in her bag: dried sweet potato flakes, biltong, peanuts, roasted cassava. She accepted an extra dress, two pairs of underwear, and a new headband.

She tied her filled water pouch to a belt around her waist, secured her knife in an inner pocket of her cloak. She'd thought of throwing the knife away, but the memory of Ramona made her keep it. It held a promise to be fulfilled.

Wakani was given a newly-made spear. It was as tall as he was, its shaft made from smooth red wood and its head from a black jugged stone. He carried what he could in the sack they gave him, also politely refusing what would be too heavy for a long journey.

Nasomi walked the sleek black stallion, which was hers now, a gift from the prince. He said the horse's name was Nhema, which meant midnight in the old language. It was at midnight that the Goddess awoke from her sleep to grant the prayers of her children, to protect her people, to grant strength to her warriors.

"Majiyo Mushae didn't deserve the horse," Tebula had said to her when presenting Nhema. "May Nhema not falter when you ride hard paths, may he carry you through hard weather, and may he ride down your enemies."

"Those are sweet words, My Prince," she had replied. "I am sorry that I cannot stay."

"I know you will always be with me, and come to help me when I am in trouble. I am no longer afraid."

"You are a strong and wise boy," she said when he embraced her. "You will be a great king."

After another mile, much of the group went back. The remainder continued singing praise songs about Nasomi, composing more as they went.

> *The Heart of Mohale is filled with mercy;*
> *She saves those who cry to her.*
> *She sees with her thousands of sky eyes,*
> *No evil person will escape her gaze.*
> *She goes riding on the back of midnight*
> *To draw the curtain of dawn over the world.*

She and Wakani were to be accompanied by a warrior called Buyechi. He smiled and joked often, but Tebula promised he was the greatest warrior in the kingdom. Nasomi had tried to refuse his company, saying she felt bad about taking away two of the kingdom's horses as well as their bravest warrior. The prince, the Daughters of Mohale, and the Elders insisted that it was all beneath what she deserved.

My dreams have led me here, she thought, as she contemplated the huge crowd singing behind her, the two warriors walking their horses a little ahead of her (yes, to her, Wakani was a warrior), and Kanguya running with Tebula way ahead. The two were running into bushes and picking up stones, comparing them and discarding those they both agreed were bad.

Look at me, she mused. I am like the warrior queens in the stories Father used to tell me.

> *A woman should have the heart,*
> *The Heart of the Goddess;*
> *Strong, kind, and unafraid,*
> *The Heart of Mohale.*

Another mile and most of the people said their goodbyes and trekked back home. Wakani ran ahead to bring Tebula and Kanguya back. Everyone stopped for the final goodbyes. They embraced and spoke sweet words to each other, making promises, wiping off tears.

Tebula dropped the stones in his hands into a basket carried by a manservant. His collection contained peculiar stones of all shapes and colors, pieces of iron and iron ore, broken eggshells, empty snail shells, cowries, leather pouches, strings.

"Whatever are you going to do with those, My Prince?" she asked.

He shrugged and embraced her. "I will build a large tower with them. Goodbye, Heart. May the Goddess protect you and get you where you need to go."

"Goodbye, My Prince. May the Goddess give you all the wisdom to rule Mifirhana. I will return with shiny things for you." She smiled for him "Kanguya, say your farewells to the prince."

The kowasa wagged its *no* tentacle.

"He is staying with me," Tebula said.

Nasomi's felt a sting in her heart. "Wha...?" Her voice caught; her throat was a burden. "Kanguya, you are staying?"

Yes.

"Kanguya! You don't belong here." But even as she said those words, she knew she had no idea where he belonged. And she had no authority over him. "Well, you must be happy here."

Yes.

Nasomi held back a tear. Even with the two men to go with her, she felt she was going the journey all by herself. But if it had to be this way, then she would accept it. There was a strong bond between the kowasa and the prince. They were perfect for each other.

"Goodbye, then, my friend. Be good. Protect the prince the way you did me."

She watched them go, waved at them repeatedly. When they were out of sight, she turned and got up on her horse, led him at a gallop. The men rode hard to catch up. She rode until she felt the horse tire out, and she herself was out of breath. She didn't stop moving, only maintained a brisk pace.

Her heart and breathing settled and Nhema seemed to demand more. She rode hard again, following a path she had been told would bring her to a number of villages.

When she and her warriors came into the first village, she couldn't bring herself to stop. She rode on, passing men with hoes on their shoulders, women with bundles of sticks on their heads. She rode on until she was alone again on a winding path.

Her bag was an increasing weight; her cloak threatened to pull her off the horse. Her back and thighs ached. She stopped when Nhema stumbled. She got off and sat under a tree, took out some food to eat, gulped down some water, and took breaths to calm herself.

The men found her dozing. Wakani sat next to her as Buyechi stood watch a few feet away. "My Lady, I can't believe I will be the one saying this. I got fond of the kowasa. I miss watching him dash ahead of us, pick things."

Nasomi gave a weak smile. "I miss him, too. Wakani, you are not bound to me."

"I know, My Heart."

"You have a family. They're waiting for you. You need to go back to Nari."

"I will go tomorrow, My Lady. Get some rest now. Dream the dreams that will show you which way to go. We will watch over you."

The two men sat firmly beside her, saying nothing. She slept.

Tambo and Reema were making their way to Tunkambe, trying to keep a good distance from their pursuers. Ramona was a sad girl, always sitting alone, longing for something. Meron had made some rowdy

*friends and they were bullying young boys in the
streets of Nari.*

She awoke with a start. The sun was low in the
sky. She got up, demanded that they continue riding. It
was well into the night when thick clouds covered the
moon and they couldn't see what was ahead that she
said they could rest some more. She ate some food and
fell asleep under the men's watchful eyes.

*The vengeful sorcerers led by Chonse the jackal
divined which direction Reema was headed, and they
pursued tirelessly. Nasomi followed Reema and Tambo
from afar to keep from being sensed by Reema. The
Bride knew she was being chased by the sorcerers and
she pushed Tambo and the hyena to move faster.*

She awoke the next morning thirsty and aching
all over. She took some water, ate a breakfast of dried
sweet potatoes and peanuts. She was riding again, and
walking, and riding. Through a cold valley, over a hill,
through a knee-deep marsh. Past a number of human
settlements. Into a savannah of jutting limestone rocks.
She decided they would spend a day and night
when they came into the next settlement. She bought
food for her, the warriors, and the horses. When she
took to a hut to rest, she fell into a dream as soon as her
body lay down. She found herself in a strange telling:
Tambo was alone, tying the beams of a shack he was
building that looked like the one they once lived in Nari.
He was whistling to himself. Everything twisted and
sprung, and he was hiding in Ituntulu's cave. Insects
came toward him and he screamed and kicked them
away. They crawled all over him.
"I'm in his dream!" Nasomi said, and Tambo
stopped thrashing. He looked at her.
"Nasomi?"
"Tambo? You can see me?"

He came to her, smiling, as the world spun away and they were in their old home. Meron and Ramona chased each other between them, and a little dog followed after them.

"My sunshine," Tambo said, hugging her. She saw his form embrace her, but she couldn't feel it. "Of course, I can see you."

"Tambo, it's me, Nasomi. Your wife. I am in your dream and you can see me."

"I have an errand to see to. Come eat with me before I go."

He turned and another Nasomi came through a door. He looked from one to the other. "What is the meaning of this? How can you be two?" He laughed.

"Tambo, you're dreaming," Nasomi said. "Look at me. Remember." As the dream started to change, she said, "You're with Reema, she has you under a spell."

"Yes, I remember." The dream world became nothing but blackness. "I remember! They're after us, Nasomi. Reema did a bad thing."

"I know, my love. I saw it."

"And she can feel you. Though she hasn't these past days. She says you gave up. You're never coming for me. She tells me she is all I have."

"I'm coming for you. I have followed from afar so that she cannot feel me."

"I am scared."

"I know. Tambo, I am in your dream. I can talk to you like this."

"Is this happening? You're here with me?"

"It is happening."

"Where are you Nasomi? I miss you terribly."

"I was held in Mifirhana for a while."

A tear ran down his cheek. "I couldn't do anything."

"It wasn't your fault. I am coming. I will find you."

"We're near to entering the peninsula. Reema wants to go find the wise men in Ndinge. She says they have knowledge that can make her beautiful again. It's all she wants, Nasomi. She wants to be beautiful like she was before. Then she says she'll be happy. She's failed, you know. Everyone she's gone to, from Arwo to the Kingdom of Bones, says it's impossible what she wants. But she's stubbo—"

The world rocked.

"She's stubborn. She won't lis—"

Nasomi was pushed out of his dream into the real world. She found herself looking at Reema waking Tambo up.

"Why are you crying, my love?" Reema said. "Bad dream? Come, we must go. I can feel them catching up with us. We will be safer on the other side."

Reema stood and looked around. She sensed Nasomi.

"You're here, dream witch? I thought you'd given up. Leave us be, we have important things to do." She waved her hands in the air and Nasomi was pushed further away.

Reema whistled and Gweuka came into view. He crouched down. Reema and Tambo got onto his back, and he bounded away, faster than any natural hyena can run.

Nasomi awoke and forgot she was on a tree. She flopped and swung, and was prevented from falling to the ground by the ropes. She arched her back, heaved her body until she could get herself back in place. She undid the knots and climbed down.

She could communicate with people through their dreams! This changed everything. She could get in touch with Tambo, talk to her children, the people in Mifirhana. And Naena. She's missed Naena much. She had so much to tell her.

CHAPTER 27
TAMBO'S HEART

Nasomi's days and nights became a routine of four things: riding, walking, resting under trees and eating little food. Her strength began to wane easily, her daily distances decreased. There was a pain in her bones, her skin itched, and she stank of sweat. Buyechi had a tiny flute similar to the one Mihide in Mishi had. He blew on it often, making sweet reedy sounds that seemed to come from anywhere but the flute. The sounds soothed her, made her forget her troubles for a moment.

She was losing sleep despite being exhausted, and the little she could catch bothered her with dreams of world events that mattered little to her: Refugees from Micha made a slow exodus northward. A tattooed group of mercenaries along the Gold Road went on a crusade to terminate the Gaula in Ao'Pan.

The dreams that mattered brought her no comfort. Tambo was still too far from her reach as the Bride sped him away to get away from her enemies. Nasomi spoke to him through his dreams, but he wasn't entirely convinced it was truly her he was talking to and not a conjuring of his dreams. He told her where he was, where they were going, what Reema was doing. She encouraged him to hold on to hope, to stay alive.

"I am coming," she told him. "I am coming."

Her son Meron was now a mage. He had saved Prince Keyula's life by pushing him off the path of a runaway wagon that would have killed the prince. The king was so pleased he announced right then that Meron would be the new mage. Kaan and Thorro were not pleased and whispered their sentiments against the decision. The king was adamant.

"You two are getting old," he said rather loudly in the public. "This is what you have always wished of me. We need honorable people like this boy to protect the royal family and to be the next generation of the Mage Council. Teach him everything you know."

Many a night, Nasomi watched Meron poring over tomes, scrolls, and tablets of Majen under dim firestone light. She was ashamed of seeing her son in a heavy grey robe, practicing how to move objects with his mind. She blamed her absence, hated herself for it, pushed herself beyond her limits to catch up to Tambo. But she never went into the boy's dreams, nor his sister's. She wanted them to get to know the real her when she got back. Not this thing she had become. Oracle. Seer. Dream witch. Dreamwalker.

On the twenty-fourth evening of her journey, exhausted from riding over twenty miles and in need of sleep from having eaten too many num-nums and raw mushrooms the warriors had picked in the woods, she fell into a dream of Tambo and company surrounded by their pursuers.

The jackal had an expression on its snout that looked like a smirk. The old man held a rather small spear. One of the twins set the toddler down from her back, and he sat on the ground and played with dirt.

"We've caught you at last," the jackal said.

"What do you want from me?" Reema said. "Go away or I'll kill—"

"Let's see you try," the jackal replied, springing into action. Reema made a defensive stance and the jackal was caught in an invisible snare.

Tambo ducked as the old man threw his little spear.

"Fight, Tambo!" Reema shouted as her shadow, oily, darker than night, expanded toward the jackal. Tambo engaged in an exchange of fists with the old man, though his face showed he would rather be running away. The old man was stronger than he looked. He gave Tambo a punch to the jaw that sent him to the ground. Tambo rolled away from the old man's aimed stomp.

Gweuka and the lynxes rolled on the ground, biting and scratching at each other. One got on Gweuka's back, biting at his neck. But the hyena had grown into a big beast. He shook the lynx off. Gweuka slapped away its companion with his paw, bound at it, tore off a chunk of its flesh.

The Bride and jackal were going at each other with their shadows, exuding a power that threatened to knock Nasomi awake.

The toddler faced away from the battle, etching silly symbols on the ground with a twig, unbothered by anything.

The young women clapped each other's hands and patted their thighs as though they were playing a childhood game. Then they turned to face Reema, cupping their hands as if they held stones in them. They hurled the invisible stones at Reema. They hit her with real force, and her temple was bleeding as she fell down.

Reema stretched out a hand toward the twins as they faced each other to conjure more magic, shoving them away, but they gathered themselves and resumed the hand clapping.

The jackal bit into Reema's hand. It would have snapped it off if her shadow didn't elongate to slap it off. The shadow sprung to where Tambo and the old man fought over the spear. Even as Tambo kicked away the old sorcerer, Reema's shadow yanked the spear off Tambo's hands, thrust it toward the twins. It went through one's back and out of her chest.

The other screamed as her sister fell, thrashed and died. She came after Reema, physically pulling at her hair and slapping her. "Leave her to me!" the jackal shouted. His shadow grabbed the girl's feet, pulled her to the ground and away from Reema. "Leave her to me!"

She scampered away, went to the body of her companion, and wailed.

Gweuka was ripping the remnant lynx apart. He had so many scratches on his body he looked like he had a fur coat of red stripes. He slashed at bit at the lynx with such fury that if it were possible for Nasomi to close her eyes in this form, she would have.

After the lynx lay in gory pieces, Gweuka came after the old man who had Tambo in his grip. The old man let go of Tambo, summoned the spear, which came flying into his hand. He and the hyena circled each other.

"You lied!" the weeping twin screamed. "You said she was a nothing, but she's powerful. Look what she did to Arize. Look at the size of her hyena."

"Go then, coward," the jackal replied. It was clawing against an invisible cage the Bride had conjured.

Reema's veins bulged, making her look uglier, as she concentrated on keeping the cage potent. The jackal slashed hard and Reema was thrown backward.

"I will get all the glory myself, and shame you all!" the jackal screamed.

The young woman heaved up her dead sister and carried her away from the scene.

"Are you going to run, too, Malwi?" the jackal asked the old man, who shook his head and walked away in the same direction the twin had taken.

"And you, Kamo? Will you be a coward, or will you lend me your power?"

The toddler stood up, and there was an eerie buzz in the air. "I will help," he said. Even his voice was that of a toddler. With every tiny step he took toward the battlers, the buzz increased in the air. The shapes he had been drawing in the sand were moving. Thrashing like cut-off tails of lizards.

Reema's shadow wobbled and drew back toward her. Her face was twisted in shock. "Help me, Gweuka, Tambo. I can't move!"

Gweuka made to charge at the toddler but was caught mid-air and thrown hard to the ground. Tambo started to scream and pat his thighs like something was squashing his legs.

There was a *whoosh,* the sound of shattering terracotta, and Reema's shadow was no more. She flopped to the ground. The jackal bawled in triumphant laughter. It sauntered to Reema, placed a foot on her chest. "You thought you could have the best of me, Chonse the Jackal, first disciple of Ituntulu. I will have my vengeance. Bring me the spear, Kamo."

Gweuka stood up, turned about as though chasing his own tail. He let out a whoop. "I am free. I am free!" He took a few steps as though to confirm this.

"Finally, I am free. We're free, Tambo."

Tambo examined himself, wiggled his fingers, moved his legs. "We're free," he said in disbelief.

Gweuka bound away, giggling. But then he stopped and looked back.

Tambo was hesitating. He watched as the toddler picked the spear, walked back to the jackal. Reema couldn't move, and she tried hard to.

"Stab her," Chonse said to the toddler. "Stab her good, let all the power she's gathered flow out of her." He was grinning down at Reema. "Then I can eat her."

"Tambo, no!" yelled Gweuka as Tambo dashed at the toddler. He grabbed the spear off the tiny hands, kicked the toddler away and threw the spear at Chonse. The spear didn't fly straight, but as it turned, its shaft struck Chonse in the snout.

That was enough for Reema. She jumped up and all her power returned. Her shadow thickened. It bulged out, caught and pinned the jackal down. Reema reached into her upper garment and brought out something shiny. A large golden coin. She pressed it on Chonse's head. "You're mine now!" she said.

The toddler made to run away, but Reema's shadow took hold of him, lifting him by the leg and bringing him toward her. She placed the coin onto his forehead, claimed him. He became as obsequious as a sheep.

Reema went to Tambo, threw her hands around him, pecked him on the lips. "I knew you still cared. Thank you. Thank you so much, my love!"

Gweuka came timidly before Reema. He flashed an angry look at Tambo.

"You're still with me, Gweuka," Reema said. "Until I get what I want."

She turned to the two sorcerers as she put the coin back into her bosom. "I can kill you all, right here. But my husband has seen enough killing today. He may think evil of me. You are under me now, and you will pay for trying to kill me." She pondered. "You will do only what I tell you. I want something, a magic of youth and beauty. You will help me find it. Everywhere. You will never rest until you find what I am looking for. You hear?"

"We hear," said the jackal grudgingly. "As you say."

"Go, now. Leave my presence before I change my mind and kill you."

The toddler climbed onto the jackal's back. When they were out of view, Reema held herself and sat on the ground. She breathed. "I thought I was surely dead."

"I told you death will come for you."

She smiled. "But you rescued me. I see I still have your heart."

"No, you do not. Free me. You owe me everything now, and I must be the one to demand things."

She spoke softly. "I only want to have myself whole again, my love. My quest continues, and with you by my side."

"So, I am still bound to your whims?"

She gave me a pained look. "I still need you, Tambo. I trust you; you should know that. I can't trust this hyena here, but don't feel bad if it seems I am treating you the same. Look, it's been a hard night. We need to rest to have enough strength for tomorrow. Come, help me up. Let's find shelter."

Nasomi watched as Tambo helped Reema walk to a ditch of a dried-up river. At her request, he ripped part of his breeches and bandaged her bleeding arm. Nasomi watched them fall asleep.

She went into Tambo's dream. "What were you thinking?"

He sat on a throne, dressed in a heavy garb trimmed with gold, and all his fingers glimmered with moonstone rings.

"Nasomi?" He looked confused as the world about them turned to blackness and he was a simple man in tattered clothes.

"You were free! You could have run away!"

He looked down. "I am sorry. I don't know what I was thinking."

"You don't know what you were thinking? I can't believe you, Tambo. Do you know how much I am suffering just to get to you? You had a chance. We would have been coming to each other finally."

He sat down, scratched his hair.

"Why didn't you do leave her, Tambo?"

He didn't answer.

"I am asking a question. Why didn't you leave her?"

"I don't know! I don't know!" He stood up, turned away from her, but she appeared in front of him. "I don't know. I wanted to go. Right there, I had the freedom I have been longing for, but when I saw she would be killed, I don't know what led me... I couldn't have let her be killed."

"Do you still have feelings for her?"

"What? No, no, no. You shouldn't be thinking like that. I want to come home to you. I think of that all the time."

"Be honest with me, Tambo. Is it because she is next to you and I am not?"

"Well, you're not."

"Tambo!"

"You want me to be honest. Every night I dream I am talking to you, but how can I be sure? I love you, Nasomi. I love only you. I did not want things to turn out this way. I fear I may die out here. I fear I am going mad with dreams of talking to you."

"It is I, Tambo. You're talking to the real me."

"Forgive me, Nasomi, my wife. I am in pain, in anguish. I think my death will come soon, out here in the wilderness."

"You could have run. I told you I am coming for you."

"Should I have let them kill her? Should I?"

It was her turn to be silent. They didn't speak or face each other for a long moment.

"I have to wake up now," he said. "I need to make some water."

She was pushed out of his mind. She watched him get up, look at the sleeping Bride and the hyena, sigh, and stand to go to a bush. When he was done urinating, he turned and was face to face with the hyena.

"Ah! You scared me, Gweuka."

"You're a fool, that's what you are!" the hyena said.

"Look, I know. I misjudged. I let my humanity get in the way and I rescued her."

"I wish I could eat you right now. We were free! We would be on our way to our homes right now, but you... you... what is your problem?"

"I am sorry, beast! You're angry with me, my wife is angry with me. I will run the next chance I get, is that what you want to hear?"

"This is it, fool. Your other chance. Are you ready to do it right this time?"

"I can't take the coin from her. How many times should I tell you? She's too alert. She probably can hear what you're thinking right now."

"She's exhausted, bleeding. She's in deep sleep. She won't hear you. I need that coin, Tambo. You need it."

"Very well," Tambo said, with resolve. "I will get it. Let's end this."

He crept back to where Reema slept. She was snoring lightly, looking peaceful where she leaned against the edge of the ditch. He lowered himself with as little noise as he could make. He knelt before her, stretched his hand ever so slowly, toward her bosom.

She opened her eyes. "My love," she said. "Is it morning yet?"

He withdrew his hand. "Not yet. I failed to sleep."

She stretched and yawned. "I am awake now, and hungry. I have an idea, as well. We can use the fur of the lynxes to make some garments. I would so love a cloak. It may be cold where we are going."

"Let me get to it right away."

"Sit, rest. Do it in the morning. Where is that hyena? Gweuka!"

The hyena showed itself from a bush.

"Fetch us some foo—" She examined him. "Come here, Gweuka. I can sense something is off."

"Nothing is off."

"Come here, I said!" She prodded him with her eyes. "There have to be no more secrets between us, Gweuka. I know there's a part of your mind you have hidden from me from the start. I can sense it burning in you. I want to know."

"There is noth—"

Her shadow whipped out arms, gripped the hyena's limbs and neck, dragged him closer to Reema. "Tell me this desire of yours you have never wanted me to see."

The hyena struggled for a long time but soon gave up. "We wanted to kill the dragon and take his place. I and Loshui."

The Bride squinted at him for a while and then burst into laughter. She laughed so hard she held her ribs. She clutched her stomach and stooped as the waves of laughter faded.

"Don't kill me with your jests."

"I am not jesting," Gweuka said. "The dragon is real."

She laughed again, a little more controlled this time. "Is that so, my dear idiot? Where then would you say he is, if you believe he exists?"

"I don't know."

"I want the truth!" the Bride yelled, her shadow spreading around the hyena's body.

"I speak the truth. Look inside. I have opened myself."

The Bride put away her shadow. She sat down next to Tambo, taking in breaths to calm herself. She was quiet for a long time, pondering.

Tambo said, "I hope you are not having a bad idea right now."

"No," she replied softly. "Tambo, have you ever considered that I really loved you? And still do? That all this is just for you to see that?"

"Reema, stop."

"You must see this. There's nowhere I wouldn't go — nowhere I haven't gone — to prove my love for you. I will show you, when this is all over. I will give it all up, all this power, just because I love you and want to be with you."

Tambo looked away.

"Gweuka?" the Bride said.

"I am listening," said the hyena.

"Help me with my mission. When it is done, I will give you your freedom, and you can go hunt your dragon all you want. Say that you're with me."

"I am with you."

CHAPTER 28

INTO TUNKAMBE

Nasomi's posse passed through Ozomboe, a settlement on the verge of an arid piece of land. They were
moving too slowly for her liking, and she found herself
expressing her agitation through biting and clicking her
fingernails together.

Buyechi's horse took an illness, could hardly walk
half a mile without stopping to lay down and groan.
Buyechi had not ridden it for the past three days, choos-
ing to run by its side. They both often lagged by far and
Nasomi and Wakani would have to wait for them.

"We can sell the horse, My Heart," Buyechi said.
"The locals might want its meat before it becomes too
sick."

Nasomi nodded. "And if we find no horse here?"

"Then I will ride with Wakani."

"My horse can carry us both," Wakani said, offering the best reassuring smile.

They know I'm impatient, Nasomi thought.

They were still a very long way from catching up
to the Bride, who had already gone into Tunkambe
through a dark forest and over a wide part of the river
that separated the Peninsula from the continent. Reema
used her shadow magic to hold some logs together to
make a crude raft, and to propel it over the river. Even
Tambo said he was impressed by her ability.

Gweuka was now big enough to carry both Reema and Tambo on his back. He was strong and tireless,
too, propelled by Reema's increasing powers.

Reema was quick and could make her way
through and over obstacles that would give Nasomi

trouble. Nasomi had to take the longer route, and even though she and her warriors rested little and rode as fast as their horses could take them, she was still a long way from catching up.

As dry as it was, Ozomboe abounded with so much life. Nasomi and her warriors moved among clustered and haphazard buildings with narrow alleys in between. Children romped and chased each other, and several of them begged to be lifted unto the horses. Huge clay pots boiled with stews over fires; people pounded food with mortars, drew water from deep wells, shouted greetings at each other from first-story windows, followed and gawked at Nasomi's posse.

She asked if anyone would be interested in buying a horse. No one seemed to have enough wealth to do so, even when Nasomi said, "Any amount will do. Food and water for a long journey ahead," and even though it was for a sickly horse.

She was directed toward the northern end of the town, to the "Wise Ones" who had a lot of silver and gold and, camels. Where the mashed architecture ended, a rocky patch of land began, with sparse cottages and dozens of massive gapes in the ground.

From the nearest cottage, a man dressed in a flowing robe emerged and came. "You can't go any further," he said.

"Why not?" From her high view on the horse, she saw what she thought was a stairway leading beneath the closest gape. She glimpsed hints of pillars and engravings on the walls where the light of the sun touched.

"It's only for the worthy, the chosen. And we never let foreigners in there. You have come far enough. Head back to the homes."

"We only came to sell a horse, for food and water if money won't be found. We were told the Wise Ones would buy."

After looking at the horse pensively, the man said, "Wait here." He went back into the cottage.

As they waited, the men started guessing what was down the holes.

"Piles of treasure," said Buyechi. "Lots of gold."

"Then the town wouldn't be very poor," Wakani said. "I say snakes. Big, big snakes that they feed."

"For what damn purpose?" bawled Buyechi. "Those are latrines. Look at them."

"What?" said Nasomi, bursting into laughter. She realized she hadn't laughed or smiled since confronting Tambo in his dream.

"The whole population has a day when they line up and take a dump in there and then go back home. Maybe after each one is given some water to drink after the deed is done. 'Bless you,' a Wise One will say. 'For your holy duty.'"

"Buyechi!" Nasomi said, bending forward in mirth. "How do you even think like that?"

He grinned. "These are strange people, My Heart. Strange people."

A taller man came with the first one from the cottage. He appraised the horse and said it would make good meat. More Wise Ones came forth, bringing dried fruits, bread, and gourds of a thick sour brew that sent a shudder through Nasomi when she tasted it. She thanked the Wise Ones, asked for the directions toward Tunkambe.

"Go east," one of them said, indicating. "You will come upon the Yukani caravan. They are going in the direction of Tunkambe."

"Caravan?"

"Nomads. This year they are going to Nkole, next year they travel back to Nkani."

She thanked them once again, and she and her warriors rode away. They soon saw a long wall of dust in the distance. But she was now too tired to go on. She said she needed to rest for a bit.

Buyechi and Wakani constructed a makeshift shelter using a large piece of cloth, to shelter her from the burning sun. When she slept, she was inside one of the great holes of Ozomboe. They were temples, upside-down temples. Staircases and pillars had been hewn from solid rock, leading down into three stories. Some of the pillars were shaped into human and animal forms, and all the walls were etched in symbols she couldn't make sense of.

The Wise Ones walked from wall to wall, reading the writing out loud. She hovered over them as they discussed the shifting of the world about six hundred years ago. How the sun moved from its original position; east was no longer east, and the days and nights became longer. How the continent broke up as the world quaked, and pieces of the land floated away. How the land folded to make the mountains of God's Teeth; how strange creatures emerged from these mountains: the undying dragon, lions with scorpion tails, kowasa, the inkanyamba. How seasons changed.

How the land here used to be green and fertile, and wars and drought turned it into a desert, but soon a new rain would fall and the land would be full of life once again.

Nasomi realized there was nothing in the world that could be hidden from her. But she didn't care about the world; not its history nor its future. All she desired was to find Reema and take Tambo away from her. So, she floated up and out of Ozomboe, went eastward until she found the Bride and company.

A horde of sorcerers attacked them, but Reema was undaunted. She was more powerful than the attackers' combined effort. They fell to her magic, and of those who tried to run away, Reema screamed to Gweuka, "Hunt them down. Kill them. Kill them all!"

It was too much gore and death for Nasomi to stomach. She awoke, and her posse went on again. The Yukani caravan was a train of camels pulling wagons and carrying impossible luggage. Nasomi could see neither the end nor the beginning of it.

The Yukani were not a hostile people. They let Nasomi and her men ride among them, eat of their food, listen to their stories. The caravan rested at night, but Nasomi tried to make as many miles as she could. The going was slow. She couldn't push the horses to a gallop, what with the lack of water and dry weather. Hard dust winds often blew, and the horses had to be stopped and shielded from them.

Nasomi and the men were invited to spend some nights in the wagons as their horses recuperated. Nasomi tried to keep her mind off the creeping journey, by participating in the Yukani women's gossip, wearing their clothes, telling them of the goings-on in Mifirhana. They were sweet people, these, and she liked their folklore, particularly the story of Onyezi, a bright goddess who lived in a mountain, bringing sunshine upon the world. Many men tried to court Onyezi, but they always fell back because of her brightness.

One man convinced her he was the source of her brightness, and she believed him, fell in love with him, did all be bade. The man became king of the world, and all bowed before him as he was the one who had conquered the bright woman. Unsatisfied by his wealth, children, and accomplishments after he had subdued Onyezi, he tried to kill her. But in her final dying moments, she remembered who she was, and she shone so bright her light engulfed him and the entire kingdom. The man couldn't contain the glory. He died, and his soul became so dark he tried to destroy Onyezi's light. But she rose to rule in the sky. He followed after her, chased after her, him being the night and her the day, but never was able to catch her.

The caravan crawled for a month, and Nasomi's impatient was as glorious as Onyezi's ascent. She felt she was going to go insane if this journey took one more day. She decided to walk into her cousin Naena's dream, for she remembered the comfort Naena used to give.

It took a long while to get Naena to focus on Nasomi from the rest of the kaleidoscopic dream.

"I am sorry to invade your privacy, Nae," Nasomi said when the dreamworld became black and she was alone with Naena.

"You're my sister, you can come to me anytime," Naena said. She looked about, confused. "Why is everything black?"

"Please forgive me, Nae."

"For what?"

"For not coming back soon."

Naena suddenly remembered. "You didn't come! Nasomi, you didn't come!" She gave Nasomi a slap, even though Nasomi didn't feel it.

"I deserve that."

"Two years, Nasomi! You've been gone for two years."

"I will return, Nae."

"Where are you?"

"Would you believe me if I told you I'm in Tunkambe?"

Naena snorted. "No." She gasped. "The children. I did my best. But I wasn't their mother, and they do remind me every day. They... they..."

"I know, Nae. It's all my fault for leaving."

"Mona, she likes being by herself, won't let anyone talk much to her. And Meron... Oh, Somi. Meron was made a mage. It was the king's decree. I couldn't talk him out of it."

"Would you tell them for me that I love them and will still return?"

"Oh, I know that promise! They'll hear it until they are old and grey."

"No. With all seriousness, Nae, I will return. My dreams—"

"Swallow your dreams, Nasomi! I wish you never had them."

"You think I don't always wish that? You think I want this? I'll promise you this one thing, Nae: I will not care how many of these dreams I have once I have Tambo back. I will stop—"

The next words she had been about to say were, "paying them attention," but she cut herself off because she realized what she was saying.

"Oh, *Mara*! I'm becoming just like Reema!" She fell to her knees and cried into her palm. Naena came closer to comfort her.

Nasomi didn't hear what Naena said, as she was being awakened by Wakani. "My Lady, we have arrived at Ndora." She wiped off the tears flowing down her cheeks and he pretended not to notice.

Ndora was another dusty city, but the good thing about it was it was only six miles to Kawana River, which separated Ao from Tunkambe. Her posse reached the river in quick time, the horses having gained their strength back.

She paid for passage across a large raft and wasted no time in driving Nhema and the other horses at their full speed. She allowed herself and her warriors little rest, but they didn't complain about it. They made jokes and told stories, and Buyechi played his flute during those times.

In three days, the Badjom town of Kedjaki spread out before her in its own time. She wasn't even excited to finally be there because she knew this was less than half the journey of where she was going. Reema was still far off. But she was glad she could stay there for a few days, pack some food for the way.

The hustle and bustle of Kedjaki was a welcome sight for Nasomi. It felt good to be among people busy buying and selling and exchanging fruits, vegetables, fish, fabrics, beads. It reminded her of Nari.

Unlike Nari, though, the goings-on in Kedjaki was rather... serious. Everything was so orderly as though rehearsed: exact steps from one seller to the other, and none of these shouted their wares at the top of their voices or tried to out-hustle each other. A seller would smile at a buyer, mention the price of his or her goods, receive the money, wrap the purchase meticulously and hand it over, smile for the next customer. If someone didn't buy, they would apologize and move on. The seller wouldn't make a fuss about it.

She was buying plantains from a rotund boy when a girl, in the ubiquitous black garb plus a turban the women around here wore, slammed into her, spilling away the coins and plantain in her hands. Nasomi found her balance, but the girl fell and the turban flew away from her head. The girl picked up Nasomi's goods as she scrambled up.

She would have run if Buyechi didn't grab her. "*Zje'gei!*" the girl yelled in the Badjom language and then in Ao'Mu, "Leave me!"

"Should I kill her, My Heart?" Buyechi said, pointing his spear at the girl, to whom he said, "Do you know from whom you steal?"

I'm nothing like Reema, Nasomi thought. "Let her go."

"Bring her to us," a voice said, and Nasomi turned to see a group of robed men. The one leading them said, "Thank you for catching this thief. We will take her now to justice."

"See what you did now!" the girl shouted to Nasomi as she was being taken away. "You let them catch me!"

"Keep quiet, Djina! This is the last time you will be tolerated.

"Wait!" Nasomi shouted, following after them. "What did you say her name is?"

"Djina."

Nasomi laughed, looking the girl over. "I wondered when I was going to meet you." To the robed men, she said, "I'd like her back."

"She's a thief who must be put to trial."

"I'm not asking," Nasomi said. Wakani and Buyechi took the cue and threatened the men off with their spears.

Nasomi offered the girl a hand to help her onto the horse. "What do you want with me?" Djina asked.

Nasomi was going to say she didn't know yet, but said instead, "What was going to happen to you if I let them take you?"

"They would have cut off my hands." She still looked doubtfully at Nasomi.

"Good for you that is not happening. Do you know the way to Ndinge kingdom?"

"The way, yes. I haven't been there. You want I show you the road?"

"You're coming with us."

CHAPTER 29
SHAPES IN THE DARK

She followed Reema and Tambo in her dreams. They moved in more or less silence, their days uneventful after the Bride's triumph over the sorcerer horde.

Tambo was irritable, and in his dreams, of which Nasomi stepped in every few days, he said he had had enough of this and he wanted to go home. He was willing to kill the Bride if he had the chance.

The Bride, on the other hand, seemed anxious about finding what she desired. She said it as much: "If the Ndinge Mfundae cannot give me what I seek, I don't know what I will do next."

Tambo had replied to that with a grunt.

They soon came into a forest of verdant jacaranda trees. Each tree was spaced about eight paces from the other, as though deliberately planted thus. Given the sparse undergrowth, one would think it was so. Sunlight striking through the purple crowns gave the whole forest a dazzling dreamy view, as if walking into a dreamy world. The little flowers rained from the trees in the soft wind, laying thick violet carpets on the ground. Even Tambo enjoyed kicking his way through the flower blankets.

Nasomi was hiding in Tambo to keep Reema from detecting her, even though Reema gave a subtle gesture as if she suspected. She said nothing about it. Maybe she was sure Nasomi could do nothing but suffer as she watched the Bride control her husband.

"Sometimes I am grateful I've been through all these trials," the Bride said. She breathed in the scent of the flowers, closing her eyes for a moment. "The places we've seen, the different cultures... the world is so vast. Let's not forget the power I have amassed. I would have still been a sad little housewife in Nari, married to your insufferable brother. But I was brave enough to step out."

"You mean wicked enough," Tambo said.

She gave a mirthless laugh. "Tambo, my love, I'm not in the mood for that."

"Well, I am." He smirked. "I'll never get tired of insulting you."

"I guess I have to get used to it." She turned around to face him, walking backward. "But you have to revert to what you used to call me when all this is over."

"I don't remember," he pretended.

"'My Radiant Beauty' was my favorite." She turned back around. "I really do promise you that I will give up all this. Then you and I can settle anywhere we like, and have lots of children... a happy family."

He sighed. "You'd have killed me by then because of my stubbornness."

She chortled. So did the hyena. Gweuka slunk back, a predatory look on him.

"Why would I kill the man I love? I know you love me, Tambo. If not *still* then *anew*. I can see it in your face. You're warming up to me."

"Don't flatter yourself." But there was no anger in his voice as before, only tiredness.

"I have a gift for you, my love."

"Gift?" He looked about. The hyena was not in sight. "Where is Gweuka?"

"Don't worry about him. This is a sweet moment between us."

He stopped walking, gave her a suspicious eye.

She sashayed to him. "You have been with me through these years, Tambo. By my side, through much trouble. I make your legs move when you don't want to, but you have still been by my side. And you even saved me. You know what they say about people who experience hardships together."

He shook his head.

"They develop a deep fondness. I have always liked this coyness of yours. It's one of your attractive elements, did I tell you that? Now, as to my gift, I am giving you freedom." She knelt, untied the cloth on his leg, stood up and showed it to him.

His eyes were so wide they would have popped out. "What is this? What have you done to me?"

"Nothing, my love. I want you to trust me. I also want to trust you."

"You have set me free? I am no longer bound to you?"

"Only through your heart."

"Why?" He still looked about like there was something bad about to happen.

"As I said, nothing can compare to the bond we've shared since I got you back." She was smiling at him.

He slunk back from her and she made no move, only smiled wider. He backed away further from her, she still did not move. He watched her for a moment, and then sprung for his life.

"I see your folly!" the Bride yelled.

The cloth magically floated from her hand and flew toward him like an angry bee.

Strangely, Nasomi's perception followed after the cloth as it hunted Tambo among the trees. It was close by, matching his running speed, teasing him.

She became him again. He was determined to get as far from the Bride as he could. He was not going to let his freedom be taken away again. He was going through his options: Hide? No, the Bride would sniff him out. Fight? He heard the giggle of the hyena. He knew how strong Gweuka was, how quick. No wonder he'd hidden. Both he and the Bride were playing this game on Tambo.

He had nothing else to do but run.

Gweuka appeared beside him, and he veered away. The hyena jumped in front of him. He dashed another way. He kept his direction till Gweuka was almost upon him, then he banked aside, and the hyena hit into a tree. "Ha!" he yelled in triumph.

The dead flowers and leaves underneath thickened, making his running cumbersome. He didn't notice the creek until his foot didn't step upon ground but dipped into water, and he sprawled into it. He didn't take the time to check himself. He was up immediately and running again. He didn't mind that he lost both his sandals.

He dodged an aimed bite from the hyena, feinted and dashed another direction. He ran toward a fallen tree; it had space underneath enough for him to crawl under. He dove, but he hardly started crawling when a hyena bit into his leg and dragged him back.

He kicked with his free leg. When Gweuka let him go, he scrambled under the trunk. When he stood up on the other side, he was facing the Bride. Her black shadow was writhing beneath her.

"Come now, enough of this," she said, as the cloth floated from under the trunk and wrapped itself on his right thigh. His will was gone from him, and he fell to his knees.

"Swallow you, Reema! And you too, stupid Gweuka. May the depths swallow you both."

"No need for curses," the Bride said. "It is clear to me you still want to return to the dream witch." She offered her hand and he took it. She helped him up. "You need to forget about her, my love. I know you will when I am all you will have. I think she must die."

"Reema, no!"

"I have been good to you. But you keep despising me. She doesn't know you as I do. She must die, my love. I will help you through the grieving. I will cry with you. When it is over, you will have no one in your heart but me. I am so sorry."

"I will kill you if you touch her. I swear—"

She touched his lips. "Shhhh. I know, I understand. But you must understand me, too." She beckoned Gweuka. "Whom can we send?"

ENOCK I. SIMBAYA

The hyena giggled. "Ooh, the Toddler, send the Toddler!"

"And the jackal, too, to make sure it is done."

Nasomi jerked awake, found Wakani the only one awake by the fire of the little camp the made for the night. Buyechi and the girl were asleep.

There was a crack behind her. She jerked her head and saw the Toddler, silhouetted among some bushes, watching her. But it turned out to be a tree stump. A shadow flitted in the trees. An animal. Or a conjuring of her imagination.

She stood and went to sit next to Wakani on the fire. "Keep an eye out," she said, her heart fluttering at shapes in the dark being that were not being what she perceived them to be. As the fire warmed her face, she faced her fear. And then being afraid didn't make sense anymore.

"I am the Heart of Mohale," she said, more to herself.

"Yes, you are, My Lady," Wakani replied.

How would the Bride send the Toddler and jackal after her when she didn't know where Nasomi was? It's a gimmick, Nasomi realized. To break Tambo's heart. When he grieves, she would be there for him. Also, to scare me into not coming after her. Cunning witch.

"She doesn't know me," Nasomi said. "I am the Dreamer, the Seer. I will find her anywhere she goes, and I will get to her no matter how long, how far it takes me."

"And I will be there to fight with you," Wakani said.

"Wakani..."

"I know what you want to say, My Lady. Let me take you to the Bride, then I will go back."

"I don't know what's ahead, what danger it is to you. I will not forgive myself if something bad happens to you. Think of your daughter Khuya."

"I always do. But I will not say to her, 'And then I abandoned My Lady to go face the witch by herself.' She will want to know the end of this."

As the dawn chased away the darkness, the posse was riding out again on the road to Zjala. Nasomi and Djina rode on Nhema, and the two men took turns riding the other horse and running.

"You thought to steal my bananas," Nasomi said to Djina, when they slowed to a walk as a new night encroached.

Djina laughed. "I was hungry. Sorry. I didn't know you would be the one to save me."

"I do hope you won't try to steal any more from me."

The girl sighed. "I am ashamed this is the image of me you have. I need to reintroduce myself properly."

"So, who are you, Djina, if you're not a thief?"

"I am the daughter of a priest and priestess in Kedjaki. The man you got me from, who wanted to see me come to justice—that's my father."

"*Eh?* Your father? And he was quick to condemn you thus?"

"According to him, it was after many warnings. I gave him much trouble, unlike my brothers and sisters."

"You don't sound contrite."

"Believe me, I am. But it's just so hard. Sometimes I think there's something wrong with me, or maybe I don't belong here. I see things, shiny things, and I just want to take them. Also, when I feel happy inside, I can't help it but sing and dance in places I am not supposed to."

"Is that what they wanted to punish you for? Singing and dancing?"

Djina laughed. "At 'inappropriate times.' And there's plenty of those. Foreigners like you get to do what they want, and your ways are just beautiful. Full of freedom. I have always wanted the freedom to do what I want."

"And the stealing?"

ENOCK I. SIMBAYA

"There are few things which are not sacred in Kedjaki. It's all confusing: you can't take this on the first day, you can't touch that when the moon is out. My people can be such stiffs. Good thing I am leaving, with my hands intact. Why did you take me after hearing my name?"

"That's a long story. Your name, is it common here?"

"Common enough. Why do you ask? You rescued the wrong girl?"

"That shall be seen." Djina squirmed. "Stop that, Djina. You'll fall off the horse."

Djina did it twice more. "Nasomi! I've seen something! It looks like... like a child riding a dog."

Wakani gave a cry, and Buyechi shouted, "What in the name of Mohale is that?"

Nasomi whipped her head to see the Toddler and jackal catching up to their side, going past the astounded warriors. She just kicked the horse into a gallop when the Toddler stretched out its tiny hand. An unseen heavy hand threw her off the horse. She was rolling on the ground, spinning in dizzying disorientation, hearing the horse bray and the girl scream.

They found me! The Bride had indeed sent them!

Her head hit into something, and the world continued spinning even when she stopped. She didn't know whether she was whole; she was too panicked to feel her own body. She didn't even know whether she tried to get up or just lay there.

Someone was screaming. Was it her? No, one of the men. "Let me go, you stupid witch!" Wakani screamed. Nasomi heard him grunt and then there was a sickly *fft*, and he made one more scream and went silent.

What have you done to Wakani? Nasomi shouted but wasn't even sure her voice came out of her mouth.

Invisible arms took hold of Nasomi, clasping her hands and feet. She could feel a burning all the way inside her.

242

"Is she the one?" the jackal asked. His muzzle blocked the moonlight. He was looking down at her with fiery red eyes.

"She smelled right," the Toddler said in his toddler's voice. He came into view on her other side, and for a moment she remembered the days when baby Meron would frolic all about her when she lay in bed.

"We have to be right, I am tired," the jackal said. "We've come too far to waste time."

The Toddler put a hand on her forehead. It was soft, but far from endearing. It was like a stone weighing on her head.

"She said she was one of them, with some magic inside. I don't feel anything."

Nasomi's heart, already a wild drum, spiked. Djina, the warriors. What was happening to them? She jerked up into a sitting position, her motion pushing the sorcerers away like a storm.

"She's the one!" the jackal shouted excitedly. "And a fighter, too. Do your thing quick, Kamo."

The Toddler faced the other way, flopped down onto its buttocks, started writing on the ground. Nasomi could feel her soul inside begin to fade. The unseen hand pushed her head back down. The jackal placed his paw on her chest, grinning.

"I am hungry, Kamo. I may start before you're done."

"Remember to leave the head for the Bride to see."

Another figure came into view over the jackal. Buyechi, with his spear raised in both hands. Blood streamed from his forehead, covering one of his eyes. He hit the jackal, who yelped and sprinted away.

"Buyechi, you must run!" Nasomi was able to sit up again. When she stood, her left ankle burned with pain.

But the warrior was adamant. He charged the jackal with the spear as it turned back around. The spear was yanked off his hands magically and the jackal came for a bite.

Nasomi threw herself at the jackal, bringing it down with her body. It threw her off.

"My Heart!" The warrior couldn't move, held by an invisible web. He shook and fought, broke free and lunged onto the jackal once again. It jumped at him, bit into his thigh.

A stone flew and hit the jackal. Djina picked another one, threw it. Chonse let go of the screaming warrior and turned toward the girl. Djina stood where she was, perhaps petrified, perhaps out of stubbornness.

A mighty force pushed Nasomi back to the ground. *Djina!* she screamed, unsure whether her voice actually came out or not. *Don't die here with me!*

Her vision caught the Toddler standing up and turning around. With that motion came a palpable darkness, a dark oily column that spread and encompassed her, and she was lost in it. She could not move, could not fight, could not access the power of her tellings. She was like a helpless child, while the Toddler seemed like a giant coming to crush her with his legs.

She saw Djina backing away, the jackal stalking her. She saw Buyechi dive onto the jackal, saving Djina from a nasty bite. A spear flew, lodged into the jackal's hide.

The darkness closed in; the madness came. Pain, grief, tormenting memories. All of Nasomi's soul was being taken away, stripped, broken apart. What pended was physical death.

But she wasn't all gone, was she? She could feel a finger, her right pinky. And that was sufficient to recall herself. She was Nasomi, Seer, Oracle. She was "one of them", the ones with magic inside. She was the Dreamwalker, the ghost that could travel the world, Heart of a goddess.

She clenched her pinky, and all fingers followed. She raised her fist in the air, in the enveloping darkness.

"I have you conquered, dream witch," the Toddler said. "You cannot fight this." He was still coming toward her, his baby steps rocking the ground.

Nasomi tried to speak, and it came out as a strained whisper: "I am not afraid."

Thud thud thud. He was next to her now.

"I am not afraid of you." She raised another fist. "I am not afraid of you!" Her voice was stronger, louder. She could shout, she could yell for all the world to hear. "I am not afraid of you!"

The darkness broke, flaking off into pieces of light and color. Nasomi raised herself from the pulling shadow. She faced the Toddler. He blinked, surprised. She pushed him away, and his power dissipated.

Wakani was – Wakani! He was alive, but bleeding heavily. He was stabbing the jackal repeatedly with his spear, grunting in disgust. It just wasn't dying. No blood but puffs of dark smoke poured out from its wounds. The spear was magically yanked from his hand. It spun in the air. It stabbed into his heart.

Nasomi screamed. She stood up. "I am not afraid of you," Nasomi said to the Toddler. She stood up, as a wind from inside her blew away all the nasty witchery the two had wrought. She swung her hand; she gave him a mighty slap. He fell away, and he lay unconscious.

The jackal was whimpering now, trying to get up. Without knowing what she was doing, Nasomi went to get the spear from Buyechi. When she stabbed the jackal, it shriveled up, like a scorched plant. It coughed, fell limp and lifeless.

"Arrrgh!" the Toddler cried, and Nasomi turned to find him awake and upstanding. "Look what you've done!"

"Go away, you beast!" Nasomi shouted. "Or I will do you like I have done the jackal."

The Toddler crawled away into some bushes.

CHAPTER 30
THE SECRETS OF BEAUTY
AND LOVE

Wakani was dead, stabbed with his own spear. He sprawled grotesquely on the ground, a strange expression on his face like he was saying, *It is well, My Lady. I will go home tomorrow.*

A tear ran down Nasomi's cheek. "Not like this. It shouldn't be like this." Fury and hate burned hot inside her. "It shouldn't end this way!" she said at the top of her voice. "What am I going to say to Khuya?"

She hated her dreams even more. Wakani had not been in her returning dream because he was going to die. "Why in the depths do these dreams have to be right? I told him to go home. I told him... What will I ever say to Khuya his daughter?"

Buyechi had a deep wound in his thigh. He couldn't get up to walk and fever caught him. Djina used one of Nasomi's extra dresses to tie around his wound, but the blood soaked through.

Djina had a cut on her forehead and a number of scratches all over her body, but she was otherwise whole. She knelt beside Nasomi to comfort her wordlessly.

When Nasomi stood, she discovered she had a sprained ankle, and stepping on the ground with her left leg sent a fever and weakness all over her body. She stood still to let the feeling pass. Djina offered a hand but she brushed it away, and limped toward where Nhema the horse lay on the ground with a pool of blood forming around him.

Nhema had hit his neck against a tree trunk and fallen onto some sharp rocks. Sometime during the fight, he had got up and run on ahead, but had fallen and could not move anymore.

As the sun was rising, Nhema was grunting his last breaths. "I don't know what to do," Nasomi said, to herself. "I am tired of losing."

Djina came next to her. She had salvaged Nasomi's bag. "That's the scariest baby I have ever seen."

Nasomi only gave her a look.

"What are you, Nasomi?"

Nasomi thought for a moment. "One of *them*."

"Eh? I don't get."

"Apparently there are people in the world who possess some gift or other. I haven't met anyone like me, though."

"Magic, you mean?"

"If you want to call it that. I can see things in my dreams."

"You defeated those... things. The baby and the jackal." She shuddered. "I still feel tingles about all of it."

"They're powerful sorcerers, both of them... Well, were. Their type of magic has strange effects on them. I fail to imagine how the Toddler got that way. Some most powerful ones choose animal forms: jackals, lynxes, hyenas."

"But you defeated them."

Nasomi looked at her hands, as if she could see in them the power of her tellings. "My ability can undo their magic. Djina, my journey is no good thing. There's danger. And death."

"I will follow you wherever you go."

"Don't be silly, Djina. I cannot protect you. You must remain at Zjala, make a new life for yourself."

"I am coming with you, Nasomi. I have a feeling I should be with you."

Nasomi told her about the dream she had had many years back, of returning to Nari with Tambo, a girl named Djina and a dragon named Mdua.

"Eh? A dragon?"

"I could have misremembered that part. Maybe it was somebody who likes to think he's a dragon."

An ox cart trundled their way from the direction of Zjala. The two men in it jumped off, came to them. One whistled when he looked upon the gore. He spoke in Djom with Djina, who told them what happened. He switched to Ao'Mu when he studied Nasomi.

"I have not heard of witches attacking people on this road before," he said. "Dark times we are living in."

The other man had a staff in his hand. He used it to poke the injured horse. "A mighty fine horse this was," he said.

"His name was Nhema," Nasomi replied.

"He will make some fine meat."

"Are you insane? No one is eating my horse. I will bury him."

"*Zjala ne djuka,* woman. Why waste to the earth what can remain and sustain a good number of people? Your horse died so that we can live. How much would you have?"

"Just do whatever you think you need to after I am gone, please. Some food and water," Nasomi said, and there was a tear in her eye. "And your staff."

He clutched it to himself. "It is quite sentimental."

"I have a bad leg. It will help me walk."

"Give the lady the stick," the other man said, slapping his friend on the back. "Your son can whittle you another one."

The man gave her the staff, as well as pieces of flatbread, a water gourd and some balm to use for their injuries. The two men helped her dig a grave and bury Wakani. Buyechi played a sad tune on his flute, and Nasomi spoke solemn words over Wakani's departure.

I can't take them with me anymore, Nasomi realized. She regretted telling Djina about the dream. It's dangerous. They will all be killed by Reema. They will all have to stay behind.

Nasomi said it was time to move on. Buyechi rode Wakani's horse while she and Djina walked. The going was slow, imbued by a solemn silence. They moved for over three miles in this manner, and they all became too tired and hungry to move on.

"Let's sit here and eat," Nasomi said.

Djina laid Nasomi's cloak on the ground, helped Nasomi to sit on it. They ate the bread and drank the water and applied the balm to their wounds.

"Every one of your people seems to speak my language well," Nasomi said to Djina.

"Ao'Mu is easy to learn," Djina said. "I could speak it well when I was two. My language is something else. It has so many depths of expressions. I am still learning it, can you imagine."

"It must be a tough language."

"The fundamentals are easy to grasp. *Djom* means thing. A thing in general. The plural of that would be *djombo*. What else can I teach you? *Zje* is you, *zji* is me, *zju* is him or her. So I can ask: *Zje'kdjin?* Meaning, what is your name?"

"So, *Djina?*"

"*Djina* literally means 'girl's name'. But it has some sacredness attached to it. So it's a word that depicts the glory and beauty of a woman. Eh... *li* is to walk, *lo* to crawl or move slowly. We have a saying: *kedlak zje'li kedlak zje'lo um:* You cannot walk without first crawling."

"Teach me something vulgar."

Djina gawked at her, then smiled wickedly. "*Zje'pi toov.* It says—"

"Please don't tell me what it means. I just want to be able to say it to someone when I meet her. *Zje'pi toov.*"

Djina laughed. "Nasomi, you bad girl."

Djina attempted to teach Nasomi some more Djom, but Nasomi was in too much pain to comprehend it. She soon fell asleep.

She had a telling dream. Tambo, Reema, and Gweuka were in Olonge, followed at a distance by its curious denizens.

Tambo looked sick, exhausted, stooping as he walked. The Bride's spell on him sapped his health. But he followed after her, like a dog on a leash.

The Bride sashayed through an avenue of people backing away. The cloak on her back, of lynx skin, was tattered at the hem. It was heavy with the blackness of her power.

Three men dressed in bright orange and red robes emerged from the entrance of a massive edifice. The elder one was the tallest, his hair so white it almost glittered. The shorter one of the three was portly and torpid. The other was also pot-bellied and had a slack countenance.

"What do you want?" the white-haired man said.

"Only to ask a few questions. May we do this privately?" The crowd was thickening.

"We do not answer to your demands, witch. We have heard of what you did in Siloka village. We do not look lightly upon terrorism on our people."

"It was because they couldn't get me what I wanted. I was being nice, but they were mean and insulting. I tried not to kill them, but they left me no choice."

"Here are your choices from us: leave, never return, or face a trial."

Reema smiled. "Will the trial include you giving in to my demands? I have heard you are wise and know many things. The great Mfundae, the ones who know everything."

"There is nothing for you here," replied the Mfunda.

"I want to know the secrets of beauty and love."

The Mfundae looked at each other, whispered amongst themselves. The shorter one replied to her.

"Love comes from the heart and beauty - well, one is born with it."

"Do not let my looks fool you. I was born beautiful and still am beneath this ugliness imposed on me by some fools." Gweuka cowered when she scowled at him.

"I want to reclaim it, and also the love that others had for me. Tell me how I can have this magic."

"There is no such thing as magic for beauty and love. If you're as powerful as you claim, you should understand that. Please leave."

She approached. "I have come a long way and traveled many years. I cannot accept that answer. If it was that simple, why did you confer among yourselves before you answered me? Tell me what I want to know."

The white-haired Mfunda shook his head. "There are things even the most learned Mfunda cannot know. Those are mysteries even our gods cannot tell us."

"You lie. Show me to your magic records and items."

"You are mad!" the average one said. "Have you no respect? Who are you to demand such a thing of servants of the spiritual order?"

A power radiated from the Bride's cloak, like wisps of black smoke. The shadow on it fell to the ground, and the cloak billowed from the lightness. The shadow expanded towards the Mfundae as she approached.

They took the challenge. Retrieving handfuls of golden dust from pockets, they came at the Bride, blowing the dust off their palms. It swirled in the air, materializing in the form of a thin pellucid wall that dragged towards the Bride.

But her shadow passed under the wall, unperturbed, still expanding. She didn't break her walk and the wall shattered when she came in contact with it. The Mfundae were wide-eyed, and before they could run, black tentacles shot out of the widening shadow and grasped and wrapped around them. It pulled them down.

As the lazy-faced one struggled, a tentacle squeezed about his neck until he was pale and out of breath. He sprawled lifeless onto the ground. The shorter Mfunda wailed as the shadow engulfed him too.

The older Mfunda was calmer, his arms raised in submission. The denizens of Olonge were screaming and stampeding away.

"Tell me what I need to know," Reema commanded.

"We have told you. There's no such thing as—"

An appendage shot out of the shadow, grabbed at the man's neck, yanked him down. The hyena put a paw on the old man's chest.

He panted. "There have been legends– Tell your beast to step off me."

"I will not. Speak, like the wise man you are."

"The Tunka gods - they had the power to grant beauty."

A smidge of uncertainty swept over the Bride's face. "The Tunka?" she said, a shaking in her voice. "I hear they are ugly scum. What can they ever do for me? I want to know what you have!"

"We have nothing. I speak the truth. The Tunka lost their grace, yes. Their gods exiled them when they apparently let us Ndinge and Badjom people settle onto their land. They are left distraught and barbaric, deprived of all beauty and civility. There's an ancient city called Dunia. It was the Tunka capital before their gods banished them to the oceanside. There is word that an ancient power lingers there, the power of their old gods. But it is an angry power, and no one goes there."

"You could have saved yourselves all this trouble if you had told me this in the first place."

"Eh!" the Mfunda screamed. "You are mad, woman. The Tunka are wild and dangerous, they kill and eat anyone who gets close to them. Your daring will get us all in trouble—"

"I didn't say I am going there, old lunatic. Since you're now in the mood to talk, come, show me your vast knowledge."

She walked toward the building, and her shadow dragged the screaming, thrashing Mfunda toward her. Tambo and Gweuka followed as she entered. They stepped into a large hall lit by sunlight boxing in through large square windows near the roof. The hall seemed to want to hold on to a grey gloominess, though.

On hundreds of plinths in the hall that stood to the height of the belly were thick tomes. Some were open to random pages.

"Which shall we start with?" the Bride demanded.

"*The Wise Teachings of Mfunda Fomara*," the Mfunda croaked. He pointed to a tome.

The shadow dragged him across the floor. "Begin to read."

CHAPTER 31

THE MFUNDA

When they finally got to Zjala, Nasomi's posse filled their bags with foodstuffs for the rest of the journey, even though Nasomi was making a plan to go alone. She'd brooded over it, and trying to convince them to stay in Zjala didn't work.

"I go everywhere My Heart goes," Buyechi said. He was walking better now, but she could tell he was masking the pain. "I fear no witches."

"I will not risk your life anymore, Buyechi," Nasomi said over and over again.

"It is only pain I feel. My leg will be better, and I will fight for you again. For me to honor my duty as a warrior."

Djina said she, too, wasn't afraid of witches. "Out here, even though it is dangerous, is where I feel more alive. I will come with you."

She stopped trying to convince them, but the same notion she had had in Nari was overwhelming her: It has to be me to do it. Alone. This is my burden.

They rested in Zjala for the night, finding accommodation in an inn atop a hill. Nasomi and Djina had one room and Buyechi another. As she drifted to sleep, Nasomi said an apology to the *Mara* for the life of Wakani and Nhema, for the injury of Buyechi, and for taking away the girl Djina.

"They died for me," she whispered. "They were hurt for my sake. I will not become like the Bride who lets others die for what she wants. Forgive me."

"Mhmm?" said Djina, who lay on a pallet near Nasomi.

"I'm sorry, Djina. I was talking to myself. It's a habit I inherited from my father. I'll be quiet now."

"Please, if you want to talk to yourself, go ahead. It is healthy, especially if it helps you relieve all the tension within."

"Some would say it's insanity."

"What do some know? I talk to myself when I am in distress, I remind myself that things will turn for the better. There is much you can learn from yourself."

"I thank you, Djina, for your words. I will sleep now."

In the telling Nasomi had, the Bride sat on a rock, warming herself over a fire. There was a tome burning in the flames. The Bride was quiet, deep in thought.

She got up, walked away from the other two, into a field of corn stalks. From there came cursing and shouting, and sobbing.

"Maybe she'll let us go this time?" the hyena said.

Tambo let his hand fall to the ground languidly. "I have no more strength, Gweuka." His voice was weak, whispery. "I wish she would kill herself right now and let this be over. She will never find it."

The hyena grunted where he sat. He flopped his head onto his paws, slept. Tambo stared for a long time at the field of corn into which the Bride went.

Nasomi awoke, judging it a good time to slip away from the others. She got up from the straw pallet and tiptoed to where Djina slept, stretched her hand to get the bags that were by the girl's head. As she slid the first bag to herself, Djina opened her eyes. "Is it time to go?"

Nasomi sighed. "For me, Djina. You must stay."

"You were trying to abandon me?"

"Yes."

"You told me you dreamed I was with you when you went back to Nari."

"That was a long time ago. Things can change. And I can go and come back for you. You needn't go thousands of miles for nothing."

"It's not for nothing, Nasomi. This is what I want."

"I need to get to my man quickly. He needs me."

"I promise I won't slow you down. Look, I have money." She took out a small pouch from under her garment. "We can afford to travel together."

"Djina, I hope you didn't steal that."

"It doesn't matter where it came from." Djina stood and took Nasomi's hand. "We're going together, that's the important thing. I will not try to get in the way, or try to get killed." She grinned, kneading Nasomi's shoulder.

Nasomi could pretend to go to sleep and try again later, but Buyechi might awake at any time. "We are going now, without the warrior."

"Why?"

"Because I say so. Are you coming or not?"

Nasomi picked up one bag and peeped outside the door. The night was quiet, and a cold breeze greeted her cheeks. She tiptoed as quickly as she could away from the inn to where they had tethered their horse, and Djina followed.

She helped Djina onto the horse, got onto it herself, and wasted no time in riding the horse to the road that led away from the town.

They rode through the next morning and into the afternoon, taking little rest and food. They walked in the evening to let the horse gain its strength, and they slept a little in the night. The next morning, they were out riding again, and morning turned to afternoon and evening and night. And again. The days and nights were long, and the road wound, meandered, stretched, dipped, turned, disappeared, appeared, rolled, widened, narrowed, rutted, smoothened... and they came into Ndinge territory.

"I've always been fascinated by Ndinge customs," Djina said, as they rode through a village. "I always knew that if I ran away, I'd come here and live the rest of my life with them."

"Now you can."

Djina laughed. "You're still trying to get rid of me. But I am with you now, and I know that whatever lies ahead is a thousand times better than if I stay here."

"Even if it is pain and death?"

"Even. My religion teaches that when we walk in the path the gods have set for each of us, we will come into a glorious end at our death."

"Well, I wouldn't be quick to call you pious."

"In my own way, I am. You're part of my strange but glorious spiritual journey, as I am yours. That's why you dreamed me, years before you met me. The Ndinge have a saying. In Badjom it goes *Zjala ne djuka, djuka ne zjala*. In Ao'Mu it says 'All is nothing, nothing is all'. I don't know how I can explain it to you, Ao'Mu is strange to translate to."

"The man who bought Nhema said that."

"It's a Ndinge philosophy which means all things are equally sacred. But that's the first meaning."

"Nothing is too precious to hold on to, maybe?"

"That can be another way of putting it, and that's one way my people interpret it. The Ndinge take it to mean two things: As everything comes from a formless nothing, everything is sacred. The blade of grass is as sacred as the leaf in the tree. And all things being sacred or important, then nothing is sacred or important. All is nothing. Nothing is all."

"That can be confusing."

"That's just the beginning. Holiness would be regarding everything as sacred. And it would also be to regard nothing as sacred. Here's a question for you, which I always challenged my father with: If taking someone's thing is sinful, isn't it equally sinful for the first person to possess it?"

"Perhaps. If everything is the same, then it belongs to no one. But that doesn't excuse you taking from another. It wouldn't make sense if someone could shift their family into a house I built with my own sweat. Or take my husband."

"My father would give you a hug for saying that. 'We're not Ndinge!' he always tells me. 'We have our own teachings!' We had a Ndinge prisoner some months back, a Mfunda. I talked much with him and he explained the philosophy. 'All is nothing, nothing is all' means everything is a part of and an expression of the formlessness from which it comes. They call the formlessness the big 'nothing'. The nothing from which everything comes. All form, that which we can hear and see and feel and experience comes from the nothing taking up different shapes out of its potential to do so. I can take a piece of clay and form a doll or a brick. It's a brick or it's a doll, but it is clay. And clay is water and soil, and water and soil are forms of a substance that molds them. And perhaps that substance is the nothing we're talking about or yet another of many forms of a preceding nothing, and on and on that way. You see where I am going with this? That means while I am me right now, I am also made of the same substance that makes the sky, the water, the stones I pick up, the cob I eat for supper. I am me, I am this horse, I am the warrior Buyechi, I am you."

Djina continued talking, but Nasomi's mind had latched onto that last statement. She mulled it over, lost in the edifying noesis of breaking and merging things ad infinitum. Objects, colors, sounds. To this thing called nothing that was behind everything. Maybe that was why, through her dreams she could be anyone anywhere, while asleep somewhere.

When they rested again, Nasomi sought out the Bride. Tambo and Reema and Gweuka were awake in the same spot they'd burned the book. The fire was dead, the remaining ash being fondled by a breeze. Tambo sat in the same position, holding his head in one palm.

"I have made up my mind," the Bride said.

"You're as foolish as ever. It is over. Learn to recognize when you've lost."

"I can't, don't you see?" She flopped to the ground, lay down facing the sky, hands on her belly. "I have to try."

"You heard what they said. You're leading us to our deaths if we go there. The Tunka are not like any people we've met. They're savage—"

"There are no people I've met that I can't best."

"That's what you want to prove?"

"I have made my mind. We go tomorrow."

Tambo stood up. He was breathing like a bull about to charge.

"You're the stupidest woman I have ever known, you know that? You're selfish, big-headed, you never listen to anyone. Nothing is not worth sacrificing until you get your way. And you go blaming others, making them suffer for your own childish desires, things that don't even make sense. You've got what you deserved, and now you want the whole world to pity you. To suffer for you. No one wants to be with you unless you force them. You've broken up families, murdered innocent people, destroyed ages of wisdom. All because you don't like the way your face looks! You're stupid, you're evil, you know that? You're a snake in a hen pen, a fly in the soup. I can never love you if you were the most beautiful thing in the world, if you were the only woman—"

"Tambo, I am tired." She said it coolly, but her shadow wiggled slightly. "I want to sleep. Sit down, keep quiet."

He sat, kept silent. He faced away from her, lay on the ground. Only Gweuka and Nasomi got to see a tear run from the corner of Reema's eye. Down her temple. Over the ear. Onto the ground like a raindrop.

Reema clicked her fingers and a shimmer shot out of the ground, surrounding her, Tambo and Gweuka into a protective dome. It shoved Nasomi away, waking her up.

Nasomi thought she had the territory in her mind, as she had seen in her last telling dream. She led Djina into a north-easterly direction, saying it would take them toward Ashge quickly. Tambo and company were perching near Ashge, Tambo's legs unable to move after walking through the night. The Bride spoke little, brooded on her choice much. She once told Tambo and Gweuka that she had decided it was time to give it up, but changed her mind again and sent Gweuka ahead to Dunia to reconnoiter it.

As Nasomi and Djina blundered through some woods, the trees became closer and larger, the grasses taller and thicker, and the ground softer. A quarter moon beamed in the cloudless sky at night, helping their visibility, but soon a mist rose, obscuring the ground ahead. The smell of many decaying things hung in the air, and nocturnal insects began to chirp and bite.

The trail was presently lost. All they could do was move forward as they had been doing, skirting obstacles, wading through ankle-high murky waters, slapping and swatting at stinging insects. Nasomi spied a large shadow sweep by and she clutched Djina's arm to stop and listen. The forest was alive with tweets, creaks, groans and the whistling of a breeze through the trees.

Djina began to tell Nasomi a tale of the ghosts said to live in the Ndinge swamps, but she stopped when Nasomi didn't acknowledge if she was listening. Throughout the night, things dashed below the tree, creatures' eyes stared at them from the shadows, and a cold touched their bones even though they covered themselves thickly. When they came to a peaceful clearing, they both had trouble sleeping, and Djina whispered a song.

At dawn, as she tried to get up on the horse, Nasomi missed a footing and she fell down, twisting her ankle again.

"Swallow the Bride!" Nasomi cursed. She attacked a shrub that was before her, striking it with her staff. Shredded leaves and twigs flew about. She slashed at the grasses, shouted out one more curse, hit the lower branch of the tree they had slept in.

Djina touched Nasomi's shoulder, and before she realized what she was doing, Nasomi turned and pushed her away. The girl landed on her rump.

Nasomi felt ashamed. "I am so sorry, Djina. Are you fine?" She winced when she tried to turn her foot. It stung as though she had stepped on fire. She sat down.

"I am fine." Djina got up, dusted herself and picked up the supply bag that had been slung over her shoulder before the push. "Is it bad?"

"I think I'll be able to walk after a while."

"Was it a dream?"

"It's always the dreams!" Nasomi said, too loud.

"What has the Bride done now? Is Tambo alright?"

"These tellings. I hate them!"

"But they will help you find your husband."

"Will they, Djina? They only show me how incapable I am of doing anything! All I have are my dreams. He's dying, my Tambo is dying and she knows it, she's killing him. Her power is terrible now, but she's still insisting on going to Dunia. Will I keep chasing them till I am old and toothless, watch him die? I have come all this way to see him die. I will feel everything, see everything. Do nothing."

Nasomi realized she was wheezing. She tried to compose herself, ashamed by it, but the thoughts were terrible in her mind and it got worse.

"You're a liar, Nasomi," Djina said.

"Wha...?" Nasomi breathed to find words. "What did I say? What did I lie about?"

Djina burst into laughter. "It does work, after all." She laughed some more. "I just wanted to disturb whatever was going on with you."

"What for? I'm not in a good mood, Djina."

"Yes, that's why. My father – as much as I have wronged him – taught me that you need to shake yourself from an entanglement of thinking, remember your calm and face your problem with a clear head."

"This is not the time to remain calm."

"It more especially is. Let me show you what I mean. It will help."

She sat before her, took Nasomi's hand in her own. "Close your eyes... go on, close them."

"Djina, please—"

"I can teach you some things, Nasomi. Close your eyes."

Nasomi reluctantly did.

"Now, breathe. A slow intake... hold it... now, breathe out. Let's do it twice more. In... hold... out. In... hold... out. Keep doing that, even as I speak. You have lied, Nasomi. To yourself."

"About what?"

"About who you are."

"I know who I am."

"Take that which you've said you are. Hold it in your mind like you would hold sand."

"I don't—"

"See it in your mind. Now, toss the sand away. Watch it spread, some of it falling, some of it flying away like dust. See it as it spreads out, get lost in everything. Breathe in strength. Breathe out the tension. There is an urgency in your mind."

"Of course there is."

"Breathe it out, let the urgency float away. To a place where you can find it later, but not here, not now. Here and now, breathe in peace."

Nasomi remembered the way the mage kept his mind like a home, with the perfect spots for everything. She tried that, putting her urgency on a shelf in the kitchen of her mind.

"More urgencies are showing up, demanding attention. Send them away, and the next, and the next, until you are left empty. Just a breathing calm being."

Nasomi broke apart the thoughts in her head, sent them flying everywhere her mind dared to expand.

"There's a deep peaceful feeling at your base, isn't there?" Djina prompted.

Nasomi had a feeling. It was the one that preceded the telling dreams: a tug, a pit of warm peace, lifting through her body.

"There is, but I'm not sure it's the same feeling you're talking about."

"As long as it is gentle, demanding nothing from you, but giving you much, then we're talking about the same one. Here's what I have found: It has no name, but it names everything. It has no shape, but it forms everything. That is the deep nothing, what connects you to all. Feel it. Call it up."

As Nasomi focused on the feeling, something flashed into her mind. A moment. A vivid vestige. For that brief instant, she was someone else, looking out a window, longing.

A telling.

She opened her eyes, found Djina looking at her sweetly. "You look peaceful now, full of light and ready to take on the world."

"I want more. Lead me into it. I felt something, saw something."

"Let's use the staff," Djina said, lifting it off the ground. "We'll use it as a reminder, as a door if you may. You know how when you smell something, it brings to memory a happy childhood moment? Or when you see an object, and you remember something fond? For me, it's the smell of fish. It takes me back to when I went to the river with my grandfather. Sunshine, happiness, so much to eat. And the rain. I love the sound of it. It brings all the wonderful times I was at home, watching the rain, taking hot beverages and listening to my grandfather tell me stories."

Nasomi smiled. "I know what you mean."

"This staff will be your reminder of the deep calm feeling inside you. Take it in your hand and think of nothing but the... the nothing."

Nasomi took the staff in her right hand, closed her eyes, let the feeling come up again. The same window came to her mind, the same feeling of longing. Longing for someone to return. A city spread outside the window.

"When it vanishes," Djina said, "let go of the staff and do it again. All we want is the picking of the staff to remind you to remain calm."

Nasomi set the staff down, closed her eyes. When she picked it up, she fell into the telling.

Outside the window, a group of children played with a leather ball. Beyond them, towering over trees and other tall buildings, a wall through whose slits the sun poked through. Nasomi knew this place. It was her city Nari. She also knew this person. Her daughter, Ramona.

Nasomi opened up her eyes, dropping the staff. "Did I fall asleep?"

Djina shook her head. "It can feel like that sometimes. Also like a heartbeat is as long as a watch. Time doesn't seem to matter."

Nasomi took the staff again, closed her eyes, focused on the feeling. Nari formed before her, through Ramona's eyes. Nasomi tried to float her ghost from her daughter, succeeded after the third try. She went through the roof out into the sky, saw her home city as she had left it. She was in Nari's sky as well as sitting on the floor of a forest miles and miles away.

She was aware of both circumstances, unlike in Mifirhana where she had eventually fallen asleep. Also, unlike in Mifirhana, she was not in any emotional upheaval to have this telling. She'd just calmed herself all the way into it.

"Djina," she said. "Teach me more of this. Teach me all you know."

Djina giggled. "That's all there is to it. Only more practice. I must say, you look much better. You learned this faster than I expected."

"You're a wonderful teacher. Wiser than you portray in many cases."

"I'll take that as a compliment."

"It is."

"I am your Mfunda," Djina said, laughing.

"Thank you. You've helped me see a part of my gift I never imagined I had." She picked up the staff, whipped through the world in search of Tambo.

CHAPTER 32
UNBRIDLED TELLINGS

On the way to Ashge, in moments of rest, Nasomi slipped into tellings whenever she put her staff into her right hand.

Djina asked for every detail. "What is the Bride doing now?"

"How are the children?"

"Didn't you say some of the Michans want to settle in the Kingdom of Bones?"

"Have you seen the Tunka boy again?"

Nasomi indulged her, describing everything in detail. It was her way of keeping herself sane, keeping her mind and soul and body in one place. Nothing seemed solid anymore, as though the ground, the trees, the jugged hills ahead would break apart into a million pieces and coalesce into other shapes. Reality was a dream.

But she also talked to Djina because she loved Djina's company. She was glad Djina came after all. It felt good to know that there was someone there for her. She and Djina were like mother and daughter, friends, sisters even.

On the eighth afternoon, they came into a Ndinge village having a festivity after the successful hunt of an elephant. There was much eating, dancing and drinking. Nasomi and Djina tasted some of the village's banana beer, ignored all inhibition, and imbibed to their fill. They were giddy and chatty through the night and next morning when they stumbled away from the village. They jumped into a stream, splashing in the water like little children.

Nasomi laughed much that day, and the joy settled down in her, rather than disappeared, as the journey went on. She was different, clear-headed, peaceful. Ready to face anything with equanimity and knowing. The tellings were with her through night and day, unbridled from the need to sleep to experience one.

"I teach you to stay calm, and you learn to see the world without dreaming. Nasomi, you fascinate me," Djina said.

When she took the staff in her right hand again, she was in Nari. It was night there. She found herself floating above the new aqueduct Tambo had taken her to see, having a strange feeling of someone being in trouble. She looked about and saw a figure moving in the aqueduct.

She drew closer and saw it was her son Meron. He was moving up against the rushing water, pushing himself up with his hands on the sides of the duct.

Meron! she called, but he couldn't hear her.

She went into his mind, and learned why he was up there. He was running away for his life; the other two mages were looking for him. They had sent warriors after him and had the gates of Nari closed. The only way he could get out was to go up the duct and hope no one would find him.

Nasomi felt ashamed that she was not there for her son, that his life was in danger and there was nothing she could do about it.

She persisted in calling him, hoping he'd hear her the way Kanguya had. *Meron! Meron!*

The boy was shaking in his hands, and looked like he couldn't push himself further. If he let go, the water would push him down and he could die.

Go on, my son, she said, *Don't let go.*

The boy closed his eyes as if resigning himself to his fate.

Don't let go!

He snapped his eyes open, looked around. "Who is there?" he said. But in his mind, Meron thought, this is silly. I am imagining things. There's no one here.

Nasomi spoke her ghostly words with increased fervor. *It is me, your mother! Go on, son, put strength in your arms and don't give up.*

Somehow, that gave him the will to go on. He pulled himself forward with all his might. Nasomi followed him all the way to the beginning of the duct, where the gigantic wheel poured water in. Meron mustered himself and jumped onto the wheel and let it take him into the river. He swam to the bank, and knelt down to cry.

You're strong, my boy, Nasomi said. Meron jumped up as though he actually heard her. He ran until he came to the path that led to Mishi. He stopped short when a dark figure appeared at the end of the path. A dark man in all black clothes, and eyes blazing red. Nasomi recognized Nin, the man who had vanished.

"I knew it was you," Meron said as he stood his ground as the man approached. "You are the one who stole the potion."

Nin grinned. "It is I, indeed."

Pebbles rose from the ground at Meron's feet. They circled him.

"I am not fighting you, Mage," Nin said. "I know what happened. I can protect you."

"Why would you want to?"

"Because I know you, more than you think. I have been watching you, Mage. I know we can fight on the same side. I could use your strength. Come, as we speak, there's a group of bewitched soldiers coming this way."

"If you are tricking me, shadow man—"

"Nin. Call me Nin. Take my hand, young Mage."

Nin led Meron to a darker spot, embracing him.

"Hold your breath!" He jumped to the ground, dissolved into it like he was one with the night. Not a single hint was left that they had been there.

Nasomi shifted her staff from her right hand to her left, opening her eyes. She stood in warm daylight. Djina was watching her, solemn, patient. Nasomi nodded to her, tossed the staff back into her right hand. She concentrated on the deep feeling as she closed her eyes, inaudibly chanting, "Ramona, Ramona."

She came to a room in the Kepe palace. Ramona sat on a stool, carving symbols into an egg-shaped stone. She jerked up, as though she could feel somebody was here.

The door opened. Her grandmother, Tambo's mother, came in. "What are you doing, child?"

"Trying to write a story."

"What about?"

Ramona shrugged. "So far, it's about a boy who can talk to the kowasa."

Her grandmother smiled. "You should tell me about it. Come, supper is ready."

Ramona followed after her into the long opulent corridor. "I will go and see my aunt Naena tomorrow. I have something to tell her."

"What is that, child?"

"Mother is coming back."

"What?"

"I can feel it, feel her. She's coming back with Father."

Her grandmother embraced her sideways, smiled and said, perhaps out of pity. "Then we will make a feast for them when they come."

"Ramona has become like me," Nasomi said to Djina when she let go of the staff. "I don't know if she dreams things, but she has intuition. She senses things."

"You still won't visit her dreams, explain everything to her?"

Nasomi shook her head. "I still feel it won't be right. She is safe at the palace. As for Meron, I will walk into Nin's dream, tell him to protect the boy. He's a good man, Nin."

Nasomi and Djina walked fifteen miles to a mining village. As they rested in the afternoon, Nasomi took her staff again and searched for the Bride.

The Toddler was reporting his failure.

"Fools, fools!" the Bride shouted, flailing her hands and making angry sounds at the sky. "Can no one do a simple thing as killing the dream witch?"

"Simple? She killed Chonse. I have never seen natural magic like this before. She almost took all my power. Give me my freedom that I may replenish my power." Give us the dignity of freeing us."

The scowl she aimed at him sent him folding into himself.

"I'm undone. I will be laughed at by everyone. Free me," the Toddler said. "Please. I have nothing more to give you. Don't send me back to her." He whimpered.

"Go," Reema said, dark smoke wafting from her. "You are worthless. Take your freedom and don't cross my path again."

He turned to leave but Reema made a pained sound of realization. "Ah! Come here, child!"

"I am not a child!" the Toddler shouted, even as he turned and came back.

"You're young! How can that be? I want to know what divinations you used."

The Toddler whimpered again. "Leave me alone. I am exhausted from your errands, and now you mock me. Do you think I wanted to be this way?"

"Know to whom you are talking, Kamo, and answer the question."

"Same as everyone I know. Human bones, chicken bones, innards of a hyrax. Sacks of gold. A few drops of enemy blood. Sang the song of lightning."

"I know all that! I have tried it. How does it make you young and do nothing for me?"

"It does different things to people. Chonse turned into a jackal, Andini shriveled till his bones popped out his skin. Others go mad, others die. I have searched for a way to get back to my former self." He wept. "I hate magic!"

Reema dismissed him. As he went, she turned and ran, till she was alone behind a tree. She bit her knuckles, ground her temples, elbowed the tree.

"Worthless, worthless powers!"

She stopped and listened. Then she flailed her arms about as though she was attacked by a swarm of bees. "Dream witch! I feel you. I will find someone stronger to kill you. You know I will. I won't let you see me defeated."

She stomped away, Nasomi followed. Tambo had a smirk on his face.

"Are you going to give up now?" he said.

"Never. Wipe that stupid smile off. We're going."

His face contorted into foulness. "Going? I am ill, Reema. I cannot move. Are you trying to kill me?"

"Here." She placed a hand onto his chest. "I have given you some of my power. It will keep you long enough until we get where we are going, and you regain your health. It leaves us vulnerable, but we can handle it."

"You could do that all along? And you didn't?"

"Tambo, please. You keep thinking I am evil when everything I do is for you. I am not a healer, the magic I have is not for that. If I keep this long enough on you, it will take from you more than it gives."

"Well, if you haven't noticed—"

"This is no time for your quips. Start moving."

"Gweuka hasn't come to report about Dunia."

"You forget that I can always feel Gweuka's mind. There's nothing at Dunia."

Tambo sighed. He moved when she did. The Bride looked up, sensing Nasomi was still about. She clapped once, twisted her hands into fists, jerked them open. A barrier closed, shutting Nasomi away.

Nasomi floated toward Gweuka. The hyena was at Dunia, and it was ancient and crumbling and cracked by vegetation. The great stone edifices looked odd among the flora, as though the forest had been here all along and someone tried to build a city without disturbing it.

Nasomi went into Gweuka's mind as he skipped over protruding roots and plants that sought to prove they could grow through stone cracks. On either side, he looked up at temples looming over him, each with its own deity represented by a statue at the entrance. A laughing monkey, a curving fish, a naked woman, a naked man, a charging rhino and an elephant with an upraised trunk.

Dunia was teeming with life: birds flitting and tweeting, snakes crawling by ever so slowly like the world belonged to them, spiders weaving webs across the buildings; little rodents that scuttled all over; monkeys jumping in the tree boughs. Gweuka could smell moss, herbs, rot, and possibly a herd of antelopes running away from him.

Dunia was also a dead city. Of humans, there were none. Of the power of the old gods that the Mfunda at Olonge mentioned, there was nothing. The Bride will be disappointed, thought Gweuka, but he knew she was here in his mind. She knew what he knew.

He dashed off to hunt an antelope before he had to go back to the Bride.

CHAPTER 33
THE DRUMBEAT OF THE
GODS

Nasomi and Djina joined a long train of people going into Ashge. Women carried bundles of fruits and vegetables on their heads. Men wielding machetes swatted away flies from chunks of meat hanging on poles over their shoulders, some dripping blood. Boys and girls dragged live goats on leashes, and some of them beat drums and sang songs. Spontaneous dancing broke out at intervals, and people would form circles, sing and dance, break apart again to continue the journey.

Djina was entranced, jumping off the horse to join the dancing circles.

"In Kedjaki, there's no dancing in public," she told Nasomi. "It's unholy."

"But dancing is an expression of joy."

"Tell my people that, please!" She laughed and went to join another dance. Nasomi lost her in the crowd.

"From Ao, am I wrong?" a young man said in bad Ao'Mu, stepping up to Nasomi. He offered perfume in a small gourd, blinking seductively. "Smell like a flower, guaranteed. It will make every man want you."

"I like the way I smell for now," she said.

"You're here to see the Wenga?"

"The what?"

He gasped as though it was taboo to not know. "The Wenga A'onze. The biggest celebration in the world. To celebrate the coming rains, the new planting season, the new families coming together. There's so much dancing and eating. The girls of age pick up their baskets and choose boys they will marry and the people throw fruits and mud at them and then there's drums and singing all night and eating again and the dead people also watch."

He told her the Wenga A'onze was an annual festivity and mass wedding among the Ndinge. No wonder the place was bustling. Even more so as they entered the town. People from other Ndinge towns nearby and far were traveling to Ashge, which boasted the biggest version of the Wenga A'onze in the entire Ndinge kingdom.

"All I want is the food," Nasomi said to the young man, walking away from him. She took the staff in her right hand, searched for Djina. She was at a stall, bargaining with a wine seller. Nasomi paid the young man to take care of her horse, and made her way to where Djina was.

"They gave me some of the wine for free because of how I danced," Djina said, laughing. She hugged three gourds to her chest. "I love this place!"

"Djina, the Bride is here."

"Where? Let's get her."

"I don't know. Every time I try to find her, she deflects me. I must find her, before she goes too far. But I don't kno—"

A girl ran by, bumping into Djina, who almost dropped the gourds.

"Girl! Look where you run!" Three more children dashed past, but Djina saw them coming, stepped away in time.

"Djina. Watch over me. I know what to do."

Nasomi switched the staff to her right hand, and her consciousness whipped into the running girl. The girl was determined to reach the stall of salted peanuts before her friends could catch her, or else she would have to let them pinch her. Nasomi looked through the girl's eyes as she ran in between masses of grownups.

Nasomi jumped into a woman carrying a bundle on her head. She was counting how much she would make if all her cassava was bought by tonight. The Wenga was good for business.

Nasomi jumped into a man. He was drunk, feeling rather happy with himself. His daughter was marrying today. He'd raised her well.

She jumped from person to person, saw their memories, felt their emotions, understood their aspirations. Peddlers, children, fathers, mothers, brides and grooms, happy people, sad people. Everyone was her eyes and ears. Until she found Tambo and Reema, walking away from a fish stall. Nasomi went into a fisherman.

Reema turned abruptly and looked at the fisherman. She sensed Nasomi was here. "Is anything the matter?" the fisherman asked. Reema pointed a finger at him, then poked the air. Nasomi felt being shoved away.

"What are you doing?" Tambo asked.

The Bride poked again, and Nasomi was hurled from the fisherman, as though a giant hand pushed her. She came into herself with such force that her body was thrown down to the ground.

Djina shrieked. "Nasomi!"

Nasomi picked herself up, touching the back of her head. People made a circle about her and some looked from her to the wine gourds Djina held. They must have thought she was drunk.

"I'm alright," Nasomi said. She picked up her staff with her left hand. "Djina, come on!" She broke into a run.

"The wine," Djina said as she ran awkwardly to catch up.

"Drop it! We must get to them. I promise I'll buy you some more."

She heard the gourds fall and break, and Djina gave out a pseudo-whimper.

Nasomi stopped by the fisherman's stall, looked around. Reema was pulling Tambo by hand into a garden. "There!"

Without her hyena, the Bride wasn't fast enough. Nasomi and Djina closed up, blundering through an unattended field. The pumpkin leaves were yellow. The sweet potato leaves were ravaged by insects. The corn stalks were stunted and flopped toward the ground. They stepped into rotten pumpkins and a horde of flies buzzed into the air.

"Nasomi?" Tambo shouted when he turned and saw them coming. "You're here?"

"I am here, my love. Stop, Reema! This has gone too far enough."

The Bride made a sweeping motion in the air. Nasomi and Djina hit into an invisible wall. Nasomi hit her knee against this barrier, and feverish pain coursed through her.

"She broke my tooth!" Djina said, touching her bloody mouth.

A series of drums began to beat throughout Ashge. People shouted in joy.

Nasomi called up the fearlessness in her, and approached. The wall shattered. "I fear you no more."

"And I don't fear you, dream witch. Come to your death."

They charged at each other. Nasomi dropped the staff, retrieved the knife from her inner cloak pocket, lifted it in the air and aimed for a killing stab. She knifed into a wall, and while it shattered, it protected Reema. Reema punched her in the belly, slapped the knife away from her hand.

Reema gripped her hair, but let go as though she had touched fire. "What is this?" she said, shocked.

"I can undo you, Bride," Nasomi said, letting a smile on her face. She took a step toward Reema, and Reema took a step backward. Reema waved her hand and a wall came in between them. Nasomi walked through it. Reema kept backing away and casting protections into the air. As Nasomi walked through them, it felt like wading through water.

She heard Djina scream behind. She turned to see the hyena coming at her.

"Yes, Gweuka!" Reema shouted. "It's about time!"

Djina moved away from Gweuka's way, but he turned toward her. Instinct made Nasomi run to the girl's rescue. Djina stumbled backward. The hyena sank his teeth into her shoulder. Nasomi reached down and grabbed her staff. In her right hand...

She shifted into a telling.

She was a dancing mother of a groom, as men about him played drums and sang. The groom was smiling, happy about his upcoming wedding, and he rose to serve another round of drinks to the dozing family members...

Nasomi wrenched herself out of the telling. Gweuka shook Djina violently, threw her to the ground. Nasomi bound at the hyena, raising her staff. A strange sensation was flowing through her body, into her hands. It was pure; it was like water, and it was like fire. It was everything she was, her past, her future, what she could be, her true self. It was the breaking of everything that had limited her. It was energy, it was color, it was beauty, it was light, it was limitless, and she was transferring it through her staff.

When she hit the hyena, the beast froze. And exploded. Into bands of blinding light and color and a loud humming sound. The bands rippled like water waves, coloring everything, brightening everything. They rose up into the sky in thick columns.

When the brightness died down, and she could see well again, Nasomi fell to her knees beside Djina. Djina was coughing blood and thrashing. There wasn't anything left of the hyena.

"Djina, no!" She took the girl's head in her hand. "This can't be right, Djina! The dream... The dream. You were with me. You should be with me."

Djina tried to speak but she only coughed, her eyes fluttering. She became limp. Her head lolled to one side.

Hurt burned Nasomi's belly. It was heavy in her chest and she couldn't cry it out enough. Her throat was a boulder, and her body trembled as she wailed. When she turned her head, she saw the Bride being carried away on Tambo's back.

"You're my Mfunda, Djina! Don't die!" Nasomi pleaded. "I have places to go with you... Djina, no! Djina please! Not you, too!"

She picked up the staff and went into Djina's mind. Djina's consciousness was expanding. It encompassed everything around her, the sky above Ashge and the ground beneath it: the wet clouds dragging through the sky, the worms squirming in the soil; the birds in the air, the roots seeking water in the rocks deep in the ground. It went on and on, making Ashge small, its people as tiny as ants, growing above the clouds and below the deep rocks into a place that was molten iron.

The oceans were now like pools. There were other landforms, not only Ao and Tunkambe; other peoples. The world became a ball, floating in a sea of the power that drove Nasomi's tellings. There were other worlds!

The sun was a ball of fire. There were stars. Uncountable, everywhere. Up, down, left, right, all around. The *Mara*. She was looking at the *Mara!* And they were watching over more worlds than her own. And then she was above them, watching everything shrink into a spiraling snail shell of worlds and stars and suns and magic. And more shells and more spiraling.

Nasomi whipped back into herself.

She wept.

People gathered about her. The drumming in the town had stopped.

"What are you doing?" she said. They were picking Djina up.

"It is done, Nha," a man said. "Nhaye and Mzaye pleasure in her death. We take her to her place among the blessed departed."

"Look!" someone shouted. "The crops!"

The tomato and pumpkins looked lively, the pumpkin leaves and sweet potato leaves a lush green. There was no sign of corruption or insect infestation, and some flowers were blooming even as Nasomi looked at them.

"What is going on?" several people asked.

"The god and goddess are among us today!" someone else declared. "Mzaye and Nhaye bless us today! Didn't you hear their drumbeat? Didn't you see their light? Now see how they turn rot into life. Our Wenga is blessed, our season is blessed. Let us celebrate!"

Cries went up, and the drums resumed. Djina was placed on a large cloth, carried away. Nasomi followed after them, saying nothing. She heard as the tale of the drumbeat of the gods spread. She learned that the blessed departed were people who died during the Wenga A'onze period. They were considered fortunate. They were placed in an open area near to where the weddings took place, and people threw flowers and sang praises their way. And after the days of the Wenga passed, a large funeral would be held for them, equally grandiose, where only good things would be said.

Nasomi touched Djina's forehead when they placed her among other dead people.

"I led you to your death. I thought the dreams would always be right. Now I am not sure of anything anymore apart from this: I will avenge you."

She took the staff in her right hand, searched for the Bride. Found her and Tambo tired and panting in a field of termite mounds outside of Ashge.

She ran after them.

CHAPTER 34
ALL HAS BEEN REPAID

She caught up to them in two days.

As she approached, the Bride turned around to face her. The Bride's shadow bulged out like a splotch of dye, giving a deeper hue to the ground. It grew till it came to Nasomi's feet. Nasomi stopped.

Then she took a step forward, stepping onto the shadow. It dissipated from her foot. The Bride, who had grinned at her show of power, frowned.

Nasomi unfastened her cloak, letting it fall as she charged forward, color trailing her, sweeping away the blackness. The Bride also ran toward her.

"Today I will kill you, dream witch!"

"Not if I kill you first, witch!"

"Reema, stop!" Tambo shouted.

"Keep quiet, Tambo!"

The Bride jumped at Nasomi, threw her onto the ground, and the staff flew off Nasomi's hand. She straddled her, administering multiple slaps. Nasomi hurled her off, and where the Bride fell, the blackness returned to the ground, for Nasomi's presence had ebbed it away.

The Bride laughed as she got up, aimed a kick. Nasomi grabbed the foot and threw the Bride down.

Nasomi got up hurriedly and reached for her staff and hit the Bride in the ribs when she was almost upon her. The Bride shrieked and jumped backward. Nasomi was satisfied with the fear in Reema's eyes. She dared Reema to return. She did, wiser now. She ducked Nasomi's swing and threw herself at Nasomi. The staff fell and the Bride kicked it away.

As they tussled and scratched and pulled each other's hair, there was a back and forth splotching of color from Nasomi and shadow from the Bride.

"It wasn't enough that you destroyed my life!" Reema screamed. "You had to come and take more and more from me!"

Nasomi punched Reema in the jaw. "I can't believe I felt sorry for you sometimes."

"You have forgotten this is all your fault, you husband snatcher." She retorted with a punch, a scratching to the face. "I have been with him. I know him. I protect him from enemies. I've been by his side, gone thousands of miles for him. You dream, you come, easy for you. I've had nothing, I've had to fight. I've had to face evil and conquer it."

She called up her shadow, which surrounded and gripped Nasomi with arms that formed from it. Nasomi felt the hopelessness that she had felt when the Toddler did a similar thing.

But she broke through it. "Then you're a fool. You can't force people to love you."

"Will is nothing without love. He just doesn't realize he loves me."

Nasomi had to laugh. "You're a child in your mind. I don't care how powerful you have become. You don't think straight." She spun the Bride and pinned her to the ground.

The Bride bit into Nasomi's arm and freed herself, pushing Nasomi away.

"Look at me! Do you see my face, my skin? How ugly I look? You have done this to me. I did nothing to you, but you came—"

"Enough of this! You're a liar, a murderer. You... you... you killed Djina. You killed Wakani."

"And how many of mine have you killed? My hyenas. My jackal! Do you know how much it cost me to get them to be mine?"

Like a feral beast, Reema jumped at Nasomi with nails, teeth, and madness. She scratched and bit and slapped.

The kick Nasomi gave the Bride emitted a strong unnatural thud, and a wide area under both of them was freed of the blackness. The Bride fell to her knees, weakened, grimacing. "What is this? My power..."

The Bride grunted angrily, and the black returned, thicker than before, almost alive, riding in waves.

The ground bulged under Nasomi, throwing her off balance. She fell backward, but the bulging followed her, faster and harder this time, tossing her in the air, and she fell down hard.

The soil was gnawing at her skin, like a multi-mouthed creature was tasting her before consuming her. The bulging up and down of the ground nauseated her and she was on the verge of unconsciousness. She could hardly move by the time the rocking ceased and the Bride was over her, holding her staff, examining it.

"I thought there was magic in this thing, but it was a trick, wasn't it? It's all in you, you undeserving wretch. But I'm not afraid."

Nasomi couldn't reply. She couldn't get up. *"Zje'pi toov,* evil Bride!"

"Ha! You think you can deter me with a little insult? I know a bit of the language, dream witch. *Zje'piwane toov!"* The Bride raised the staff to strike Nasomi.

Tambo appeared behind the Bride, and he brought something sharp down at her back. She shrieked and turned about, backhanding him across the chest. He fell to the ground, sprawled. She dropped Nasomi's staff and picked the sharp rock. It was tipped with her blood.

"What are you doing, my love? How did you...? Some will, isn't it?" Then her voice turned ugly. "You're just like her! If I can't have you, then she won't either.

You have made me do this." She raised the sharp rock at him.

But she hesitated, threw it away and fell to her knees. She began to cry.

"I can't! I love you. I love you so much. I am such an idiot! Me, the one who conquered the witches of Arwo, leveled Olonge, killed Ituntulu and enslaved his coven. I am weakened by a simple man." She emitted a self-deprecating laugh.

Nasomi got up and picked her staff. She mustered all her energy through it, and touched Reema with it. Blinding light and rippling colors hummed from the impact, just like with the hyena at Ashge, spreading far and wide and above.

When the light and hum ebbed, the ground was covered in colorful, sweet-smelling flowers and graceful grass. The air was pleasant to breathe. The shadow was nowhere in evidence. Lightning flashed in the horizon, tearing the sky in a dazzling crack.

Reema was still there, where she was kneeling. She studied her hands and touched her face. The wrinkles were gone. Her face was as dark as mahogany, as smooth as it had been many years back. The gold bands on her neck and arms glittered in stark contrast to her skin, and looked as new a fresh from the jeweler.

She was youthful again. She repossessed her intimidating beauty.

Nasomi poked her with the staff, and for a brief moment, Reema looked up at her. Tears were streaming down her face. She averted her eyes, staring in fearful wonder at her hands.

Tambo coughed as he struggled to heave himself up. Nasomi bounded to him and embraced him. She was trembling, unable to contain the bursting joy. She helped him up.

He took off the cloth around his thigh and tossed it. He closed his eyes, as he moved his limbs of his own will, cracking his neck, taking deep breaths.

"I promise I will never be weak again," he struggled to say.

"You have held on all this while."

"I missed you so much. I have loved you always."

"I know."

"I have meant to return home. On a good day."

Nasomi laughed. "Today is a good day then." She brought her lips to his. His lips were soft, beautiful to taste. He returned the kiss with equal passion.

Thick drops of rain fell upon their foreheads.

"What are we going to do with her?" he asked, indicating Reema with a raise of his chin. Reema was still entranced in her regained form.

"I don't know. I have undone her magic."

"How?"

"Remember when the mages told us there are two types of magic? Mine is able to undo hers. All has been repaid."

"Nothing is repaid until she's dead." He managed to pick up a pebble and toss it at Reema. It hit her on the forehead, making a small cut. But she did not move. She didn't even look in their direction.

"Tambo, enough killing has been done. I wanted nothing but to kill her all this while. But now... I don't know. I thought she would disappear like the hyena."

"That's what she wants. For you to feel sorry for her, then she'll return with witchery to take revenge."

"She won't. I can feel it. All her power is undone."

"So, she's not dangerous anymore?"

"Not anymore."

"We can't leave her to her own devices. We must take her with us, back to Nari. To face the king's judgment."

Nasomi's heart leaped, shattering again over Djina's death. The dream... Djina, not Reema, was the one who was supposed to return with her and Tambo back to Nari. Had she misremembered the dream?

Tambo, more from his regained freedom than strength, ripped apart Reema's cloak and bound her hands. "There's a large hole some way back," he said to Nasomi. "We must shelter there to let the rains pass." He pulled Reema up on her feet. "Walk!"

The rain washed down in a wild torrent when they were safely in the hole. It was like a tunnel, with enough room to move through in a stooping position. It sloped downward and then horizontally, and stopped dead. It told no stories of where it was to go, or what it had been for. Nasomi hoped some wild beast wouldn't come tromping through seeking shelter.

Reema sat when she was told to sit. She leaned against the wall when she was told to. She drew her knees to herself, said not a single word.

With nothing to do but wait, Nasomi stroked Tambo's hair as he lay on her lap. She had set her staff to her left side on the floor. Throw it away. That was the idea coming into her mind. It had served its purpose. There was no more need for a telling. Everything was as it had been. Tambo was in her arms again. Reema was only threatening through her beauty. Once they got back to Nari, and Reema was judged, life would be complete again.

She fell asleep, hypnotized by the whoosh of the rain, the *drip drip* of water into the hole, the peace of having finally done it. She dreamed, and it was an ordinary dream. It was a messy dream: an animal with bright red fur, long wistful tail, and long innocent snout jumped from spot to spot, coloring the world. Here some blue, there white. People emerged from the colors. Nasomi was a tall tree, singing a song, bleeding sweet chromatic emotion. But it was an ordinary dream, and she awoke from it with a smile.

Reema was gone. The cloth used to bind her lay on the ground. Nasomi picked up her staff, switched it to her right hand and searched for Reema.

She was under a tree, sheltering from the rain, a few miles east from here. Reema snorted a sad sound.

"You are watching me again, aren't you, Dream witch? I can feel you. All my powers are gone, but I can tell you are here. Or perhaps I am imagining it."

Reema walked out into the rain. "Keep him, peasant girl," she continued. "He has a small heart, I see that. I have seen that, but my own heart... Well, he loves you, the *Mara* know why. I don't care anymore. And to think I loved him so much. But he would never want me."

She wiped off rain from her forehead. "Isn't it funny, how I have searched hard and killed many for even a hint of beauty? But you, my enemy, you gave it back to me. And I have been running away."

She forced a laugh. "Go. Go home and be happy in your miserable little lives. The world is not for me. I am too good for it. You will never forgive me, but I forgive you. Yes, I forgive you, dream witch. I will die here; I choose to die here. I go the way I want."

When she returned to herself, Nasomi sighed, a deep inhale and exhale. She was still for a long moment. Tambo awoke.

"Where is she?"

"Gone, Tambo. She freed herself."

"She must face the king's justice in Nari!" Tambo said. "She mustn't be let loose."

"There is nothing more we must do to her," Nasomi said. "There's nothing more we must do for her. She has made her choice."

If Reema wanted to die here, Nasomi would let her. She was certain Reema would never show up again with more terrible powers and a dozen hyenas to her command. Nasomi had her journey to think about. She had Meron and Ramona to think about.

She looked at her staff. Well, nothing was as it had been. The tellings were now part of her. She also had Djina to think about.

"My love," she said. "I must look for someone."

"Who?" asked Tambo.

"A friend, a teacher, a sister. She is a lot of things to me."

"Where is she?"

"Well, she died."

He narrowed his eyes. "I don't understand."

"I have so much to tell you, so much to make you understand. Right now, I want you to watch over me. I will be as though I am asleep, but I'll be looking for her. Her body is not yet buried. I want to bring her back."

"You can do that?"

"I don't know. I can only try." She wrapped her right hand over the staff, closed her eyes.

CHAPTER 35
WALKER OF THE SPIRIT WORLD

Djina!

She called her name into the far reaches of existence. She searched for her through the vast corporeal plains, through an unending ocean of what could not be seen; shouted her name into fields of ever-changing substance that she couldn't fathom, where light and darkness were one thing, nothingness and form coalesced into each other. She persisted, and she called in all the places Djina's soul had gone to, grown into. There were other people she knew, too: Father, Mother, Wakani. But they were too far gone, too melded into the fabric of everything. But she expressed her love for them, and she felt their love for her.

Djina heard and answered. *Nasomi? Isn't it all beautiful?* Her voice came from everywhere and everything.

It is.

You came to take me back. A solemn statement, not a question.

I need you, Djina.

I can see and feel everything. But I am not sure I can come back.

"Follow my voice. I am going to your body."

Piece by piece, from as far as she'd gone and become, Djina's essence came together. It was a beautiful thing for Nasomi to experience. She led and Djina followed, until the girl got sucked back into her body and jumped up amidst dead bodies.

There was a ring of fire around the Blessed Departed, who had been put in a sitting position, supported by stakes in the ground, and nearby a throng of Ndinge people danced and imbibed and spoke at the top of their voices.

"I am back!" Djina shouted, and burst into laughter. "Oh, wonders! I am back!" She raised her hands but a pain stung her shoulder and she winced. She prodded at the deep wound with a finger, sucked through her teeth. Then laughed as though it didn't matter.

A silence swept through the celebrations and the people looked at her with awe as she came toward them.

Nasomi came to herself, jumped up. "She's alive, my love! She heard me." She threw her arms around the confounded Tambo. "I did it, Tambo! I called her back."

"What is happening, Nasomi?"

"I will explain on the way. We must hurry now to go meet her."

She told him everything as they journeyed to Ashge. He listened intently, asked a lot of questions, interjected with parts of his tale that she didn't see in her tellings. If he were a scribe, he would have written it all down. Twice the first night as they rested on a bed of leaves, she awoke to find him staring at her. "I'm finally with you," he whispered, stroked her cheeks.

The next day, Nasomi decided it was finally time to walk into her children's dreams. Ramona was at the Kepe palace. "Mother," she said, as she looked around the blackness, over which sparks like stars began to environ. "I have been thinking of you."

"I know, child. I am with your father now. We are coming home."

"I knew it! I've had these... feelings."

"I have so much to tell you about them." She thought of explaining that this was no mere dream; the actual Nasomi was talking to Ramona, but she knew this was reassuring enough for her daughter.

"I will be waiting for you. Meron..." She dropped her gaze.

"It is fine, Mona. I know what happened. I will find him and speak to him."

Meron was asleep in Mihide's house, the one made of bamboo sticks, in which she herself had been and met the young Azuku. When his dream, in which he was on a throne, turned black and he saw Nasomi, he only stared at her.

"Meron."

He approached her. He said, "I remember your face now. I had forgotten."

"It is truly me, Meron. I am here with you, and I will return."

"You left me!" he shouted. "You let this all happen. I have done bad things now."

She approached him, but like in all other dreamwalks, she couldn't touch him. Her hand passed through him like he was air. "I am so sorry I had to leave. Words cannot mend what my absence destroyed. I will do it right this time. Please forgive me."

He looked up at her. "Mona said you're coming back."

"I know it is hard for you to believe, but I am truly here talking to you. I am with your father, we are in Tunkambe. We are coming to you. Meron, I will always be watching over you."

He woke up, placed his hands over his eyes in deep thought. Nasomi returned to herself, and told Tambo that the children were safe and expecting them.

She and Tambo reached Ashge on the evening of the third day, found Djina surrounded by a mesmerized crowd. They held on to her every word as she told them about what it feels like to come back from the dead. It took two days to pry her away from them, and they had made up a dozen songs about her.

Djina the Awoken, the Joyous One, would never be forgotten among the Ndinge. Even though Nasomi urged her to understate Nasomi's role, an equal number of songs and legends spread about Nasomi the Caller, the Walker of the Spirit World, the One Who Sees All. They had devotees all along the journey from Ashge. Nasomi had to insist that she could not do it again when they asked her to call to their dead loved ones. They followed still, even if all they did was gaze at her in admiration.

Djina's wound slowed them down as well. She tired quickly and developed a high fever. But nothing could dampen her soul. She talked and laughed like the pain didn't matter. Even when she slept, there was a smile on her face.

She often said, "I feel as if some part of me out there." She made a wide arc in the air with her hand. "Being here, back in my body, is like waking up from a sweet dream, starting to forget what it is like. But remembering only the good feelings. Ever since, though, it's like nothing is... big anymore. Nothing bothers me. I'm just happy. I feel like dancing and singing all the time."

They perched in Olonge for five days, to let Djina heal. Because of their new reputation, they were offered the best accommodation the village could give, at no charge. They dined in the Chief's kraal and his best medicos attended to Djina.

One night, Nasomi awoke from a dreamless sleep, her bladder pressing. She sat up and lifted herself from the sleeping mat. Out of habit, she picked up her staff. She warped into a telling.

Reema lay on a small patch of ground from which she'd cleared the grass. She had curled herself tightly against the cold. Nasomi melded into her, and realized Reema wasn't asleep, but was trying hard to. She was cold, hungry.

Reema started, sat up, squinted around into the night. There was a shape approaching. Two, three. More. They surrounded her.

She made out barely-dressed tall bony people wielding spears, and Nasomi recognized them as the Tunka people she had seen by the ocean shore. Among them was the boy she'd been, who had swung dangerously in the tall trees. He stared at Reema with big curious eyes.

The man in the lead pointed his spear at Reema. Nasomi felt she needed to go back, to give Reema a private death, but she lingered. "*Wenda? Ke banga?*" the man said, in a sharp thin voice.

"I don't understand," Reema said, shielding herself with her arm as if it could stop the spear if he thrust it.

The man turned to his companions, instructed them something. Two dashed away, quick as hyenas. The man turned to the boy. "Mdua. *Tonya we pa. Bela mpa.*"

The boy's eyes widened in fear, then came, knelt before the man. "*Ne pekane*, Mungu," he replied, quite unwillingly as far as Reema could tell.

The boy turned his spear, held it at the head and brought it to his chest. He bit his lower lip, closed his eyes, made a slow slash across his chest. Blood trickled down. The man placed a palm on the blood, rubbed it.

He turned to Reema, grabbed at her neck before she could flinch, lifted her off the ground. He was stronger than his gaunt looks suggested. He said something.

At first, all she could hear was him repeat, "*Tuka... tuka,*" as though it was a chant, and then, as if something unlocked in her mind, she, and Nasomi within her, could understand him. "Speak."

He squeezed her neck tighter.

"Please, you're choking me." Reema's eyes widened. "I can speak your tongue! How is this possible?"

"How many are you?" he demanded. "What do you want in our land?"

"I am alone, lost. Please, all I want is some food."

"If you lie to me, we will find out. I have sent two to scout. We will kill anyone we find trying to hide."

"Stop choking me. I have told you I am alone. If you won't feed me, then kill me."

"Tell us about the pillar of light we saw in the west."

"Pillar of light? I don't..." Then she remembered her fight with Nasomi. It seemed these people all the way here had seen the effect. "That was caused by the dream witch."

"Who is this dream witch?"

"Some simple farm girl who has the ability to find anyone in the world."

"This is another sign, Mungu," someone said. "The gods brought her into our path for this."

The man let go of Reema's neck, and she flopped to the ground. As he turned to confer with his companions, she realized she'd lost the language. She got the gist of it, and a few words stood out. Their language wouldn't be a difficult one to learn, she conjectured.

The man got hold of her neck. "Can this dream witch of yours find Uzegwenya?" She could comprehend the language again.

"Who is Uzegwenya?"

A woman answered, stepping around to be in Reema's sight. If she wasn't afraid for her life, Reema would have scoffed at the girl. She was thin and knobby, starved, looking ridiculous with such a big spear in her hand. "The great beast. Shaker of mountains, destroyer of cities, breather of fire. It will make us stro—"

"That's enough talking from you," the man admonished her, giving her a stern look. She cowered back.

"I have heard of this beast," Reema said. "The dream witch can find it."

"You will take us to her." He dropped her again, and someone came forward with a rope.

"At least give me food if you're going to tie me up."

A hand on Nasomi's cheek brought her back to her body. Tambo was up, staring at her. "Are you alright?"

She smiled. "I was only going to make water. Go back to sleep."

"You had a telling?"

She nodded. "Reema."

"Again?"

"Again. I will tell you about it when I return." She stood and went outside.

A cold breeze greeted her, she shivered but paid no mind. She would be back in warm covers soon. The sky was moonless and dotted with so many stars it looked alive. She gazed upwards. She had been up there, out there, with the *Mara*, seeing everything.

As Djina said, nothing felt big anymore. Nasomi had a constant joy with her now, rooted within and nothing could faze her anymore, not even the telling she just. Whatever trouble Reema and the Tunka horde were bringing was not worth losing sleep over. Not even the prospect of a mountain-razing, fire-breathing beast could scare her anymore. She would be ready for them.

She had a long journey to think of. Perhaps there would be new discoveries to make between here and Nari, new adventures. She needed to apologize to Beyuchi for leaving him without warning; she needed to see Tebula and Kanguya again, needed to dance once again in Mifirhana, this time with Tambo by her side. Marvel at the trees of the Redland. Admire the stars watching over Nari.

And she had so many things to tell her children.

ABOUT THE AUTHOR

Enock I. Simbaya is an Electrical Engineer by profession. He loves to daydream and create stories; he believes stories have the power to inspire people and to effect change in a way other things cannot. He lives in Lusaka, Zambia, with his wife and son.

For more exciting Sword and Soul, visit our website www.mvmediaatl.com